HEARTS OF
BRIARWALL

ALSO BY KRISTA JENSEN

Miracle Creek Christmas

HEARTS OF BRIARWALL

PROPER ROMANCE

KRISTA JENSEN

SHADOW
MOUNTAIN
PUBLISHING

Library of Congress Cataloging-in-Publication Data

Names: Jensen, Krista Lynne, author.
Title: Hearts of Briarwall / Krista Jensen.
Other titles: Proper romance.
Description: Salt Lake City : Shadow Mountain, [2022] | Series: Proper romance | Summary: "Lydia is fascinated by the freedom afforded by the new motorcars, and Spencer is a forward-thinking entrepreneur, looking for investors to support his chain of auto-supply shops. Lydia and Spencer's love of motorcars and their quick, witty banter leads to instant romantic chemistry, but their relationship is threatened by the traditional expectations of marriage and the needs of a free-spirited woman who is determined to create her own future"—Provided by publisher.
Identifiers: LCCN 2021062765 | ISBN 9781629729961 (trade paperback)
Subjects: LCSH: Man-woman relationships—Fiction. | Automobile mechanics—Fiction. | Women automobile drivers—Fiction. | Nineteen hundreds (Decade), setting. | London (England), setting. | Albury (Hertfordshire, England), setting. | BISAC: FICTION / Romance / Historical / 20th Century | FICTION / Romance / Clean & Wholesome | LCGFT: Romance fiction.
Classification: LCC PS3610.E5685 H43 2022 | DDC 813/.6—dc23/eng/20220207
LC record available at https://lccn.loc.gov/2021062765

Printed in the United States of America
PubLitho, Draper, UT

10   9   8   7   6   5   4   3   2   1

For Laurel, Mara, Marci, Donna, and Sherrie

My Wendy-birds who taught me how to fly

CHAPTER 1

Lydia Wooding lounged at a nearly upside-down angle on her great-grandmother's settee, her head hanging off the blue jacquard cushion, her feet propped on the raised end, a book clamped in her hands and hovering above her nose, blissfully forgetful that she was both expecting company and had nearly reached twenty-one years of age, a point of life where such postures were frowned upon.

Violet Whittemore entered the room and tilted her head. "I believe you've misinterpreted the design of that piece of furniture, my friend. You look excruciatingly uncomfortable."

Lydia drowsily turned the page, reluctant to stop reading. "If you believe *this* to be the picture of discomfort, you've lived far too sheltered a life."

Violet sighed and dropped down into a Louis XIV chair opposite the settee. "I can't argue that one. You do realize your feet are supposed to rest where your head is?"

Lydia removed a hairpin and slid it in the book to save her place and slowly maneuvered upright. "I began that way, but by chapter four I was like this."

Her friend squinted at the cover. "Good heavens, what are you reading?"

She held out the book. "*Love Among the Chickens*. It's the latest from P.G. Wodehouse. I believe I'm in love."

"No chickens involved, I hope." Violet took the copy and perused it.

Lydia shook her head. "Just silly fun. Wodehouse makes me laugh."

She took a moment to observe her friend. Violet always dressed smartly and conservatively yet often included a touch of the old, extravagant prosperity she came from in some whimsical form. Lately she'd been wearing the jeweled insect brooches she'd inherited from her maternal grandmother. Today, a large emerald stag beetle sat pinned at the waist of her deep blue skirt.

Violet handed back the book. "I shall read it next, then. I could use some silly fun."

"You've come to the right place." Lydia checked her gold watch pinned to her slightly crumpled blouse by a bar of pearl doves. "Is it time already?"

"I'm a bit early. Mama dropped me off on her way to a fitting at Beaumont's."

Lydia gave up on smoothing out her blouse and reached behind to straighten the bow at the small of her back. "However did you get out of it?"

"I told her we'd been reading Oscar Wilde."

"You did not."

"I did. She went on and on about him until we arrived. She's simply obsessed with the man. For a moment, I feared she would invite herself here, but instead, she nearly shoved me out of the carriage, admonishing me to have a brilliant time and report back to her. Oh, let me." Violet stood and pulled on Lydia's bow, straightening the folds and giving an overly firm tug.

"Oof." Lydia turned with a frown, smoothing her skirts. "What was that for?"

"For putting the Wendy League at risk. If your brother had walked in here and found you askew on the settee, he would've forbidden you from reading. And how could we hold a 'literature club' if you weren't allowed to read anything?" Violet's gray eyes challenged her beneath arrow-perfect brows and a silky, golden-brown coiffure—arranged today in a Psyche knot.

"Pooh," Lydia said. "Andrew would never. He'd more likely forbid me from sitting." She gave her friend an impish grin, daring her to argue.

On the verge of laughter, both girls turned at a commotion in the morning room's entry. Florrie Janes swept in, a vision in pink, her blonde tendrils bobbing beneath the biggest hat Lydia had seen her wear. Nibs, Florrie's small Jack Russell, yipped at her heels.

"What sort of cad would forbid you from sitting?" She eyed Lydia, pulled a hairpin out of her tiny silk bag, and then jammed the pin into Lydia's updo. "There."

"Ouch." Lydia winced and sat back down, patting her skull. "With friends like you, who needs a lady's maid?"

"You do," both girls answered together.

Lydia frowned, knowing they were right. "Well, I have one."

"Yes," Florrie said as she seated herself and picked up her dog, now happily wagging his tail. "And she earns every penny."

At that moment, Mrs. Parks brought in tea. "Will that be all, miss?" she asked Lydia.

"Yes, Mrs. Parks. I'll pour out."

When the girls were left to themselves once more, Florrie

reached for a biscuit for Nibs. "Now, who is forbidding you to sit? As in Parliament? Or just sitting in general?"

"Andrew," Lydia answered.

"Andrew is forbidding you from sitting in Parliament?" Florrie looked to Violet, who was laughing, then back to Lydia. "This is a scheme of yours I've not yet heard. Though I wouldn't put it past you. You do realize, don't you, that you'll need to go a little further above your brother to reach this new goal of yours?" She sipped her tea, eyes sparkling.

"Parliament is *not* a goal of mine," Lydia stated. "Only the *vote*. If I'm important enough to govern my home, then—"

"—you're important enough to have a say in how you're governed," they completed for her in unison.

She narrowed her eyes but continued. "I was merely lounging upside down on the settee, and Violet warned that Andrew would forbid me from reading if he found me in that pose, and I told her he would sooner have me never sit again. That is *all*."

"Oh, well, that clears up everything." Florrie gave Lydia a charming half-smile, mischief in her blue eyes. "Are you certain you don't want to run for Parliament? Papa would finance your campaign, I'm certain of it."

Lydia shook her head at her friend. "Your papa would tell us to settle down and then offer to send us to Paris for a fitting at Worth's."

Florrie's eyes grew wide, a look Lydia had seen a thousand times. "Oh, let's tell him! I *adore* Paris!"

"Tell whom what?"

All three girls turned as a petite, walnut-haired beauty entered the room.

Florrie leaned forward in her chair. "Papa is sending us to Paris because Andrew is forbidding Lydia from running for Parliament and sitting upside down." She tilted her head at the dog. "Or was it reading books?" Nibs tilted his head in return.

Lydia answered, "Sitting," as Violet said, "Reading books."

Ruby Burke stared, eyes round. "So, we are going to . . . Paris?"

Lydia bit her cheeks as Florrie nodded enthusiastically and Violet soberly shook her head. A rush of affection for these delightful girls coursed through her veins.

Ruby took a breath, settling her shoulders. "Shall I go back out and come in again?"

Violet folded her arms. "I believe that would be wise, yes."

Ruby turned without another word and left the room, her heels clicking on the parquet floor in the corridor.

The three remaining girls looked to each other, quickly composing themselves.

In another moment, Ruby reappeared in the doorway. Lydia, Violet, and Florrie stood.

"Ruby," they said together, "you're here!"

The customary clasping of hands and kissing of cheeks were exchanged, the door was shut, and tea was poured. Violet took up a notebook and a pencil as Lydia stood.

"Ladies," Lydia began, "welcome to the eighty-and-ninth weekly meeting of 'The Wendy League.' Do you swear to secrecy and silence?"

"We do," the other girls answered.

"Florrie, will you lead us in the motto?"

Florrie stood, bouncing Nibs in her arms. After an eyebrow lift from Violet, she set the dog down and straightened her shoulders. "Like Wendy Darling at the nursery window, we seize the opportunity to fly."

The others stood and, chins lifted, repeated the motto. "We seize the opportunity to fly."

Just as it had for almost two years, warmth washed over Lydia at speaking those words. And just as they had for almost two years—ever since they'd attended the magical play *Peter Pan* by J.M. Barrie at the Duke of York's Theatre together—the four girls grinned at one another.

They were not *The Wordsworth Ladies*, the name she'd used to convince Andrew to allow them to hold their official meetings in this seldom-used morning room. They were *The Wendy League*.

And while the odd novel was mentioned, and book titles were tossed about for the ruse, more important things were discussed. Courage, aspirations, community, womanhood, and . . . men. It could not be denied that while Peter Pan refused to grow up, the boys who had caught the eyes of the Wendy League certainly had.

Long ago, the girls had decided that Wendy's brush with the boy who could fly changed her forever, for the better. She must've sought out adventure after soaring in the skies, must've been fearless after facing pirates, and must have had a better understanding of boys after finding homes for the Lost Boys.

Was Wendy's heart broken when Peter chose to stay in Neverland? Did she try to find someone like Peter? Or somebody very different? Did she wait for the boy to change his mind and come for her? Or move ahead steadfastly without him?

Only two of the four friends could claim a broken heart: Lydia and Florrie, though Florrie wouldn't reveal any details. That was no help at all and highly suspicious considering Florrie had been breaking hearts since she'd been in braids. And Lydia questioned if her own heart truly had been injured, or only her pride. Nearly four years had passed since Lydia had put more meaning to a young man's attentions than he'd intended. The lesson of unrequited love had been a confusing and bitter pill at the tender age of seventeen. While young men had approached her or she had sought them out in the years since, the dance remained an enigma. So, it only showed wisdom for the League to discuss boys. And the men they became. And hearts in general.

Not surprisingly, this was a subject with which they floundered.

Lydia blinked and directed her thoughts back to the present. "Please, be seated. Violet, read us the highlights from last week's meeting."

The girls sat, and Violet tilted her notebook toward the spring sunlight pouring in through the window. "My mother's suffrage meeting took place Monday evening as usual while Father was at his club. Only Ruby was able to attend with me. Mrs. Blanchard proposed a march on the first of May."

"But that's May Day," Florrie said.

Violet nodded, setting down her notebook. "Precisely. Ruby, tell them what we learned."

"Oh." Ruby took a deep breath and kept her eyes on the tea service. "Well, it is believed that, centuries ago, May Day began as a celebration of . . . fertility." Her cheeks pinked.

"Of *women*," added Violet.

"Mrs. Blanchard thought it an appropriate addition to the celebrations taking place in the park," Ruby continued, "to wear our sashes and pass out nosegays with a note for our cause."

Violet nodded. "A quiet sort of demonstration." She quirked her brow.

"And are the organizers of the celebration aware of this quiet sort of demonstration?" Florrie asked.

"As much as organizers are ever aware."

Florrie raised her brow in return.

"I've always loved May Day." Lydia shrugged. "That sounds perfect. All in favor of participating?"

Four hands were raised. Violet made a note.

"Next?"

"Florrie reported that the wife of one of the farmers on their estate had given birth to twins and were in need. It was decided to put a food basket together and collect nappies and blankets for the little ones, along with a milk goat. This was carried out on Thursday. Florrie also suggested they might name the girl after her for such an endeavor."

The girls looked to Florrie, who pouted. "They did not. The poor thing is called Myrtle. *Myrtle*." She was met with half-hearted sounds of sympathy. "She's a pretty little girl, though. I suppose she'll carry it off."

After sufficient reassurance that the child would survive bearing such a name, Florrie grew flustered. "That is not all. Myrtle is darling, and I'm sure I shall take a special interest in her as she grows, but no, the awful—the most humiliating thing—"

"What is it?" Ruby asked, placing her hand on Florrie's arm.

Florrie faced them and lifted her chin, though she avoided their expectant gazes. "They've named the *goat* after me."

After a heavy pause, Lydia threw her hand over her mouth to stop her laughter as Violet bit her lips, her shoulders shaking. Ruby grinned while rubbing Florrie's back.

Violet attempted to speak. "I'm sure it's a testament to how much the gift meant to them, dear." She snorted and pressed her lips together once more.

Lydia nodded vehemently, trying to compose herself. "Yes,

without a doubt. After all, Miss Florrie will be providing the extra sustenance needed for two babies."

More giggles erupted, even from Florrie, who dabbed at her eyes with a handkerchief. "My reputation shall be ruined!" she exclaimed, and the girls broke free of the last of their composure.

"At least," Lydia said between hiccoughs, "you didn't gift them a pig."

At the height of their laughter, the door opened, and the girls swallowed their impropriety at the appearance of Lydia's brother, Andrew.

Lydia shot out her arm to retrieve her book and opened it quickly.

"Ahem," said Violet.

Lydia quickly turned the book right side up.

"Excuse me, ladies."

Lydia blinked up at her brother. "Oh, Andrew. I did not hear you knock."

"I did knock. It's no wonder you did not hear me." He nodded curtly to the other girls, his censure apparent.

Florrie primly nodded. "The girls were merely offering me comfort over a most distressing . . . er . . ."

"Goat," Lydia said, and Violet snorted once more.

"Yes," Florrie said, her eyes wide with innocence. "A most distressing goat."

Andrew cleared his throat. "Yes, well, I wish you the best with the . . . goat situation, Miss Janes." He ignored the suppressed giggles and addressed Lydia. "I'm leaving. I'll return with our guest before dinner. I've the basket from Cook. Oh, and I've informed Warren and Latimer of my absence should the calving begin. Shouldn't be a problem."

Lydia nodded. "Very well." The cattle were a newer undertaking at Briarwall, with seven new calves anticipated this season. To her surprise, Andrew had allowed Lydia to witness the births last year, and she looked forward to it again. Seven was a lucky number, after all.

"You remember that the Piedmonts will be dining with us on Friday?"

Lydia stifled a groan and forced a smile. "How could I forget?"

"Good." He paused another second. "Do try to conduct your meeting with more decorum."

"Of course. I assure you this was an exceptional circumstance."

He glanced at the group once more, nodded, and left, leaving the door conspicuously open behind him.

Violet leaned closer to Lydia. "At least you weren't upside down."

After several moments, the girls managed to gather their decorum.

"Who is your brother bringing home?" Florrie asked after a sip of tea. "Dare I suggest it is a woman?"

Ruby choked on her tea and quickly patted her mouth with a napkin.

"Quite the opposite," Lydia said. "He is bringing home a school chum."

Violet's brow rose. "Andrew had 'chums'?"

"Apparently so. And that means, bafflingly, that *he* was also a chum."

"Is this chum handsome?" Florrie brought them back around to the crux of the matter.

Lydia set her teacup down with a shrug. "Last I saw Mr. Hayes, I was a girl of eleven and he was a gangly boy of eighteen with an exuberant amount of hair, rather bony elbows, and spoke incessantly of mechanics. I recall an obsession with clocks."

"Hmm." Violet sipped her tea. "Too bad it wasn't motorcars. Then you'd have been smitten."

"That, my friend, is sadly true—tall hair, elbows, and all."

"And how long is he to stay?" Florrie asked, feeding Nibs another biscuit.

"I'm not sure. Andrew has been fairly tight lipped about the thing. My impression is that the visit is predominantly business, and the outcome might determine how long Mr. Hayes stays."

Violet winced. "Doesn't sound very chummy to me."

"Well, as I said, I don't know the details, except that he's from Birmingham."

"Birmingham?" Florrie asked with a wrinkle of her nose. "Perhaps you needn't worry about *all* the formalities. What does he do?"

"I've no idea."

"Really, Lydia, it is entirely within your realm to ask questions and expect answers."

"When it comes to a houseguest, anyway," Violet murmured.

Ruby lifted her brow in agreement.

Lydia shook her head. "I wish you could all stay with me for the duration. I'm bound to make a bungling hostess. We've seldom had guests. Aside from the Piedmonts."

Andrew had made her practice some scenarios at dinner during the last week, but it had only made her realize how inexperienced she was at being the lady of a house. No amount of rushed lessons could take the place of actual experience.

"Invite us to dinner," Florrie said. "Or host an outing. You needn't face this alone. We shall be at your beck and call."

Lydia nodded, relieved by her friends' support. "Perhaps I

shall. All of you are hereby invited to dinner for the next week . . . or so."

Ruby tipped her head. "I'm afraid I cannot this week. Great-Aunt Margaret is staying with us."

The others nodded with understanding. As the only daughter in her family, Ruby was required to attend to her aunt's company and comfort when she visited, as Ruby's mother's nerves were no match for the woman.

"I'm afraid we're dining with the Havershams tonight," Violet said. "I should much rather be here when this clock-obsessed houseguest shows up. Bruce Haversham has taken to staring at me."

"Bruce Haversham is but fifteen years old."

"Exactly. And believe me, he is not staring at my captivating eyes."

Lydia gave her a commiserating look.

"Perhaps I can join you tomorrow, or Friday," Violet said. "I'll have to clear it with Mama."

"Come Friday. The Piedmonts will be here, and I won't feel so set upon if I have you by my side."

"Sir Lawrence tends to make everyone feel set upon. Friday it is."

"Well," Florrie said, "I'm here for you this evening. If anything, I'm curious to see our ever-austere Andrew as a 'chum.'"

Lydia breathed a sigh of relief. "Thank you, Florrie. I'll speak to Mrs. Parks. I don't know why I didn't think of it before."

"Because you buried your nose in a book as you always do when you're avoiding something." Violet smiled warmly.

Lydia shrugged. "You know me too well. As a matter of fact"—she glanced around the room—"you *all* likely know me too well. I've no upper hand with any of you." She grinned, and her friends returned it. How she adored these Wendy-birds. "Now, back to the meeting. Violet? Anything more?"

Violet moved on with her notes. "Next. Ruby was asked to give her usual report on anything useful she'd learned from her plethora of brothers. We discussed how the scent of rose water made Cyril's nose burn and lavender gave Oscar a headache, but both men agreed that orange blossom or a vanilla scent was pleasant. A bothersome scent seemed to play an important factor in whether or not they pursued the lady, no matter her beauty. It was agreed that we would think on the matter and consider our own selections of scents."

"If you ask me," Florrie said, "I daresay it's different for every man—what fragrances attract him. Why would they make a lavender scent if it drove all men to a headache?"

"Perhaps," Lydia said dryly, "they make it for women because women *like* it."

Florrie sighed. "You say that because you often wear lavender."

"Briarwall boasts an entire lavender field, Florrie. It would be treason not to wear it sometimes. And I *like* it. What a relief I'm not vying for Oscar Burke's attentions. No offense, dear Ruby."

"None taken."

"I wear lily of the valley," Florrie declared. "I'm told it suits me."

Lydia turned to her. "It does. But would you wear it if it drove a man who interested you to a headache?"

Florrie opened her mouth to respond but paused.

"I think," Ruby said quietly, "the scent is a powerful thing." Ruby seldom spoke, but when she did, the whole room listened. "At times, when Cyril, Oscar, and George are readying themselves to go out, after the shave soap and the tonic and the pomade and the cologne, I'm rather reminded of peacocks. They are off to strut and *waft* and display the feathers God—or Harrod's—granted them, and whatever females are drawn to that display are the women they consider pursuing."

Violet leaned forward. "You're saying they choose the allurements they wish to use for *themselves* and simply wait for the women who are attracted to those particular allurements?"

"More or less. Not one of them are married yet, though."

"What a novel idea," Lydia said with a smirk. "Having the audacity to choose what one finds personally comfortable and attractive and *then* waiting for the opposite sex to come to you. If that's the trend, you'll find me in breeches and rolling in cedar branches."

Violet snorted. "The foxes would adore you."

"Wouldn't that be lovely?" Lydia said, grinning. "Foxes and hedgehogs to do my bidding."

Ruby nodded with her own giggle.

"Shall we put it to the test?" Florrie asked with a look of mischief that rivaled Peter Pan's.

Violet, always the competitive one, squared her shoulders. "What do you propose?"

"I propose I take you all to Floris in London as soon as we can manage. There, we have you personally suited to a perfume, and then . . . we simply *waft*. And see what happens." She beamed.

To Lydia's surprise, each member of the League leaned forward, eyes alight with interest.

"You can't be serious," Lydia said.

Florrie turned to her, brow raised. "What are you afraid of? That the wrong man will come calling? Or the right one will?"

Violet leaned back and shrugged. "Seize the opportunity to fly, Wendy-bird."

Lydia found herself nodding. What could it hurt? Anyway, a trip to London would get her out of the manor and away from playing hostess for an entire day. "Well then." She lifted her teacup. "To London."

The others lifted their cups. "To London."

"And to peacocks," Florrie said, smiling impishly. "And their *feathers*."

The room filled with laughter.

CHAPTER 2

Spencer Hayes wasn't new to railway cars or stations or the miles in between. Yet his pulse still quickened as the brakes labored to slow the beast of an engine. After the train entered Paddington Station, he folded up the paper he'd been reading and eyed the crowded platform.

As he did, he caught the gaze of the young woman sitting across from him, the one who'd stared at him throughout the trip from Birmingham. Finally having his attention, she smiled prettily. He adjusted his derby lower on his brow and nodded politely, then grabbed his travel case from beneath his seat and rose, making his way to the nearest exit and feeling like a cad. What was wrong with him that he couldn't even make conversation with—let alone smile at—a pretty woman?

The train came to a stop, and Spencer allowed the cacophony of whistles, the hiss of steam, the shouts of porters colliding with shouts of disembarking passengers and their awaiting welcomes, and the barks of cab drivers to possible fares to muffle his discomfort over the woman on the train. He stepped off the train and made his way to a small leather trunk set on the platform with other passengers' luggage. He wrapped his hand around the familiar handle and headed out from the massive arched station toward the cabs, the horses, and the swish and step of a thousand people.

Before exiting the station entirely, he turned and looked back at the machinery that had brought him here, the big black cylindrical steam engine above wheels and pistons, the coal car behind— the mechanics of the thing pinging around in his head. How long would it be before the diesel engines ran this line? Not long, likely. Still, he admired the iron horse. It had brought him here, one step nearer his future.

Spencer's jaw tightened. So many steps. Just months ago, he'd stepped onto a ship to America in search of the education Oxford could not give him. Now, he was home, having learned more than he'd intended. He took a deep breath and let it out, then turned away from the train and the crowd and made his way to the streets beyond.

He reached Westbourne Terrace and strolled past the few motorcars waiting there, admiring the line and curve of each.

"Hayes! Spencer Hayes!"

At the sound of his name, he looked to his right and found a familiar face. "Wooding, you old man."

Andrew Wooding grinned, reminding Spencer of the schoolboy he'd once played cricket with, and shook his hand.

"How are you?" Andrew said. "It's been years. Good of you to meet me here. Worked out perfectly with the appointment with my solicitor. Come, let's get your things in the carriage and leave this smog of a city." He took Spencer's trunk and motioned him to follow without waiting for answers. He hadn't changed there, then.

"I'd think you have a man for that," Spencer said, half-serious.

Andrew glanced back at him. "He's at home, likely eating my lunch."

Spencer chuckled. It felt good to laugh. Still, the tightly wound coil inside him wouldn't relax yet. Andrew approached a double brougham and two matched bays. Beautiful horses. Beautiful carriage. But not a motorcar.

"Not a Daimler man, eh, Wooding? No TK limousine?"

Andrew heaved Spencer's trunk into the enclosed plush passenger cabin and offered to do the same with the travel case. He smirked. "I'll leave the Daimlers to His Royal Highness."

Spencer surrendered his case, and the luggage and carriage door were secured. Both men hopped up front to the driving seat.

To Spencer's surprise, Andrew pursued the subject as he took up the reins and urged the carriage forward. "I've a Singer at home. A solid tourer. Nothing splashy, but my steward suggested it would be good to have on hand if needed."

Spencer nodded, listening to what his old friend was not saying. "Excellent idea."

"You can have a go at it while you're here."

"You're certain? I have to admit, I'd enjoy that."

"Consider it at your disposal. I'll let Warren know. He's my stableman, but he's taken to the garage as well. You should get on swimmingly."

Spencer paused, deciding to wait to accept the offer of the motorcar until *after* they'd conducted their business, and only if it went well.

"Do you have any business in London before we get a move on?" Andrew asked before the next crossing.

"No."

"Good." He turned the carriage west. "I'd cut through Hyde Park, but the timing is abysmal for a day like today. Nothing but phaetons, bicycles, and suffragettes. You don't mind the detour, do you?"

"Not at all. Those bicyclists with their sashes and placards—and the chanting . . ." He threw his gaze heavenward.

Andrew laughed, shaking his head.

Both men grew quiet as Andrew focused on maneuvering the carriage away from the hub of the station.

Andrew cleared his throat. "Spencer, I know you've come here with a business proposition, and you know I'm open to hearing it. But I want you to understand, no matter what, it's good to see you, and I'm sorry it's been so long. Too long. How is your family, might I ask?"

Spencer shifted in his seat, his old friend's words a mixed bag of relief and unease. "Nell is a secretary for a medical practice in Coventry."

"Little Nell. I remember her pounding away at those typing tests."

He allowed a smile at the thought of his sister, barely three years his junior.

"Is it a good situation for her?"

Spencer nodded. "I believe so." He frowned in thought. "She was to be married, you see. But the chap changed his mind."

"I'm sorry to hear that."

"I think taking the job in Coventry—even though it's farther from Mother—has been good for her. I *hope* it's good for her. There was no changing her mind. She's a woman of five-and-twenty, and I've never seen my sister so shattered from a broken heart, and so determined to make a new start." Yes, he was immensely proud of her.

Andrew frowned.

"I apologize," Spencer said. "I've shared too much."

"No. I'm glad you did. I feel neglectful for not having kept in touch with you through the years. What has it been—five, six years?"

Spencer nodded. Life had a way of skipping over time between distant friends. Like a stone on a pond. "Six, if you can believe it." He and Andrew had kept in touch for a year after the elder had graduated Oxford. But then things had gotten . . . complicated.

"I'm sorry for your sister's disappointments. But I'm glad she's thriving."

"As am I."

"And your parents?"

Spencer swallowed, smoothing the furrow between his brows with his thumb. "Mother is well. Still in Saltley." He couldn't help the upward turn of his mouth. "Still a force to be reckoned with."

Andrew smiled knowingly.

Spencer's mother was the reason Spencer had applied to Eton and—if he was honest—that he had been accepted. She'd absolutely approved of Andrew Wooding's friendship and, despite the disparity in the boys' stations, made Andrew welcome at their modest home whenever possible without apology or simpering. She simply made the best of everything and knew she had the talent and mind to do so, and she believed the same of her children. Ironically, Spencer had never felt shame in what his family lacked until he'd been sent to school. Unfortunately, he hadn't borne the differences as well as his mother had.

But when young Andrew Wooding, gentleman-heir to Briarwall Manor, visited for the odd weekend, he was simply Andrew, Spencer was simply Spencer, and the boys filled their time with the usual bouts of ignoring their studies, practicing cricket, eating whatever concoction Mother had baked until it was gone, and playing chess, badminton, or whatever else they could conjure up in Ward End without getting into too much trouble.

"And your father? How is ol' William Hayes these days?"

This time, Spencer's frown could not be smoothed away. "I hope he is at peace," he answered quietly. He met Andrew's questioning expression. "He died last year. Failure of the heart." That was one way of putting it. Failure was, in Spencer's mind, precisely what had killed his father.

"I'd no idea."

"We kept close to ourselves for a time."

Andrew grew quiet. "My condolences. To be honest, and with all respect, I pictured your father retired after some brilliant scheme of his came through."

Spencer chuckled, the sound tinny in his ears. He simply nodded, swallowing the truth. Now was not the time. "That is a generous thought." Too generous. "Thank you."

"Did you take over the livery, then?"

"No." Hayes Livery and Carriage had been lost. "It is now called Johnson Livery and Carriage. And I wish Mr. Johnson the best of luck with it." He spoke with sincerity, but his words earned a dubious look from Andrew.

"I recall your studies taking you in that direction—taking over for your father's booming business."

Spencer nodded, staring ahead as the city thinned out. Paddington was already on the outskirts of London, and he knew the Wooding manor house to be south, in the wooded foothills of Surrey.

"That was the original plan, yes. But things change. Sometimes very quickly."

Out of the corner of his eye, he saw Andrew nod. "That, I understand."

"I know you do. It's one of the reasons I sought you out." Spencer paused. He didn't want to talk business now. He sat back in his seat, glancing around, needing to change the subject. "Do you come to London often?"

Andrew's expression brightened. "As little as possible." He tipped his head toward Spencer, allowing the change of subject, for which Spencer was grateful. "What we can't find in Albury, we can in Guilford. Our social circle is small, but I've a good club. Do you play tennis?"

"Very poorly."

He barked a laugh. "Good. I've arranged for a game the day after tomorrow. Oscar Burke and Sir Lawrence Piedmont will be joining us. You remember Piedmont, don't you?"

"Yes," Spencer answered out of the side of his mouth. He remembered young Lawrence Piedmont as an arrogant, patronizing twit.

Andrew chuckled as if he'd read Spencer's thoughts. "Ah yes, I'd forgotten how well you two got along. I assure you, the man has improved with age and his time spent in South Africa."

Spencer straightened. "The Boer War?" His imagination strained to picture Piedmont as a soldier.

Andrew nodded. "He and Oscar are good chaps. I hope you don't mind."

"And if I did?" Spencer asked good-naturedly.

Andrew shrugged, laughing.

Spencer shook his head. "You haven't changed a bit, have you?"

"If you mean I'm still devilishly handsome, somewhat conceited, and exceptionally focused, then no. Not a bit."

Spencer joined in his laughter.

"I imagine you're hungry," Andrew offered as they left the city behind.

"Starving, as a matter of fact." He'd had coffee that morning and a packet of biscuits on the train.

"I have a basket Lydia insisted Cook put together for us, just there under the seat."

Spencer looked beneath his seat to find a willow picnic basket. He pulled it up and opened the lid. Thick sandwiches, a thermos, and two large wedges of cake—carrot from the look of it—with creamy frosting. His stomach rumbled. "Ah, yes, your sister. Bless her. How is she? Still hiding behind curtains?" He reached for a sandwich and offered it to Andrew.

Andrew shook his head, taking the sandwich. "How I wish that were true," he muttered.

Spencer paused in unwrapping a sandwich for himself. The last time he'd seen Lydia Wooding, she'd been generously sprinkled with freshly mown grass and fallen apple blossoms, a smear of mud on her clothes. It had been a brief spectacle, as she was being chased upstairs by her scolding governess. "I remember her as excessively shy and always escaping out of doors."

"That's the one."

"She was your only thought when you learned—" He paused, uncertain how welcome the memory was of that time immediately following his parents' death.

"Yes. She's still one of my top priorities." Andrew gracefully diffused Spencer's concern. "Just above the running of Briarwall. She's nervous, you know? About playing hostess."

"I'll be sure to be the model guest. We'll slide down the bannister for dinner, correct?"

Andrew grinned. "Knowing Lydia, she'd most likely lead the way." He chuckled. "She'd murder me if she knew I'd told you that."

"I promise to act surprised."

Both men laughed.

After several miles of pleasant quiet between the two men, and polishing off the last of the hearty lunch, Spencer's nerves had uncoiled a great deal. The haze and crowds of the city had given way to rolling green pastures, grand estates, rustic villages, and country houses. It had recently rained, but that only brightened the newly greened trees and verges, the turned earth ready for planting. The hills of Surrey rose around them, clumped with woods.

"This is a sight," Spencer murmured. Birmingham was a center of engineering and industry. The city had overcome much of its workhouse-slum reputation and overcrowded terraced housing problems, but it was still a large, factory-powered engine, far from the serenity on display before him.

"That it is," Andrew said. "No matter how often I leave, no matter how pleasant a trip I've had, it's still a relief to return to Surrey."

"How is your humble estate, then?"

Andrew's features tightened. "'Tis a rambling old farm with an ancient manor and a fair wood," he growled, sounding more like a tenant than a landlord. He shrugged and faced Spencer, his expression clearing. "The work is extensive and never-ending. Gads, I hate it." He sighed. "And I love it."

"Depending on the day?" Spencer asked.

"Depending on the hour."

Spencer tsked. "Poor old man." He hesitated but decided he should know the answer to his next question. "Is there a *Mrs.* Wooding, or somebody thereabouts I should know of before we arrive?"

Andrew was already shaking his head. "No. And I ask you not to bring it up in front of Lydia. The girl hounds me to no end. When she thinks I would have time to court a woman, I cannot fathom. I'll marry when I'm good and ready. Some time when I don't have my head stuck in ledgers or soil that needs amending, or attending to animal stalls and woods that need managing."

"You stick your head in the soil? Perhaps you're right in putting off any marriage business. You've some strange work habits, friend."

Andrew socked him in the arm.

Spencer grimaced, suppressing laughter. "That wasn't very genteel of you."

"I slip in and out of gentility these days. For my next demonstration, I'll ask you outright. Do you have a girl?"

Spencer deserved that. The crushing hollow in his chest had faded, replaced by a numbness he now welcomed. "No, and no thank you. I've climbed that hill." And been tossed off it. "I've more important things to focus on."

One thing, actually: securing the future his father had destroyed in one terrible gamble.

Spencer Hayes was no fool for love. Not anymore.

CHAPTER 3

Lydia entered the sitting room where Florrie watched the front drive from a tall window, Nibs in her arms. The sight was both charming and unnerving, as it meant their company would soon be arriving. Still, she pushed forward.

"Will Nibs be joining us for dinner, then?" she asked.

Florrie turned. "Of course not. Ralston is taking him back to the kitchen while we dine. I've promised him a walk after."

"Who, Ralston?" Lydia said, crooking her brow. "How thoughtful."

Florrie tsked. "No, *Nibs*. Though Ralston is welcome should he need the air."

Lydia smiled and approached the window. "It's going to rain."

"Shocking."

Lydia muffled a laugh, then drew in a deep breath and released it. It did little to calm her nerves.

"You've nothing to fear, you know," Florrie said. "You're a capable woman and a natural friend to everyone."

"Who says I'm afraid?" Lydia asked.

"You're clenching your hands together as if awaiting eternal judgment."

Lydia let go of her hands. "Why do these things bother me so? I like people. I just . . . don't like *rules*."

"Bothersome things, really."

"You seem to adore them."

"I suppose I do to some extent." She grinned. "Until I don't."

Lydia shook her head. Where Florrie was known to sometimes bend the rules or make them work in her favor, Lydia's head spun attempting to recall them all. She liked ideas that *made sense*. And so many social expectations did not. "I'm glad you're here."

"As am I." The sound of a carriage drew Florrie's attention back to the window. "Here they are."

Lydia watched as the carriage rolled to a stop, her brother in the driver's seat instead of inside the carriage. She wasn't the only odd member of this family. "Should we be gawking through the window like this?" she asked, peering to catch a glimpse of their guest.

"We cannot gawk through the wall, can we?" Florrie glanced down and swatted at Lydia's hands, once again twisted in a death grip.

Andrew exited the driving seat side nearest the house, and their guest hopped down on the other side, so Lydia could not get a good look.

"I don't even know why I'm nervous. He's a knock-kneed bird-watcher, for all I know."

"You like birds."

"To eat."

Florrie took her hand and turned her away from the window. "What he's like does not matter. What matters is who he is to your brother and whether he feels welcome in your home. You only need focus on your responsibilities as hostess of Briarwall. Do that well, and the rest is up to Andrew. He is Andrew's guest, after all."

"Yes. Of course. You're right." Lydia often looked to Florrie for guidance in the ways of society.

Her own parents had died when she was six years of age and Andrew had been fourteen. As no living relatives were found, a neighbor, Mr. Markham Piedmont, had been named their guardian until Andrew was of age.

The two children had continued to live at Briarwall, while the Piedmonts provided them with nannies and servants to see to their care, tutors to provide education, and a steward to manage the estate. Mr. Piedmont had been kind, and visited more frequently than his wife did, but he was never truly the "father figure" the children needed.

As for Mrs. Piedmont, she was careful to keep a line between charity and familial connection with the Wooding siblings, preferring instead to dote on her only son.

After Mr. Piedmont's death, the only connections kept alive between the two families were a regular monthly dinner at Briarwall and Andrew's occasional social interactions with Lawrence Piedmont, who had grown up to be knighted during the Boer Wars. With some business of discovered African diamonds, he'd purchased his way out of service and returned home to his mother when word of his father's untimely death reached him.

All of which was to say that Lydia—an orphan—leaned on any female guidance she could procure. The Piedmonts had provided her with a nanny who had since passed on, a governess until she was eighteen, and a lady's maid. Mrs. Parks, their housekeeper, had been with them since before their parents died.

But Florrie had learned the skills of society from her mother, and Mrs. Janes held balls at Grantmore Hill, great dinners, and weeks-long house parties. Though the Janeses were not among the peerage, they were historically genteel, and more importantly, "wealthier than Pharaoh"—as Violet so delicately put it. If Florrie had advice to give on hosting one potentially gangly ornithologist clockmaker, Lydia listened.

"Oh pooh, we've missed him," Florrie said, once again looking out the window.

At the rumbling sound of gentlemen's voices approaching, the girls turned and Nibs barked.

"Hush, Nibs." Florrie kissed her dog's head.

Lydia smoothed the black eyelash-lace overlay against her rose-colored silk gown and recentered the garnet-and-marcasite necklace that had been her mother's, tapping it in place before clasping her hands behind her.

Ralston, the butler, appeared at the sitting room doors. "Mr. Wooding and Mr. Hayes, miss."

Andrew entered, looking cheery, which was the first thing to strike Lydia as odd. Her brother more often appeared pensive. Overly concerned was another favorite of his. The second thing was the unconventionally attractive man following him. He glanced at the portraits on the wall with a faraway smile beneath a conservative blond mustache.

Florrie leaned in. "Yes, I see what you mean," she murmured. "All that . . . tall hair."

"Hush."

Lydia swallowed, blinking so as not to stare. His hair was no longer as tall as she remembered, but cut closely on the sides with longer dark blond waves on top, pushed back. But more than that, as he turned their way, she noted his clear hazel eyes. Intelligent, observant eyes under dark-blond brows.

"He could wind my clock anytime," Florrie murmured appreciatively.

Lydia shot her friend a silencing look.

Florrie grinned.

"Lydia."

Lydia jumped, throwing her shoulders back.

Andrew looked at her curiously as he approached. He leaned forward and kissed her cheek in greeting. "At ease," he said quietly.

She let out a breath, narrowing her gaze at him.

He backed away, a rare, carefree smile on his face. He nodded a greeting at Florrie. "Miss Janes, you are still here, I see."

"Quite observant of you, Mr. Wooding. Thank you for assessing my whereabouts," Florrie said with a fluttering blink of her lashes. "Before your pronouncement, I'd no idea where I was."

Her sarcasm never fazed him. "Happy to be of service. Will you be joining us for dinner?"

"I will be."

"Glad to hear it. Ladies, I'd like you to meet Mr. Spencer Hayes. Spencer? My little sister, Lydia."

Lydia cringed at the diminutive introduction as their guest's eyes flitted briefly between her and Andrew.

He stepped forward and bowed. "Miss Wooding, a pleasure."

"Mr. Hayes," she said, regaining her breath. "I'm not certain you remember, but we've met before."

His eyes flickered quickly over her person. "Yes. It was a long time ago."

"A very long time ago. I believe the first time you came to

Briarwall, I was still hiding from Nanny, hoping not to have to eat my carrots."

A smile waited in his eyes, then he blinked and it was gone. "And the last time I visited—"

"I was still hiding from the carrots." She grinned. She'd been on the verge of twelve then, and painfully shy.

Andrew cleared his throat and gave her a warning look she didn't understand.

Mr. Hayes again darted a glance between her and her brother. "I'll make a note not to offer you any carrots, Miss Wooding."

She threw Andrew a triumphant look. "Thank you."

"It was gracious of your brother to invite me here. I hope I haven't inconvenienced you."

She had no recollection of what Mr. Hayes's voice had sounded like the last time he'd visited Briarwall, but she was sure she would've recalled such a deep timbre. His faint Birmingham accent only added to her curiosity. Did he hide it on purpose?

"Not at all. We're delighted to have you."

Florrie's elbow into her arm jolted her.

"Oh. This is Miss Florrie Janes, a very dear friend of mine. And, er, Nibs."

"Mr. Hayes, welcome to Surrey." Florrie extended her hand, and Mr. Hayes took it with a gentle squeeze and nod of his head.

Why hadn't Lydia remembered to do that?

"How do you do?" he said, releasing her hand. He crooked his finger under the dog's chin in a brief scratch. "Pleasure to meet you, Nibs."

Florrie stroked Nibs's head. "I understand you're from Birmingham."

"Yes. Saltley."

"How exciting," Florrie said. "I recall my father telling me the city had gone from an industrial cesspool to one of the best governed districts in the world."

Mr. Hayes cleared his throat. "As hesitant as I am to admit I hail from a former *cesspool*"—he glanced at Lydia as Andrew chuckled—"your father is correct. It is much improved even since my mother was a child."

"I should like to see it sometime, to experience it for myself," Florrie said. "I am always interested in improvements."

He hesitated, as if Birmingham was a well-guarded secret. "If you should ever like a tour, Miss Janes, I'm sure I could arrange it." He bowed.

Florrie beamed as if she'd been granted an unexpected queendom. Lydia wondered if Florrie had truly wished to see Birmingham ever in her whole life.

Lydia tipped her head. "Do you find Briarwall much changed, Mr. Hayes?"

He met her gaze. He had a longish face, a straight nose, and a square chin. And full lips. She pulled her gaze quickly from such a beautiful mouth.

"I've only just arrived, but for the most part, I find it unchanged."

"And what is it you find different?" she asked.

He held her gaze a moment longer, then blinked and looked around the room. "Well, for one, I recall a large hunting scene over the fireplace, and now it is this lovely portrait. Your parents, correct?"

She glanced at the portrait and back to him. "Yes. You have an astonishing memory." She'd not thought of the hunting painting for ages.

"Your parents had quite an impact on me during the few occasions I was able to visit."

"I'm glad to hear it. The few memories I have of them are happy ones." She wondered if it would be socially acceptable for her to ask Mr. Hayes to share some of his memories during his stay.

"I was terribly sorry to learn of your loss," he said.

"Thank you. Andrew has told me what your friendship meant to him."

He flickered a glance at Andrew, who gave a short nod. "I'm glad to hear it."

Ralston appeared. "Dinner is nearly ready, sir."

Andrew nodded and rubbed his hands together. "Well. Now that we all know each other, I'll show Mr. Hayes to his room so he can get settled. We'll be down shortly."

The girls watched the gentlemen leave and waited until the sound of footsteps in the corridor faded.

Lydia faced Florrie, who was just as wide-eyed. Together, they broke into a hushed flurry of speaking over one another.

"I thought you said he—"

"He's changed so much I—"

"I'd never have guessed he was from—"

"When he spoke I just about—"

Ralston cleared his throat, and the girls fell silent, quickly glancing at the butler.

Florrie led Lydia to the sofa and pulled her down next to her.

"What do you think of your ornithologist clockmaker now?" she whispered.

"He is not *my* ornithologist clockmaker."

"You know what I mean. He is handsome, though I wouldn't

put him in the same class as Andrew." She set Nibs down on the rug.

"*Nobody* is in the same class as Andrew," Lydia said with a sigh. She paused. "He was very . . . intent. He did not smile, did you notice? It was almost there, and then it wasn't. And did you notice his accent? I expected more *Brummie* and less London."

"Why do you think I got him talking? He is likely upper class. You simply must find out more about your houseguest. And if you don't, I will."

"Have at it," Lydia said.

Florrie only pursed her lips.

Lydia conceded. "He does have extraordinary eyes, doesn't he? I did not remember that from before."

"Yes, and you did well, overcoming that abysmal introduction of Andrew's. For such a sensible man, he can be quite oblivious."

"You noticed, did you? I felt all of twelve years old. And what was with all that cheerfulness? I hardly recognized my own brother."

"Never mind him." Florrie grabbed Lydia's hands. "I'm glad I stayed for dinner. This will be far more interesting than I'd hoped."

"You have that look."

"What look?"

Florrie had round, sky-blue eyes, and she knew how to wield them.

Lydia pulled her hands away. "That look that always comes before trouble."

Florrie batted her eyes with all the innocence of a lagoon mermaid. "I am simply here to support you as hostess."

Lydia narrowed her gaze at her friend, then let it go. "Thank you." She paused. "I should like to see Mr. Hayes smile, though."

Florrie gasped in delight. "Let's make it our mark for the evening."

"What, to make Mr. Hayes smile?"

"Yes. It is your duty. As his hostess." She grinned.

Lydia frowned, unsure. "Perhaps the man has good reason not to smile. Perhaps he's shy. Or has horrible teeth."

Florrie brushed that away. She leaned forward, brows high. "Courtesy of the Wendy League?"

She couldn't argue with that. "Oh, very well."

Florrie let out a yip of delight.

What would the harm be in attempting to make a man smile? As Florrie had said, Lydia made friends easily. Surely, she could find something to set Mr. Hayes at ease. Perhaps she could ask him about clocks. Or birds.

She remembered the almost wistful way he'd gazed at the portrait above the fireplace, his handsome profile a testament to how much time had gone by since he had last been here in her home. Her mouth curved upward in amusement.

"What are you thinking?" Florrie asked.

"I'm thinking about time." Lydia sighed.

"What about it?"

Lydia's brow rose. "It does extraordinary things."

"For example?"

She shook her head slowly. "Mr. Hayes is no longer all elbows."

The girls broke into giggles until Ralston cleared his throat again.

"May I get you a lozenge, Ralston?" Florrie asked as she dug into her little bag.

Lydia snorted, and Ralston gazed at the ceiling and sighed.

Poor, long-suffering butler.

Spencer slid his arms into a dinner jacket and brushed away a speck of lint on the sleeve. The jacket was new, as were the starched collar and cuffs. He rarely dressed for dinner at home, but he'd known the tradition would still stand at Briarwall. The vest was older but would do. He needed to exude security. Confidence. Trust.

He glanced in the mirror, grimaced, and straightened his tie. If only he felt as confident as he looked.

Andrew Wooding had always had confidence in spades, and Spencer had learned the mannerisms quickly from his friend. As boys, he'd believed that Andrew's self-assurance came from being a year older, and Spencer simply had to reach that age the following year to achieve the same confidence. What a naïve boy he'd been.

He took a deep breath and lifted his chin. At twenty-seven, was he any less naïve?

Briarwall Manor leaned on the smaller side of Surrey estates, but it was elegant in its simplicity. A pale-gold brick edifice with white trim and moldings sat amidst rolling Surrey hills with climbing roses and wisteria vines clambering up its walls as if the earth were saying, "Stay." Once upon a time, it had been a country home of an earl who'd had to sell off his holdings one by one. Which is how it had come to Andrew Wooding's great-grandfather, then to his grandfather, then to his father, then, much too soon after that, to Andrew.

No matter when Spencer had come to visit Briarwall, he had always been given this guestroom. The handsome mahogany furnishings in Greek lines were familiar and comforting. Deep blue draperies framed a wide window overlooking a verdant countryside—the sun lingering on the horizon below heavy clouds.

He crossed to the window and opened it. It still squeaked. Fresh, cool air brushed past him. Light rain plunked a rhythm on the eaves and leaves of the nearby walnut tree, which was much taller than he remembered it being. Distant brass rain chimes sounded from the unseen garden.

He leaned forward, almost able to picture two young men chasing the family dog—a collie named Champ—who raced them happily to the pond and always won. Spencer's few days spent at Briarwall were filled with morning farm chores, studying from any of the academic volumes from the library that caught his eye, roaming the estate to swim or to fish, or enduring another futile riding lesson, care of Andrew. Whereas Spencer's father had sent him away to learn how to better manage his family's future, Mr. Wooding—and then his steward—had made sure Andrew learned the ins and outs of farming firsthand. Time at Briarwall was full, and Spencer had always hit his mattress hard at the end of the day. Tired, yes, but also inspired.

Was it any wonder confidence came so naturally to young Andrew Wooding? Briarwall had been a refuge from both the social pressures of school and the boom and hiss of Spencer's life in Saltley.

Unbidden, Spencer's father's words came to him in his deep Brummie accent. "Don't ever let 'em see you weak. Sure, you'll feel it, you will. Life 'as a way of makin' a man feel it now and again. But shed it off, like a downpour on a duck. You'll get by just fine."

The irony of those words coming from his father at that moment dampened any warm feelings of the memory. His father's actions had become the downpour, and Spencer had awfully few feathers.

But the man had been right about weakness.

Spencer blinked at the view before him. Both of those boys had learned that lesson. Shed off weakness, or you drown.

A structure on the Brairwall grounds caught his eye, drawing him from his thoughts and sparking another distant memory. He'd forgotten about the "temple"—a covered colonnade fashioned after the Greek Temple of Concordia. Mr. Wooding had made the boys write a paper on the history of that temple, including calculating the scale by which the temple at Briarwall had been reduced and ciphering how many clay tiles were used on the roofing. But that was not Spencer's only memory connected to that building.

One summer day, Spencer had retreated to the temple with a book of Leonardo da Vinci's inventions, only to be tempted into a game of hide-and-seek with Andrew's little sister, who would run from column to column and peer shyly around the climbing wisteria as Spencer pretended to read. As soon as Spencer would look her way, the girl would gasp and run to another column with a hushed giggle. This had continued until the governess had called her name from the green, and she'd gone running.

Spencer found himself smiling, shaking his head. "Lydia Wooding," he said, unsure if he'd even known the girl's name at that point, it being his first visit and Andrew not being particularly interested in his "baby sister" at the time.

He compared that vague memory of a girl about four years of age with light brown hair in thick ringlets and a bow the size of her head to the young woman he'd just met downstairs. From the way Andrew spoke of his sister, Spencer had half-expected a youth in plaits and a sailor dress peering around the corners at him. Not the brown-eyed beauty in the pale rose-and-black gown looking him directly in the eye and asking—of all things—what had changed most since his last visit. When, at that moment, the only answer he could think of was—her.

He was ready to throttle Andrew, who obviously had no idea that his little sister had grown up quite spectacularly. Spencer would have appreciated some kind of warning that he would be staying with a beautiful young woman of age. He might've made other arrangements.

He did the math. If Spencer had been eleven years of age upon that first visit to Briarwall, and he guessed Lydia had been four—that would make her approximately twenty years old now.

He closed his eyes and groaned. No. He wouldn't do that again. He wouldn't allow his foolish little thoughts, calculations, and hopes to work their way into his head when he felt a certain attraction to a woman. He would not—did not—feel an attraction to Lydia Wooding. It was simply admiration. Nostalgia. Part of the warm feelings of returning to Briarwall after all these years.

It was almost laughable, giving the girl—Andrew's little sister, of all people—any more thought than that of respect as his hostess.

Spencer paused. No, it was not a laughing matter, because Spencer was here with a business proposal for Andrew. That proposal meant everything to Spencer, and he would not disrespect Andrew or his family or allow himself to be distracted from his purpose.

He shook his head. The last time he'd allowed certain emotions to become entwined in business had proved disastrous. Matters of the heart, he'd learned, had no place in his endeavor to secure a stable future for his mother and sister.

With that conviction, he closed the window and made his way down to dinner.

Upon entering the sitting room, Andrew, Miss Wooding, and Miss Janes stood as if choreographed.

Spencer straightened. "I hope I didn't keep you waiting too long." Truthfully, he was relieved Andrew had arrived first to join the ladies.

"Not at all," Andrew said.

"My brother arrived only moments before you, Mr. Hayes. I hope you found everything to your liking. Andrew told me you were fond of the blue room."

"Yes, thank you. I could almost imagine being on school holiday again."

Miss Wooding smiled. "I hope that's a good thing."

"As far as it concerns Briarwall, yes, it is."

Miss Janes stood nearest him, and the siblings stood in front of the hearth, below the portrait of their parents. In the low evening light, he was struck by the similarities and differences in their appearances. While Andrew favored the Scandinavian heritage—blue eyes and light hair—of his mother, and Miss Wooding favored her father's darker complexion, they were both tall and slender—and wearing the same expression of curious patience as were the people in the painting.

"If you'll excuse me. I was just considering the lovely family portrait you've unintentionally created." He gestured to the painting behind them, and they turned.

"Oh yes," Miss Janes said, stepping next to him. "I see what you mean."

While Andrew studied the painting, Miss Wooding turned immediately back to Spencer, her face lit with what appeared to be delight.

It was quite . . . gratifying.

"What an artistic eye you have, Mr. Hayes. Andrew commissioned the likeness from a photograph my parents had taken a few months before they passed. I remember so little of them. I was six when they died, you know. You'd think they'd be clearer in my memory, but"—she gazed up at the portrait—"I somehow feel like they know me when I study this painting."

Her brother tipped his head. "Do you? I had no idea you struggled to remember them."

Miss Janes leaned toward Spencer and dropped her voice. "Can he be surprised? He practically forbids anyone to speak of them."

Spencer opened his mouth to question the remark, but she shifted her gaze as the butler entered and nodded to Lydia.

She took a quick breath, then faced them all, clasping her hands. "Shall we go into dinner?"

Andrew held his arm out for Miss Janes. In turn, Spencer offered to escort Miss Wooding, who seemed relieved to take his arm.

As they entered the dining room, Miss Janes spoke to him over her shoulder.

"Is that *cedarwood* I detect, Mr. Hayes?"

He paused in the act of pulling out Miss Wooding's chair, as did Miss Wooding pause in the act of sitting. Her cheeks were fast turning rosy.

He cleared his throat. "Why, yes. My aftershave tonic." He pushed in the chair as Miss Wooding sat, feeling his own face warm at the somewhat intimate observation.

"Such a masculine scent. Wouldn't you say, Lydia? Reminds one of a walk in the woods."

Miss Wooding scrutinized her friend. "Yes. Considering the woods are where one would most likely find a cedar."

"Mm, and foxes and hedgehogs as well."

Miss Wooding pressed her lips in a thin line, giving Miss Janes a most pointed and perplexing look. Spencer didn't know whether to laugh or be concerned for Miss Janes.

He sat down and attempted to focus on a dish of cream of asparagus soup, but Miss Janes turned her large blue eyes his way. "We were discussing Beatrix Potter in our literary club this morning, Mr. Hayes."

Next to him, Miss Wooding muffled a sudden cough with her napkin.

Miss Janes paid her no mind. "Are you familiar with her children's stories?"

He breathed an internal sigh of relief for Miss Janes, her foxes, and hedgehogs. "Yes. Delightful illustrations." He picked up his spoon.

"Quite. I made the observation that Peter Rabbit was a darling little bunny, in spite of his mischief, and Lydia countered that he was a bothersome creature, and she sided with Mr. McGregor."

He turned to find Miss Wooding staring round-eyed at her friend. She blinked, her mouth opening and closing, then turned her gaze on him.

"Is that so, Miss Wooding?" he asked.

"I—" she stammered.

"I would have to agree with my sister," Andrew said, halfway through his soup. "Managing a farm, I feel constantly at war with rabbits. Miss Potter's stories are charming and serve their purpose, but any Mr. McGregor worth his pole beans would threaten to put that rascal, Peter, in a pie or a stew or whatever it was." He went back to his soup.

Spencer took advantage of the focus being off him and tasted the soup, which was as delicious as he remembered it being.

"Why, Andrew, I had no idea you read children's stories," Miss Janes cooed. "I would think them beneath your notice."

"It so happens, I enjoyed many stories when I was a child."

She frowned. "You were once a child? I cannot fathom the notion."

He gave her a good-natured scowl. "I keep up with the latest news, Miss Janes. Be it flying machines or women writing of rabbits in jackets."

Andrew and Miss Janes sparred back and forth affably, leaving Spencer to enjoy the rest of his soup.

"And furthermore," Andrew said, resting his spoon across his empty dish, "I think it apropos that the farmer is a Scotsman. Leave it to a Scot to steal a body's clothes and hang them on a scarecrow."

"I suppose you'd rather he put Peter's head on a spike? Or is that too English for a Scot?" Florrie asked, lifting her napkin to daintily dab at the sides of her mouth.

"Oh, *look*, the next course." Miss Wooding seemed overly relieved as the dishes were brought in. "Thank heavens," she murmured, "we are not having rabbit."

Spencer smiled to himself, relieved for her as well.

She turned to him. "Mr. Hayes, Andrew tells me you enjoyed stuffed bream when you visited us last."

"Indeed, I did."

"I understand it was a favorite of my father's as well. I took the opportunity to request it tonight, along with beef tournedos. I hope that pleases you."

"That is very thoughtful of you." He shook his head. "I don't know that I merit such regard."

"Of course you do," Andrew said. He motioned to the serving dish now being held at Spencer's right. "It's not every day one gets to reminisce with old school chums."

Miss Janes chortled and quickly put her napkin to her mouth.

"Are you well, Miss Janes?" Spencer asked her.

She nodded. "I'm quite enjoying myself, actually."

He served himself the savory bread and mushroom-stuffed fish, as tender and aromatic as he remembered. Though Miss Janes's company was a bit perplexing, he was enjoying himself as well. He glanced up mid-bite to find Miss Wooding studying him, her dark brows bent downward.

She immediately cleared her expression and picked up her fork. "Mr. Hayes, how do you feel about clocks?"

He looked around at all three of his dining companions, who watched him, waiting. Miss Janes wore an expectant grin, as if Miss Wooding had asked him if he'd enjoy a holiday in Shanghai. Andrew looked perplexed. Spencer swallowed. "Clocks?"

Miss Wooding nodded, smiling encouragingly. "Is there a particular timepiece you are fascinated with, or perhaps just the inner workings themselves?"

He sat back, considering not only the answer to the rather odd question, but why he'd been asked it with no context or forewarning of the subject. "Uh, I do appreciate clocks. As much as the next person, I suppose." He frowned. "Exploring the inner workings of London's Clock Tower as a boy was fascinating, now that I think on it. I have a pocket watch of my father's, but it is currently in need of repair. Is there . . . is there a favorite clock of yours, Miss Wooding?" He looked to the others for approval of his response.

Miss Janes simply watched, and Andrew merely shrugged and sliced into his beef tournedo.

Spencer eyed the footman coming around with another dish.

Miss Wooding seemed a bit disappointed in his answer. Did she expect him to wax poetic about Archimedes with his gears, pulleys, and counterweights?

"I . . . I have a pearl watch pin that had belonged to my mother," she said. "I wear it all the time, don't I, Florrie? But not to dinner. I fear ruining it. Oh." She shifted in her chair. "Perhaps you remember the mantel clock in the study, though it was kept on a bookshelf and not a mantel. A bronze griffin with his front foot upon—"

"—the timepiece," Spencer finished. "Yes. I do remember." It had captured his attention as a boy. "A very unique piece."

She leaned forward, her eyes alight. "Yes. I believe it's Georgian, though I'm not sure which George. Do you know, Andrew?"

"Third. Egyptian Revival."

"Yes, George the third. Of course."

"And you still have it?" Spencer wondered at this young woman's interest in clocks as he helped himself to the tournedo, the seared beef rounds juicy on their bed of creamed spinach.

"Yes, it's in the study. Oh, but I said that, didn't I?"

Andrew had mentioned his sister was nervous about playing hostess. Perhaps she was only reaching for conversation. About clocks. "You did. I'll have to seek it out while I'm here."

"When I was a little girl, I believed griffins were real because of that clock. I desperately wanted one of my own. I was convinced he'd get along just fine in the stable and would befriend Poppy and Treacle." She laughed, her eyes dancing. "I fancied calling him Frederick. Apparently, that was the most fearsome name I could come up with."

Spencer broke into a smile and laughed along with her.

She paused in her laughter, her expression open, studying

him. She looked to Miss Janes, who let out a small squeal of delight and clapped her hands in a short staccato.

Odd. Yet somehow charming. He cleared his throat. "I have a great-uncle named Frederick. I assure you, fearsome is one of his more prominent qualities."

"Well, Mr. Hayes, I feel both validated and sorry to hear it."

He chuckled and lifted his glass in her direction. "Cheers."

She lifted her glass in return. "To Frederick. Griffin, great-uncle, and clock."

Miss Janes happily lifted her glass and joined them in their ridiculous toast. "But not one and the same."

"So far as we know," Miss Wooding said with a wink.

Spencer was warmed by their shared laughter, letting it course through him before tamping it down once more.

Andrew studied his sister as she sipped her wine. "Had I known the clock brought you such entertainment, Lydia, and you, Miss Janes, I would've displayed it more prominently. As it is, the thing no longer works."

"Is it fixable?" Miss Wooding asked.

Andrew shrugged. "The winding key was lost. Who knows if it would still work if wound?"

Miss Janes gasped. "We should have a search for the key. We could make a game of it."

"Search if you must," Andrew said. "I know Father once inquired of the servants years ago, but no one knew of its whereabouts."

"What say you, Mr. Hayes?" Miss Wooding asked eagerly. "Care for a key hunt?"

It took quite a bit of work for Spencer to look away from a pretty woman so thrilled to be inviting him to, well, anything.

"Lydia," Andrew chided, "kindly allow us to have at least one evening of normalcy before we expose Mr. Hayes to your *unique* brand of entertainment."

Spencer flicked a glance at Andrew, who was still focused on his dinner, then back to Miss Wooding. He watched as the light in her eyes dimmed and the color in her cheeks became blotchy.

She lowered her gaze and offered a small, forced smile of apology. "Of course. Silly of me, anyway."

"Andrew, the search was my idea," Miss Janes said, her eyes still on Lydia, who was fumbling with the napkin on her lap.

Andrew finally looked up from his fork, glancing between the two women.

Spencer cleared his throat. "I should like to try to find the key. If anything, it is an opportunity to reacquaint myself with the home I have such fond memories of."

Miss Wooding peered hesitantly up at him.

"Finding the key would only be a bonus," he added.

"You need not—" Miss Wooding began, albeit timidly.

"*Thank* you, Mr. Hayes," Miss Janes said, speaking over her friend. She turned to Andrew. "And what sort of boredom will you be immersing yourself in while we adventure, Andrew?"

Andrew still watched his sister but pulled himself from whatever commanded his thoughts and focused on Miss Janes. "I was hoping you and my sister would play for us, Miss Janes."

She nodded primly. "How authoritarian of you."

Andrew sighed silently, but deeply. "If you wish a key hunt, we shall key hunt." He turned back to Miss Wooding. "I apologize, Lydia."

She lifted her gaze to her brother and nodded her acceptance.

Later, as they quietly dipped their spoons into a raspberry jam trifle, Spencer caught Miss Wooding's eye and granted her what he hoped was an assuring smile. The corner of her mouth rose a fraction in reply. That was enough for his rebellious pulse to beat a bit faster than he wished it to. She was only Andrew's little sister, he reminded himself. Though it was becoming clearer to him that she did not always relish that claim.

"Mr. Hayes," Miss Janes said, startling him from his thoughts, "tell us your thoughts on birds." She gave a small yelp as though someone had kicked her under the table. Andrew did not seem to notice, and Miss Wooding studied the chandelier.

Perhaps his earlier concern for Miss Janes was not unfounded.

CHAPTER 4

Andrew led them through the corridor with unexpected enthusiasm. "We shall begin in the study, as that is where the clock is. It stands to reason that the key would be kept there as well."

Lydia blinked slowly, willing herself to not roll her eyes at Andrew's sudden interest and command. Still, her sideways glance was caught by Mr. Hayes, who kept his chuckle silent.

Andrew threw open a door and stood aside. "Here we are."

"We know where the study is, Andrew," Lydia sighed, not completely over the way he'd belittled her at dinner. She crossed the room to the brass griffin, nestled on the shelf containing books on Greek mythology. The creature stood about seven inches tall and nine inches wide. The timepiece itself, a round, gold clock beneath the beast's front talon, was a mere three inches across, and, as Andrew had said, was frozen at six past two.

The others joined her, giving the clock more attention than it had garnered in a century.

"It is quite regal, isn't it?" Florrie said.

Lydia nodded. "Seeing it again, it occurs to me that Poppy and Treacle would not have lasted two hours with a griffin in that stable."

"Perhaps not," Andrew said, and she appreciated him not making fun of her childhood fantasy. "I imagine that a half-eagle, half-lion creature might like ponies."

"To eat," Lydia and Mr. Hayes said at the same time. Their eyes met, and she glanced away quickly, wishing the heat would fade from her cheeks. She'd already made a fool of herself at dinner. She would not make herself a fool over a man. He'd smiled. Task met. Done.

It had been a very nice smile, though, and came with a warm, soft laugh, too. His teeth, she'd noted, were *not* horrible. Indeed, when he'd relaxed, he'd become altogether alluring.

But had her triumph been worth her current uneasiness? She clenched her fists, determined to keep her wits about her during this ridiculous "hunt" and maintain whatever decorum she could muster. After all, she and Florrie had persuaded Mr. Hayes to participate in this adventure and, as Florrie said, Lydia's job as hostess was to ensure their guest was made to feel welcome in their home.

She remembered how he had attempted to ease her discomfort earlier, and she was grateful. He, at least, seemed to find her entertaining. Which was more than she could say of her brother, who currently conducted a thorough search of the large desk at the end of the room while Florrie carefully explored the mantel above the fireplace.

Nearest her, Mr. Hayes was tipping books out of the nearest shelves and looking beneath and behind them. Good idea. She started on the next shelf. The study contained eight bookcases, and she eyed them, considering this might be a days-long undertaking.

"Quite a few of them, aren't there?" Mr. Hayes asked, gesturing to the stack he held in his hand.

She nodded. "I daresay you did not imagine this as part of becoming reacquainted with Briarwall."

He shoved the books back into place and pulled out another set. "Several things have taken me by surprise."

She dared not ask him what those might be for fear that his answer would include the ridiculous dinner conversation. Instead, she studied the shelves in front of her. "Where would *I* keep a clock key between windings?"

"Perhaps we should look behind the books about clocks."

They each paused, looked at each other, then began running their fingers along spines, reading titles quickly up and down the stacks.

"I have it," he called, nearly obscured by a large fern in a Chinese vase a few shelves over. "In the mechanical workings section."

She quickly approached as he pulled out a thick volume.

"Did you find it?" Florrie called from the shelves near the fireplace.

"Not yet," Lydia answered.

"Hold this," Mr. Hayes said as he dropped the heavy book into her barely waiting arms and went back to examining the shelf.

After balancing the book so as not to immediately drop it, she opened it, searching for . . . what exactly? A secret compartment?

He pulled two more books off the shelf and began the same perusal of them. "These are the only volumes on clocks. The others cover everything from the invention of the wheel to the steam engine. Your brother needs to update his collection."

"I seem to recall you were fond of this section in particular, Mr. Hayes," Lydia said.

He paused. "You do?"

"Yes. Just a vague impression. Am I correct?"

He went back to leafing through pages. "You are. I've always been fascinated by the way things move, and the means of recreating that movement mechanically." He held up the top volume in his hands.

"*The Artificial Clockmaker*," she read aloud, "by William Derham."

"I read this one so often your father gave me my own copy as a Christmas gift."

"Truly?"

He nodded at the worn pages. "Truly. I haven't thought of it in years. Now, if your brother had some volumes about automobile mechanics, *then* you might never see me outside of this room for the duration of my stay."

Lydia stared. "*Automobile* mechanics? Motorcars?"

He looked up and grimaced. "That was quite thoughtless of me. I'm quite obsessed, I'm afraid, and I lose all sense. Forgive me?"

She blinked at him. Could it be true? This handsome man materialized in her home, took the oddest dinner conversation in all of Britain in stride, expressed his fondness for her parents, and now admitted his love for motorcars.

"You're forgiven," she all but blurted.

His brow rose.

"Truly," she continued. "I'm quite obsessed myself."

Before Mr. Hayes could respond, Florrie appeared at Lydia's side, hands on her hips. "What are you two expecting to find?" she asked. "The winding key pressed flat as a flower between the pages?"

Lydia, about to share her newfound information about her guest, held her tongue. Telling Florrie of Mr. Hayes's penchant for motorcars might open a Pandora's box to more of Florrie's pointed questions, and she was only just feeling secure about the evening. No. Lydia would keep this news to herself. At least for a little while. Her heart thrummed with the secret.

Mr. Hayes returned his books to the shelf, then took the thick volume from Lydia. "I'm not sure what I expected. Just a fanciful guess." He pushed the book back into position on the shelf. "Would've been something, though, to find it here."

Lydia nodded and glanced back toward the griffin. "It is a distance from the clock. If I were charged with winding all the clocks in the house, I would—" She paused. *A secret compartment.*

"You would what?" Florrie asked.

Lydia's excitement grew. "That's it. Mrs. Parks once told me that, years ago, in the grand houses like yours, Florrie, a particular servant would be assigned to wind every clock in the home."

"Actually, I think we *still* have a person for that—"

Lydia nodded absently. "It would take him days. And he kept all the keys together in a box or on a ring. But often, keys would have a particular compartment—"

"Inside the clock." Mr. Hayes finished her thought.

She looked to him, their eyes locking. "Exactly," she said.

After a blink of realization, all three of them rushed to the griffin.

"I say, what are we all up to?" Andrew joined them at the mythology shelf.

"Lydia and Mr. Hayes suspect the key is inside the clock."

Andrew looked at the griffin as if it had sprung to life. "That seems overly obvious, doesn't it?"

"Obvious enough for *you* to think of it?" Florrie asked.

"Well, I . . ."

"I'm afraid to lift it," Lydia whispered with a laugh. "It's a ridiculous idea."

"Let's bring it to the desk," Mr. Hayes said. "Better light over there. Allow me."

"Oh, do let me." Anticipation coursed through her. She gripped both sides of the griffin and lifted the heavy piece, carrying it with careful steps to the desk. "Here we go, Frederick," she murmured. "Just taking a little walk." She set it down on the cherry wood with a sigh.

They all bent lower, searching for a visible door or latch.

As she leaned left, Mr. Hayes leaned right. Too late to change course, they nearly collided. The scent of cedar and sandalwood on a man—on *this* man—wafted her way, and before she knew what was what, she'd silently breathed him in before they both withdrew.

"Pardon me, Miss Wooding."

"Think nothing of it." Why had she said that? Why had she not said, *"Call me Lydia. After all, we're about to perform surgery on a very old clock, and you smell of my dreams"*? Right.

Blast Florrie and her notions of olfactory witchcraft.

She took a steadying breath. "I don't see an opening. Do any of you?"

Across from her, Florrie and Andrew shook their heads.

"Perhaps underneath?" Mr. Hayes offered.

"Yes, of course." She grasped the griffin by his head and back end, her fingers supporting the uplifted wings as she tilted the clock backward.

Just as she was about to release one hand to feel the underside of the base, something shifted beneath her fingers. She gasped.

"What is it?" Florrie asked.

"Are you hurt?" Andrew asked.

"The wing," Mr. Hayes whispered.

She turned, surprised at his nearness, but nodded. Neither of them retreated this time, and she found it difficult to swallow. He barely nodded in the direction of the clock. Focusing on the griffin, she set it back down and carefully took hold of the brass wing that had moved in her grip. First, she tried a rotating motion, attempting to move the wing forward or backward with no success. Then she gently pulled the wing away from the body.

A small click sounded, and they all gasped. Florrie and Andrew hurried around the table. Precisely along the lower edge where the wing met the body, the metal separated and swung outward on a hidden arm hinge, revealing an elongated compartment where a wing joint would be.

Nestled in that compartment was a small, perfect, clock key.

"Why, Frederick," Mr. Hayes said quietly, "you sly old dog."

Florrie clapped her hands in delight. "Let's wind it and see if it works."

Lydia retrieved the small brass key and held it toward Mr. Hayes. "Would you do the honors?"

Mr. Hayes looked to Andrew, who nodded his acquiescence. He reached for the key, and his fingers brushed hers.

Her breath caught at the warm touch she felt even through her gloves, and she swallowed to cover her reaction.

His gaze flickered to hers, then away, the key in his hand. He pulled the clock closer, turning it to access the back of the round timepiece. Inserting the key into a corresponding slot, he took a breath and began to wind.

He paused.

"What is it?" she asked. "Is something wrong?"

A half-smile formed at his lips, and he shook his head. "I'm simply surprised by how eager I am for this to work."

She released a quiet laugh and nodded. "It's almost silly, and yet . . ."

"And yet." He quirked an eyebrow and continued winding. He turned the key once more, seemed to meet with resistance, and stopped. "There."

He extracted the key, lifted his hands away from the clock, and all four of them leaned in closer, an ear toward the griffin.

Tick.

Tick.

Tick.

Mr. Hayes's eyes grew large just as hers did, and they all leaped with a joyful shout. Masculine arms were thrown around Lydia, and she returned the embrace, enveloped by cedar and sandalwood. Her hands gripped broad, muscular shoulders as she laughed. So warm.

With a shock, she jumped away as quickly as Mr. Hayes did, and she immediately turned to find a somewhat disheveled Florrie, rosy-cheeked and reaching for her, eyes alight. The girls embraced, laughing unsteadily, and out of the corner of her eye, she watched as the men grinned, shaking hands, then patting one another on the back.

"After that victory, I feel obligated to display the thing in a more prominent place," Andrew said, more pleased than Lydia had seen her brother look in a long while.

"*It* has a name, don't forget," Mr. Hayes answered, laughing.

"I'll have a placard made."

When they'd settled down, Mr. Hayes knelt once more, turning the clock to the front again and using the other end of the key in a small hole on the clockface to set the hands to the current time. Andrew informed him the second the minute switched on his pocket watch.

Task complete, Mr. Hayes stood again and held out the key toward Lydia, his gaze lowered. She held out her hand, and he dropped the key in her palm. "It is yours to conceal once more, Miss Wooding."

She brushed away a tinge of disappointment that he hadn't touched her hand again.

"Oh please," Florrie said. "We are all friends now after this successful venture. Let us call one another by our Christian names. Mr. Hayes?" she said, gesturing as she spoke. "Spencer, was it? Lydia. Lydia? Spencer. Spencer? Florrie. Florrie? Andrew. Andrew? Your lovely sister, Lydia. There. Oh, don't look at me that way, Andrew. We've known each other since I was five, and you were what—sixty?"

Spencer chuckled and ran a hand through his hair. "I suppose there's no undoing that."

Andrew folded his arms, silenced on the matter.

Florrie batted her lashes at the men and walked away, head held high.

Lydia could only watch, overcome with gratitude that her friend was so very good at flying.

CHAPTER 5

Spencer woke early. He rolled onto his back and blinked at the wide ceiling.

Lydia Wooding.

He drew an arm over his eyes and growled at himself.

During the "hunt," he'd come to recognize how easy a friendship with a woman like her would be. She spoke plainly, laughed genuinely, and appeared artless in her allure. It was only a friendship that had sparked last night. But when she'd wrapped her arms around him in that embrace—an innocent, triumphant embrace—*friendship* was not the desire that had coursed through him like the rumbling of thunder.

He'd distanced himself for the remainder of the evening. He'd told himself she hadn't noticed. He'd brushed away the questioning look in her eyes. He'd avoided addressing her directly. He couldn't even allow himself the familiarity of calling her by her given name.

Ruddy mess that was. He always fell too easily, too fast. Even when he was a lad, his mother had warned him of his tendency to fall too fast for the fairer sex. His "lover's heart," his father had called it, a teasing glint in his eye. He was not a womanizer nor took advantage. He just gave his heart easily. And had it crushed often.

And while he knew he hadn't fallen for Miss Wooding, the signs were blazing that he could—and soon. And that would muddle everything.

He'd sooner flirt with the effervescent Miss Janes. That action, instinct told him, would be harmless.

But this wasn't a pleasure trip, as pleasing as his return to Briarwall had been. Today was a new day, and he would refocus. The perfect day for it, too. Miss Wooding had mentioned that she and her friends would be in London most of the day while he and Andrew attended a horse auction and lunched at Andrew's club. Tomorrow, Spencer would approach Andrew with the framework of his proposal. Though Andrew seemed content to postpone talking business, Spencer didn't feel comfortable infringing on his friend's hospitality without setting to his purpose here. Yesterday he'd been able to put it aside. Tomorrow he would be ready.

He threw off the covers and crossed to the window, drawing away the heavy drapes, allowing in the morning light still sifting through mist. A brisk walk was what he needed.

His boots crunched on the gravel path encircling the green. A solitary morning bird sang the same series of notes again and again from the woods to the north. Ahead, easterly, he spied the golden sandstone pediment of the temple and turned his steps toward it.

It had always seemed otherworldly to him, that place. As if a piece of an ancient civilization steeped in myth had been broken off and planted at Briarwall. There was a reverence about it, as though its mere design were a conduit for deep thinking and meditation. Which was what he needed.

Climbing the steps to the wide entrance, he reached out and ran his hand along a cold, fluted column. Wisteria wrapped itself around the lower section, and he thumbed the thick vining trunk where the plant followed smooth stone.

A sharp, clear bark interrupted his inspection, and he turned to meet its source.

A collie loped toward him, but he hardly noticed, his attention immediately claimed by Lydia Wooding, sitting astride a black stallion, her hair in a loose knot and as wild looking as the horse she rode.

"Is it as you remembered?" she asked.

He opened his mouth, stuttering on his reply as she dismounted without effort. She sported buff-colored riding breeches, her white blouse tucked into the small, belted waist, her tall black boots meeting her knees.

He'd seldom seen a woman in breeches, and he'd given little thought to it before. He was having thoughts now.

He closed his eyes and shook his head.

"Are you well, Spencer?" she asked as she approached him, adjusting her sable riding gloves.

He blinked his eyes open, taking in fresh, cool air to clear his head. Right. First names. "I'm well. Thank you." He directed his attention to the familiar collie, now circling about his legs. He offered a hand, and the dog sniffed enthusiastically. "Champ?" he asked. But that couldn't be.

"Champ's son, Hero. Dear Champ passed on a few years ago."

He scrubbed the dog's head and neck, resulting in great wags of a tail. "I'm sorry to hear it. He was the best dog."

"Hero is much like him, though he believes himself a puppy still."

Spencer crouched low. "Not much for growing up, eh, boy?" He leaned in, taking the dog's face in his hands. "I don't blame you," he whispered. He rose as Lydia drew closer.

"You didn't answer my first question," she said, stopping in front of him and looking over the temple, her cheeks flushed from her ride.

He forced his gaze from her to the structure. "It's exactly as I remember." He turned back with a nod. "Good morning to you, Miss Wooding."

She paused. "Good morning." She walked over to a stone bench and sat, eyes on the trailing wisteria, its clusters of blossoms hanging about her like bunches of fragrant grapes. "I love it out here. It's always peaceful, even in a thunderstorm."

"Do you often have thunderstorms this way?"

"No more than the usual, I suppose." She leaned forward, her eyes brightening. "But when we do, and if I can manage it, I come here. You mustn't tell Andrew. He'd lock me in a tower."

"Has he a tower?"

"I'm sure he'd build one somewhere just to keep me in it."

He chuckled at that, relaxing a bit. He walked farther into the temple, past where she sat. "I thought you were going to London this morning." His voice echoed faintly through the stone columns and around the roof.

"I am. 'Morning' has different interpretations to different people. So, the Janes's motorcar will be coming 'round in two hours. I wanted an early ride, and I've plenty of time. Hermes loves mornings, don't you, you magnificent boy?" She directed her question to the stallion.

The stallion nibbled grass, pausing to shake its silken mane.

"He's a beauty."

"He's particular. Fortunately, he seems to like me. Do you ride,

Spencer?" Her look held a challenge. He guessed her sternness was less about whether or not he rode and more because he'd not used her first name. She'd used his twice now.

"I'm an abysmal rider."

"I don't believe you."

He laughed. Where was the shy girl who hid behind pillars? He was both amused and mystified by this bold woman in front of him. "Believe it. My father owned a livery and carriage company, but I was sent to school. 'To be bettah than 'im,' he'd say." He shook his head. "I can harness and drive a team on the city streets, get a horse from point A to point B when necessary. But the few times I've actually ridden a horse were here, at Briarwall. And Andrew was"—he cast her a sardonic look—"a most patient tutor."

She laughed. "I'm well aware of how *patient* my brother can be."

"Yes, well, I think I've always been more comfortable sitting atop something without its own mind."

"Did you hear that, Hermes? Our Mr. Hayes prefers machine to Your Majesty's brain."

"With all due respect to Your Magnificence, of course," Spencer added, bowing in the horse's direction.

The horse continued to eat.

Miss Wooding tipped her head. "Whether or not Hermes has a brain is still up for debate, to be honest. He fights me at every jump and tends to turn home if he's decided it's time."

"Sounds to me like he has a brain, just a poor sense of chivalry."

She sighed. "It is so difficult to find a man with both."

He shook his head, smiling. He'd caught the gleam in her eye, and he refused to take the bait.

"And what are you up to today?" she asked after a moment. "I hope my brother has plans for you other than watching him worry over the price of beef and oats."

"Does he worry about such things?" he asked.

"Do you know my brother at all?"

He chuckled. "I see your point." He looked about him, as if able to see the cattle and fields of grain from this vantage point.

If Andrew was worried about the tenuous position of the farming landowner surviving Britain's second industrial revolution, it was founded. How he would like to help his friend diversify. He owed him that. He owed Briarwall that.

"We are meeting a gaggle of brothers," Spencer said. "Baird? Brooks?"

"Burke."

"That's the one. We are meeting them at a horse auction and then taking luncheon at a club in Guilford."

"Grant's."

"That's it."

"That's Florrie's club," she said offhand.

He sputtered. "Miss Janes owns a gentlemen's club?"

She looked at him as if he were daft. "No, silly, it's one of her father's clubs. Grantmore Hill is the estate, his clubs are 'Grant's,' and Grantworks Locomotive is his empire. And I promise you, if Florrie owned a club, it would not be *for gentlemen only*."

He scratched his head. "No, I imagine not." *Grantworks Locomotive.* He shook his head at the magnitude of that holding alone. "Family name?"

"Very *old* family name." Miss Wooding stood, dusting off her breeches. "Well, I'd best be off. Florrie might prefer late mornings, but once she's going, she's about as patient as Andrew." She walked to Hermes, who lifted his head and nudged her. She pulled a treat from her pocket and offered it to him, stroking his withers, the morning sun caressing both beast and woman. "C'mon, Hero."

The dog nudged Spencer's hand before trotting off after his mistress. The whole picture left him charmed.

Lydia mounted the stallion. "Do you walk every morning, Spencer?"

"It's a habit of mine, yes," he said.

She grinned. "Then perhaps we'll meet this way again." She turned the horse, and the trio cantered off toward the stables.

Spencer found himself at odds as to whether or not he'd look forward to that.

Florrie finished her animated and detailed retelling of the key hunt just as the Janes's Rolls-Royce pulled up in front of Floris perfumery at 89 Jermyn Street in London. The Wendy League exited the car with a flurry of skirts and a flock of gauze, ribbon, and rosette-adorned hats. Florrie's lady's maid, an older woman called Agnes, followed as chaperone. The driver nodded at Florrie's instruction to return in an hour and drove off.

Lydia never tired of riding in a motorcar. She was thrilled and fascinated by every part of it: the vehicle's speed, the growl of the engine, and the motions of working the pedals and steering column. Whenever she could manage it, she would lean over the back of the driver's bench, peppering Kemp with questions and memorizing what it took to operate the Rolls-Royce. She'd become quite good at ignoring the disapproving looks from Agnes. The woman wasn't *her* lady's maid.

The jingle of a shop's bell pulled Lydia's attention away from the retreating car, and she grinned at Florrie's impatient beckoning for her to join the other girls already crossing the threshold into the grande dame of London perfumeries. She entered the shop and a gathering of fragrances filled her senses. Mahogany display shelves gleamed with polish and glass, showing off crystal decanters, glass bottles, and crisp, tastefully printed boxes. Soaps, shaving creams, and tonics, and of course perfumes and eaux de toilette, each held their own space in the sparkling shop.

One of two well-dressed gentlemen behind a long counter approached across the parquet floor and bowed. "Ladies, welcome to Floris. I am Mr. Dupree. Miss Janes, we received your message yesterday afternoon. I look forward to accommodating your friends' desire for a fragrance to reflect each of their tastes and personalities."

Florrie offered her hand. "I am delighted, Mr. Dupree."

He took her hand and bowed over it, then righted himself.

Florrie introduced the girls. "My dearest friends—Miss Burke, Miss Wooding, and Miss Whittemore."

Another bow. "Ladies. If you will follow me, we have reserved a table for you toward the back." He gestured and took the lead, the girls following. Agnes took a chair near a front window and pulled out her crochet hook and thread, settling in to wait.

"I hope they haven't taken my name to heart," Violet said with a smirk. "All my life, I've received a violet-scented something-or-other."

"You don't like the scent?" Lydia asked.

She wrinkled her nose and fiddled with the aquamarine dragonfly pinned to her lapel. "I did as a child. It's very sweet, isn't it? I'm not a child anymore."

"No. You are not." She put her hand on Violet's arm and leaned in conspiratorially. "The violet is such an unassuming little flower that I've always suspected it of malevolence. Those small, bright green leaves and all that delicate purple." She pretended a shudder. "I shall help you steer clear."

Violet raised her hand to her heart. "My champion."

Lydia laughed.

The girls sobered as Mr. Dupree waved them to four velvet-cushioned chairs gathered around a narrow table set with various bottles and small squares of thick paper. As they each took a seat, he pulled a glass stopper from a bottle and touched the tip of it to a small paper card. Then he waved the card under his nose, inhaling softly.

"White Rose," he said. "Sparkling carnation and greens, with heart notes of iris, rose, jasmine, and violet."

Lydia glanced at Violet, who narrowed her gaze menacingly at the piece of paper.

"As you test each fragrance, we suggest closing your eyes and allowing yourself to *feel* it," Mr. Dupree instructed. "Note the emotions and memories it conjures, and how you relate to those sensations."

He passed the card to Florrie, who closed her eyes, sniffed, and passed it to Ruby.

"Base notes of amber, musk, and powder," he continued. "A classic scent of the ages, yet light and feminine."

The card passed from Ruby to Violet and then to Lydia.

Feeling a bit silly but buoyed by her friends' obedience, she closed her eyes and sniffed. The scent was pleasant and reminded her of Florrie's mother's rose garden in late summer. But it was not a deep connection, and she passed the card back to Mr. Dupree, who placed it in front of its corresponding bottle.

He was already describing the next fragrance as one made

for Queen Victoria for her wedding day. It included black currant buds, something called bergamot, and peach. As he listed the supporting fragrant notes, Ruby opened her eyes. "Oh," she exclaimed. She closed her eyes and wafted the card under her nose once more and sighed. "I like this one. I do."

"Excellent, Miss Burke. Remember 'Bouquet de la Reine.' *The Queen's Bouquet*."

Ruby looked pleased and passed the card on. Florrie bounced in her chair with glee at Ruby's choice.

Several more fragrances passed under Lydia's nose. They were all pretty in their way, but nothing that struck her "emotions and memories" enough to warrant claiming one as her own.

"What was this one called again?" Violet asked next to her, suddenly sitting up straighter.

"Special Number Twenty-Seven, Miss Whittemore. Specially created in 1890 for Russian Prince Orloff. But a popular fragrance for women, as well, with its geranium and orange notes and the subtle sweetness of ylang-ylang."

Lydia didn't know what ylang-ylang was, but Violet was nodding vigorously, pushing the card toward Lydia for inspection, and, Lydia suspected, approval.

"No violets," her friend said pointedly.

Lydia smiled, then closed her eyes and wafted the card beneath her nose. It did smell wonderfully of orange and fresh geraniums, with an underlying musky scent that gave it some depth. She opened her eyes. "I think this would be lovely for you," she told Violet.

"Yes?"

"Yes."

Violet beamed. It seemed the others had been won over by this experiment.

"We have several more to try, ladies," Mr. Dupree said.

Florrie gave Lydia an encouraging nod, as if she were about to meet her handsome prince and need only match the glass slipper with her own.

Lydia shook her head, smiling.

The next card smelled of jasmine and gardenia and made Lydia's nose tickle until she released a dainty sneeze in her handkerchief. The one after that was Florrie's Lily of the Valley, which smelled wonderfully and exclusively of her friend. She passed it on.

Florrie reached across and took her hand. "I know there is a match for you," she whispered.

"I shall survive if there is not."

"No, you shan't."

Mr. Dupree was still speaking, but Violet was already handing her the next fragrance. Her eyes were wide. "Smell this, Lydia. It's wonderful."

All silenced, even Mr. Dupree, as Lydia waved the card beneath her nose. She breathed in the scent of spring hyacinth and a bit of orange, but more appealing than those were how they blended with the undeniable fragrance of woods. Of moss and sandalwood. Of walking under laden branches, between rays of sunlight and over spongy paths, catching hints of something deep and sweet and . . . alluring.

"What is this called?" she asked, her eyes still closed.

"Edwardian Bouquet," Mr. Dupree answered. "One of our newest fragrances. It is a celebration of a new era." He began listing things like oakmoss and amber and yes, mandarin and hyacinth and that ylang-ylang again.

But she was only half-listening, because it didn't matter. "This is the one." She opened her eyes in surprise. "This is the glass slipper."

Violet smiled knowingly, Ruby nodded, and Florrie squealed as only Florrie could and get away with it in public.

"Lovely," Mr. Dupree said. "Now, for the final test. When a person applies fragrance, the oils warm and blend with the skin, adding an additional and more personal note to the selections we have formulated at Floris. If you please, apply your preferred fragrance to your wrist. Feel free to browse the shop, ask any questions of our staff, and as you do, consider how the fragrance is blending with your own as the minutes pass. You may be even more drawn to it, or you may ask to start again with another fragrance. We are happy to serve you."

Not one of them changed their selection. Florrie had already arranged payment in advance, so there was nothing to be done but thank Mr. Dupree for his expertise and Florrie for her generosity, then leave the shop, each with a paper-wrapped bottle of their matched fragrance.

"Remember, ladies," Florrie said as Kemp drove them to a nearby eatery for lunch, "this was only the first part of the experiment."

"Remind me what the second part is," Violet said, smelling her wrist again and sighing.

"Oh yes," said Ruby, sounding worried. "I almost forgot the next part." She bit her lip.

"I'm pleased to hear that," Florrie said, "as it proves you've chosen scents for yourselves, without the intent to please a man." She gave Lydia a coy look as if to say, "See? I was listening."

Lydia arched her brow. "I believe what Florrie is getting at is that we are to apply these new fragrant feathers of ours, confident in their representation of ourselves, and sit back to see which peacocks come sniffing."

A muffled snort came from Kemp, which he covered by clearing his throat.

Florrie tsked. "That's not how I was going to put it. But yes. I've talked Mama into hosting a house party this summer. We shall wear our scents between now and then, make our observations, and report at the party."

Violet frowned. "Isn't this a bit against our suffrage inclinations? Aren't we to have broader goals than simply entrapping a man?"

The oldest of all the girls, Violet was also the steadiest when it came to matters of the heart, inclined to let the others chase after love while providing an anchor of sorts if needed. She seemed in no hurry to find true love or attach herself to anyone. Only Lydia understood the deeper reasons behind Violet's behavior: the acerbic men in her family had tainted her with distrust.

Florrie was not discouraged. "My dear sisters, you may have the broadest, wildest, most cavernous goals you wish. In this day and age, we are learning to embrace our power, are we not? To fight for the acknowledgment that we are valuable enough to stand *next* to a man and not *behind* him. To be more than a flower on his lapel, but a fire in his eyes. Historically, we have been traded by fathers as business deals, driven out of our homes by primogeniture, and preyed upon for our dowries. Right now, American heiresses are flinging themselves at the peerage for a title in exchange for their fortunes. Lords are wedding to save themselves from financial ruin. We are not the peerage."

She straightened her back. "We are the landed gentry. And it is within our power to apply tactics in love that men have been applying to women for centuries. It is within our power to be comfortable with ourselves and demand others to be comfortable—nay, brought to their *knees*—by us. It is within our power to *waft* . . . and see what it brings us." She waggled her eyebrows.

Agnes sighed heavily with censure.

The rest of the girls stared, speechless.

"What?" Florrie asked, innocence taking over her bold demeanor. "Did you not think any of this was rubbing off on me?"

Lydia's smile grew as she glanced to Violet and Ruby, each as wide-eyed as she was. She reached and clasped Florrie's hand. Then they were all laughing. Laughing to tears.

CHAPTER 6

Spencer sat back in his chair at the club and sipped his water. Andrew had ordered everyone the cheddar soup, fried scallops, and tomato salad, which was Wednesday's lunch menu. A tray of assorted savories sat on the table they shared.

"Saw some good horseflesh today." Cyril Burke, the oldest of the present Burke brothers, stroked his trimmed beard thoughtfully. "I'm tempted to make a bid on that mottled gray."

Spencer guessed him to have two or three years on Andrew, and a more serious temperament compared to his younger brothers in attendance, Oscar and George.

"The chestnut would make a fine hunter." Oscar Burke was a thicker, beardless version of Cyril, his black hair and green eyes an apparent hallmark of the Burke name.

"You already have a hunter," George observed, pushing his long hair back and reaching for an oyster on the half-shell. His eyes were more gray than green.

From what Andrew had told Spencer, the Burkes had four more siblings at home, all very close to one another in age. Spencer couldn't fathom it.

Oscar shrugged. "I've been thinking of giving Royal to Patrick.

He's nearly outgrown Lark, and Royal takes a shine to him whenever he's near."

"It's the sugar lumps," George said.

"He doesn't take to me like that with or without sugar lumps. I believe the two would suit. Leaving me to acquire a new horse." He smiled. "What about you, Hayes? Wooding tells me your father was in the equestrian business. Conveyance, correct?" He popped a stuffed olive in his mouth.

Spencer nodded, choosing his words carefully. "My father built his own carriage company from the ground up. He had a fleet of thirty carriages—hackneys and hansoms—and a team for each serving the city and its outer areas."

"That's quite an accomplishment," Oscar said. He was the most talkative of the brothers, and Spencer had liked him right away. They all had an effortless way about them and would've fit in at Ward End as easily as they did here at Grant's. That, Spencer knew, was a hard person to find.

The thought came to him that perhaps Miss Wooding was also such a person. He recalled her windblown hair and the shape of her breeches—

"Hayes?"

He blinked at Oscar. "Yes?"

"Did you see anything you liked this morning?"

"Er—" Horses. The man was referring to horses. He cleared his throat, glancing at Andrew. "Not especially. Though I appreciated the matched set of duns." His time at the horse auction had not been as tedious as he'd imagined. If anything, it had reassured him that, though he'd spent a great deal of time away from home, he'd picked up enough knowledge from his younger days of shadowing his father that he recognized the qualities of a good horse. And a good set to pull a carriage.

Andrew leaned forward. "They caught my eye as well. I've always been partial to duns. I'm not sure why. The latest fashion is a pair of dark glossy bays pulling one's phaeton."

"Perhaps it's because they remind you of your coffee with cream," George said, gesturing to Andrew's swirling, steaming cup.

Cyril chuckled. "He always did prefer brunettes."

Spencer quirked a smile. "That is true. A creamy complexion as well."

George sniggered. "The perfect woman, then, a dun. How do you feel about big teeth?"

The brothers laughed.

Andrew rolled his eyes. "I often question why I keep company with you lot. If I wanted this kind of abuse, I would be with our sisters in London as we speak."

Oscar made a face of disbelief. "Anything but that."

Spencer recalled how much he'd enjoyed the quick—and unorthodox—banter of the ladies last evening. "I found them delightful."

George nearly spit out his food. "That is because there were only two of them, *neither* was your own sister, and they were not bent on emasculating you where you stood."

"Ah. I can see how that could be . . . not delightful."

All four other men lifted their various cups. "Here, here."

Their meal arrived with a flourish, the soup a rich gold and sprinkled with nutmeg, the bread crusty, and scallops still sizzling. The men dug in.

But Spencer turned to Andrew, sobering as he studied his

friend. "Would you like to hear my theory as to why you prefer the duns?"

"Do enlighten me." It sounded more like a dare than genuine interest.

Spencer picked up his spoon, using it to gesture. "Though you like order—symmetry—you are also not one to bow down to fashion. You would be hard-set to find better matched markings, color, and, I'm guessing, dispositions, than on that set we saw."

Andrew grunted, Spencer assumed, in agreement.

"Yet," Spencer continued, "they are still apart from what society has assigned—*this year*—as ideal. It has always been your way. To look at what society has dictated you should embrace, and step just sideways of it. And, if I might say so," he added with a grin, "you get away with it. Every time."

Andrew narrowed his eyes, humor in his expression. "Why do I get the feeling you are referring to my befriending a brash, first-year whelp from Brum who had a brilliant mind and a horrid accent and *not* to a pair of horses I must now purchase?"

Spencer tore off a piece of his bread and dipped it in the soup. "I've no idea what you're talking about, friend." He bit off a large piece and chewed, not bothering to hide his smile.

Lydia sat in front of her mirror. Fallon had tended to her dress and hair. Left to herself, she stared at the small crystal bottle of Edwardian Bouquet, recalling her friends' parting words to her that afternoon as they dropped her off at Briarwall.

"Wouldn't it work better to test it in a room full of men?" Ruby had asked. "Where do we get one of those?"

"A room full of men?" Lydia had said with a smirk. "We'd likely not be allowed in."

She'd been taken by the shoulders. "You have a sword," Violet had warned, glancing pointedly at the parcel from Floris. "Wield it carefully."

Her elbow had been gripped. "I believe our dear Mr. Hayes will have a difficult time keeping his nose from your neck this evening." That shocking comment had come from Florrie. Though the fact that it had come from Florrie was not so shocking. Neither was Lydia's full blush.

Now Lydia sighed and picked up the perfumed "weapon of choice" from the dressing table.

"You," she addressed the bottle, "are not a love potion or some sort of aphrodisiac. I chose you for *me*. Do you understand?" She set the bottle down, stacked her fists on the dressing table, and rested her chin on top. "You are a reminder of things I love and nothing more." She stared hard at the pale elixir in the crystal for several moments. "Spencer can sneeze all he wants, for all I care." She huffed, knowing that wasn't entirely true.

But shouldn't there be a happy medium? A place where what she wore and smelled like simply conveyed who she really was, and what she wanted to be, and with whom she wanted to spend time? A place where she could be herself and not some idealized projection others expected her to be nor an instrument of entrapment?

"By the world's standards, I've been considered an adult for a few years now, and it's only getting more complicated." She sighed. "To illustrate, I'm talking to a bottle of perfume and half-expecting it to answer."

She dragged herself up and looked hard at the door, then back at the bottle.

"Oh, for heaven's sake." She stepped back, opened the bottle, dabbed a drop to her finger and touched just behind each ear then rubbed the excess onto her wrists. Taking in a steadying breath, she leaned weakly against the table. "My, that's glorious."

She straightened, pulled on her gloves, and walked to the door. If the perfume did indeed have any magical power, it was that it made her feel completely irresistible. With that brazen thought at the forefront of her mind, her shoe caught on the rug. She stumbled and banged her shoulder on the doorjamb.

Wincing, she smoothed her gown. "Irresistibly *ridiculous*," she muttered. Humbled, she paused with her hand on the door. "'The moment you doubt whether you can fly,'" she quoted under her breath, "'you cease for ever to be able to do it.'"

She opened the door and yelped.

"Miss Wooding?" Spencer, midstride outside her door, jolted, taking a large step backward.

Why wouldn't he call her Lydia? "Spencer, you startled me."

"I hardly meant to. Next time, I shall wear a bell to give you notice."

"That would be lovely, thank you."

In a larger estate house, bedrooms would be in separate wings, but Briarwall had only a lovely staircase leading up to family and guest rooms on the second floor, with a shorter gallery on the west end. Therefore, Spencer passed Lydia's room while walking to and from his guest room.

He drew in a breath, arched a brow, and presented his arm. "May I escort you downstairs?"

She narrowed her gaze. "Is it something you wish to do? Or do you feel compelled, as if you can't help yourself?"

He studied her right back, his expression worried. "It is the gentlemanly thing to do, or so I was taught. If my mother were standing behind me, I suppose I might feel slightly more compelled, but I assure you, I have my wits about me." He tilted his head. "Do you?"

She drew back. "Yes. Of course. Good. All right, then." She took his arm, a nervous laugh bubbling up from her throat. "It's the silliest thing. I'm sure I'm making more of it than I should. You see, we visited Floris today—"

"The perfumery?"

"You know it?"

"I do. My mother expects to receive an ounce of White Roses every Christmas and does not let me forget it."

"I see. And do you like it? Her perfume, I mean."

He seemed to consider. "I do. I associate the scent with her. What matters is that she likes it, very much, and beams with delight when she opens the package, as if it were a great surprise. Every time." He glanced at her.

She smiled at the way he spoke of his mother. "It sounds as though she is grateful to you for the gift."

He nodded. "It was a traditional gift to her from my father, before he passed. It was something I could not let go unattended now that he is gone."

"I was unaware your father had passed. I'm very sorry. What a thoughtful thing to do for your mother."

"Were you familiar with my father?" he asked with surprise.

"No. Only I think having lost mine so early, I assume everyone else still has theirs. Isn't that childish of me?"

"You hope for others what you do not have for yourself. I would say that is selfless."

She dropped her gaze, her cheeks warming with a blush. "Or thoughtless. Anyway, your mother is fortunate to have you."

He shrugged as they reached the landing. "My mother deserves all the reasons to smile." They started down the stairs. "But you were saying? About Floris?"

"Oh." She shook her head. What would she do, ask him if he was mesmerized by her new scent? It seemed so trite after the way he'd spoken of his parents. "I was surprised by the perfumery, that is all. I didn't expect to learn anything, but I did."

"And what did you learn, Miss Wooding?" They'd reached the main floor, and he turned to face her. His expression showed true interest, his eyes patient. She seldom had received that expression from men.

"I suppose 'learned' is the wrong word. It is more that something has lain quiet inside me for a long time, and today's visit awakened the knowledge"—she suppressed a grin—"like a wood hyacinth in spring."

He smiled at the comparison. "I am intrigued."

"I had not realized how scent is so completely intertwined with *emotion*, with memories, and with people who evoke emotions within us. Try smelling something and deny it is attached to an emotion because of a memory or a person. Orchard blossoms, or roast lamb, or sun-dried linen. Perhaps even a patch of mud."

He watched her too closely, and she looked down with a subdued laugh. "Perhaps it is nonsense."

"It is not nonsense. I happen to have an excessive attachment to the smell of mud."

She glanced up, seeing the mirth in his eyes. "You mock me," she said, fighting her own laugh.

"I do not," he said, faking indignation. He shook his head,

looking off toward the study. "To mock you would make a hypocrite of me, as I now have an indelible memory to associate with the scent of . . . of you." His gaze returned to hers, and she drew in a quick breath.

As she searched for something to say, he lowered his voice. "Rest assured, your choice suits you, Miss Wooding."

Lydia swallowed, her heart fluttering at the compliment. "Thank you, Spencer."

A brief look of regret flickered across his face.

"Lydia, there you are."

They both lifted their faces to the staircase as Andrew came down, toying with his cuff. In the same moment, Spencer stepped several paces away from Lydia, his interest suddenly taken by the portrait of Great-Great-Grandfather Wooding.

"Jones got away from me before a cuff link came apart, and this new pair is giving me fits. Help me?" Andrew said.

Wordlessly, she took her brother's rebellious cuff link and attached it for him.

"Thank you. That's a pretty new scent you're wearing. Did you get that today?"

She brightened at his notice. "Yes. We—"

"Good, good. Hold that thought. I've got to take care of some business before dinner, or it will haunt me all night . . ." He was already walking away, acknowledging Spencer with a nod and disappearing down the corridor.

Spencer glanced her way.

"Well," she said, "at least he noticed." She chuckled weakly.

He nodded. "He did. And one day, he'll come across that scent, and his memory will be overflowing with you."

His words refilled the space inside her that Andrew had emptied when he'd walked away from her. "Do you think so?"

He looked back at the portrait. "I know so."

She lifted her wrist to her nose and breathed. Then she dropped it to her side again. "Thank you," she said quietly.

"My pleasure, Miss Wooding," he said.

During dinner—a quieter affair without Florrie's distinctive chatter—Ralston appeared, looking a bit ruffled. "You are wanted downstairs, sir. It's the young Latimer boy. He says it is urgent."

Lydia shared a look with Andrew.

"Excuse me a moment," he said, standing and striding from the room.

Lydia noted Spencer's curiosity. "Mr. Latimer is a tenant. He occupies the hunter's cottage with his wife and children and oversees the cattle. It's calving season, and seven of our herd are expectant mothers." She clasped her hands. "We might be in for an eventful evening."

"We?"

She shook her head. "You don't strike me as a gentleman who would pass up the opportunity to witness the miracle of birth. Am I wrong?"

His brow rose. "You mistook me. I was surprised that you included yourself in this scenario."

"Really?" She leaned toward him. "And do I strike you as a person who would pass up the opportunity to witness the miracle of birth?" She challenged him with a look.

A slow smile stole across his face. He shook his head. "Now that you mention it, no."

She grinned, her heart pleasantly thudding.

Andrew reappeared at the doorway. "I'll need your help," he said sternly. "Both of you, if you're willing."

With an exchanged glance, Lydia and Spencer stood and rushed from the room to change.

"You are not wearing that." Andrew saddled his own horse while the stable hands readied Hermes for Lydia and a tall brown mare for Spencer.

Lydia clenched her jaw but vowed to maintain decorum. "Wearing what?" Of all the times for Andrew to make a scene.

"You know very well what." Andrew's clipped tones told her he, too, was straining for decorum. "Those . . . *trousers.*"

"Whyever not?" Lydia asked lightly. "The whole of Briarwall has seen me in breeches. Ladies wear them to ride bicycles. In *public*, for heaven's sake. I'm faster *astride* Hermes than when riding sidesaddle, and"—she paused for emphasis—"riding astride is *safer.*"

He looked down briefly, cinching the belt beneath Domino's girth, but then shook his head, his face reddened in rising frustration. "I don't have time for this, Lydia. I've got *three* calves coming, Latimer's fractured his arm, and you're throwing a *fit* about wearing what women have worn for *centuries.*"

Lydia clenched her fists but kept her voice steady. "I'm not the one throwing the fit—"

Andrew whirled on her. "For *once*, would you be the lady I'm trying to raise you to be and dress as though it *matters* what other people *think*?"

Lydia flinched. The stable hushed, and everything seemed to still, even Hero. Andrew stood before her, yet it was Spencer's gaze she felt from behind. She had come down at the same time as Spencer, both rushing to meet Andrew in the stable, and Spencer hadn't even blinked twice at her apparel. They'd only shared a sense of anticipation and hope that all would be well. She'd all but forgotten about her choice of clothes until Andrew expressed his opinion.

She blinked back tears and kept her shoulders straight. Truth be told, she wanted to run. To seek solitude and weep. Heavens, she wanted her friends. Arms around her. Putting up their hands to shield her. She wanted . . . she wanted her *mother*.

She drew in a sudden breath, then released it, shuddering. Her chin lifted. "I wonder, Andrew, what your choice would be." Her voice quivered.

He drew back half a step, as if just now realizing he'd hurt her. He pressed his fingers to his closed eyes. "What?"

"Given the choice, what would you choose? To birth a calf."

He breathed deeply, his tone quieting. "To birth a calf or what?"

"No," she said, her voice gaining strength. "To get on a horse, to get *off* the horse, to get on the floor of the barn, to deliver a calf with blood and sack and birthing fluid, to be up and down, to calm large beasts and coax small babes, and when it is all over to get back up on the horse—which would you choose? One petticoat or two, in addition to your corset, a corset cover—"

Andrew's eyes flickered behind her and back. "Lydia," he whispered, likely mortified that she'd said *corset* in mixed company.

"—and then a riding skirt over the top along with a five-foot train—because how dare a woman have legs—that you have to throw over your arm to walk anywhere—" She took a breath. "Or would you choose a simple pair of breeches?" She glanced at the trousers he wore. "Thrown on over your bloomers and done? Easily repaired. Easily washed."

Andrew sighed heavily. "I would never have to make that choice."

"Why is that, dear brother? Because you're a *man*? What if you'd been born a *woman*, heaven forbid?" She lifted her arm, pointing back toward the house. "I would still be up there, changing. Making myself into a *lady* for the eyes of, oh, I don't know, Mr. Latimer and young Davey here, while you and Spencer waited and *waited*. I could have done that, yes. But I chose to hasten, Andrew. I chose to hasten to *you*, to come to *your* aid and to the aid of those animals whose lives hang in the balance right now. Right now. As we speak. As you stand there and belittle me in front of other *men*. Taking up the precious time that *I* sought not to waste. Because I care more about helping *you* than what other people think of *me*."

Her voice cracked at the end. "This is who I am, Andrew. This is who I've been *raised* to be. I put people and our future before things like clothes and status. Would you rather I be the opposite? I may not be the ideal woman, but you can be sure I will always choose to be the very best *person* I can be. Are you so disappointed in me?"

Her breath heaved inside her lungs, filling and emptying and filling like a bellows, and she wished that blasted tear hadn't spilled over. She wiped it away and walked over to Hermes, head high, and held his face and stroked his nose.

"Are we ready, Warren?" she asked the stable master, trying not to quake. "Please say we are."

Her dear friend bowed his head and handed her the reins. "Ready for anything, I'd say." He winked, then glanced behind her and straightened his posture.

"Lydia?"

She tensed at the sound of her brother's voice. Steeling herself, she turned.

He watched the ground, his mouth turned as if he'd swallowed something awful. She hoped it was his pride and that he'd choked it down.

Then, he opened his arms, and in half a moment, she was in them, enfolded. He tentatively stroked her hair. "Forgive me," he said. "You are the best person I know."

She pressed her wet face into his shirt. "I'll still wear breeches when I feel it's the better option."

She felt him chuckle before she heard it. He placed a soft kiss on her head. "I know you will."

She hiccupped. "I'd like to see you in a skirt."

"I think not."

She breathed in the smell of him—starch and leather and lemon—then pulled away. "Very well. You've held us up long enough, don't you think?" She smoothed her jacket and pushed a stray lock of hair behind her ear.

Begrudgingly, he nodded. He looked about him and reached for Domino. "Let's go, shall we, old fellow?"

She turned, still shaky, still unnerved, but better. As she did, Spencer caught her eye. In a quiet, chivalrous gesture, he placed his hand over his heart and gave her a small bow.

A smile tugged at the corner of her mouth. She turned and mounted Hermes, trying to give a name to the sensation she felt as she settled tall in the saddle and led her horse out of the stable into a dusky pink evening.

And then she realized what it was.

She felt like a lady.

CHAPTER 7

Two calves had been born in the last three hours, but the third was in trouble, and Spencer hadn't the slightest notion how to help. He'd witnessed foals coming into the world, but his father had had crew for that. A veterinarian had been called, but it would be some time before the man arrived, as he was out on another call a distance away.

"Here." Spencer offered Lydia a flask of water he kept filled using the barn's water pump. She was kneeling at the head of the cow, speaking softly, urging it to be steady. The animal had been tethered to stall posts on either side but still fought the need to lunge.

"Thank you." She took it from him and guzzled. Wiping her mouth with her sleeve, she handed it back to him. She turned to Andrew down at the busier end of the animal. "What happens if the baby doesn't turn?"

Andrew spared her a glance full of foreboding. He wore gloves all the way up to his shoulders. Latimer, his arm in a sling, stood behind him, instructing as needed though the man needed a doctor himself.

"He won't be a-turning, miss," Latimer said. "We can only hope to get his legs up and out first without damaging the mother. Mr. Hayes, if you can be ready with those ropes?"

Spencer let the flask hang from the strap across his chest and retrieved the ropes that had loops on each end.

"Now, Mr. Wooding," Latimer instructed, "you want to push the calf back into the womb as far as you can. When you do that, find its tailhead. No time to be timmersome. Shove. That's it."

Andrew was in up to his elbow, a grimace on his face.

"Now from there, follow a leg down to the hock and lever that hock forward so it brings the hoof up toward its hindquarter. Got it?"

Andrew nodded, his focus apparent.

"Mr. Hayes, have that rope ready. Mr. Wooding, you've got to get hold of that foreleg and bring it to the middle. Cup your hand over the hoof or you'll damage mum. 'Tween the two of you, you've got to get the rope over the hoof. Hold the rope taut while the same thing is done on t'other side."

Spencer knelt next to Andrew and pulled on a long glove, his attention divided between focusing on the task at hand and bewilderment at the evening's turn of events.

"I want the record to show," Lydia said as she cradled the cow's neck, "that this was *not* my idea for this evening's entertainment."

"Duly noted," said Andrew. "It is not nearly so odd as to be counted as one of your entertainments." He grunted. "I have the foreleg."

The cow bellowed, and Lydia growled, whether at her brother or the cow, Spencer couldn't say.

"Now," Andrew said.

Spencer tentatively pushed his way in, gripping the rope and finding Andrew's fist, which wasn't too deep now that the leg was positioned in the birth canal.

"The rope's around," he said, astonished that the move had worked.

"Now, Mr. Wooding, get that other leg up. Mr. Hayes, keep that rope taut else the hoof'll go right back where it oughtn't."

Spencer kept a firm hold on the rope and gave Andrew space. He glanced at Lydia.

She was bent over the cow's head, one knee resting against its shoulder, stroking the girl's neck and speaking softly. Her face glistened with sweat in the lamplight, tendrils of hair sticking to her forehead and neck. Her jacket was gone, her sleeves rolled up, her slender arms holding strong and fast.

She'd held the same position in the warm barn for the other births, not a murmur of complaint. Then she had helped care for the calves, rubbing them clean with hay until they were up and suckling. She covered a yawn. He guessed it was sometime past midnight; the sky outside the barn was black as ink. He'd always respected Andrew's work ethic, but his sister's seemed to be as impressive.

Their eyes met, and he froze as if being caught reaching for a third helping of his mother's mince pies.

"Spencer, now."

Jolted, he moved with the second rope. Both hooves were visible now, and Spencer looped the other one.

"Now, pull on those legs, the both of you," Latimer said. "Wooding, keep a hand in there. Make a way for him."

"Lucky me," Spencer grunted.

"C'mon, girl," Lydia said. "You're quite the warrior, aren't you? Give us a big push. You can rest after this. We'll get you the sweetest hay there is."

Spencer and Andrew groaned with the effort.

"There you have it, gents. He's a-coming."

And then the hips were out, the middle and shoulders, and a matted dark head.

"Put his hind legs up over the rail there. Clear his mouth as it drains."

They lifted the calf over a stall rail so it hung upside down. As Andrew stroked the calf's throat and scooped his mouth, the cow nudged and lowed, attempting to get closer. Lydia stayed with her, but her eyes were on the calf, who wasn't moving yet.

"He'll live, won't he, Latimer?" she asked.

"He's a better chance of it now, hasn't he?"

Andrew continued to try to clear the animal's airway. Spencer picked up handfuls of hay as he'd seen Lydia do with the other calves and began rubbing the smaller body down from belly to limbs, over and over again.

"Is he breathing?" Lydia asked.

Neither men answered, though they exchanged a glance.

Andrew pulled back. "I think he's gone."

Spencer paused, eyeing the calf as if that would stir something in it.

"It was a good attempt," Latimer murmured.

"Keep trying," Lydia demanded as she pushed past her brother. She met Spencer's gaze over the calf and nodded at the handful of straw he was holding. "We must keep trying," she urged.

At the same time, they both bent to work on the calf, rubbing, scraping, cajoling.

"Lydia—" Andrew said.

She shook her head and smoothed one hand along the calf's throat again as she attempted to clear the airway with her other. "It's too soon to give up."

Spencer rubbed the straw vigorously over the calf's middle, figuring if anything would help, it would be circulation.

"Come now, little one," Lydia murmured. "Your mum is waiting."

Spencer rubbed harder, though his hope waned. He glanced at Lydia, who closed her eyes and whispered, "Please."

Then, a weak bleat was heard.

Lydia gasped, her wide gaze finding his. "Did you hear that?" she said, rubbing the calf more vigorously along its neck.

"I did," Spencer said. He turned to Andrew as if he needed to support her claim. "I heard it."

Andrew came forward again, watching, waiting.

And there it was again, sounding a bit perturbed.

"Well done!" Latimer cried. "A fighter, this one. Let's get him down and dried off. There's still some tending to for the mother, remember."

Andrew dropped his head, shaking it. "You never give up, do you?" he asked his sister.

She reached up to muss his hair, and he swatted her soiled hand away. "Someday you'll learn."

Together they brought the calf to his mother, and when all seemed well, they stood back. In her fatigue, Lydia stumbled into Spencer's side, her body unexpectedly warm and soft. He instantly drew his arm around her to steady her, and she smiled her thanks, rendering him speechless.

Though she stepped away after a moment, and his arm slid back down to his side, she stayed close. Close enough that her warmth still pervaded his senses. With the three of them standing in the dimly lit barn, among sweat and hay and babies, Spencer couldn't help but feel a part of something. A part of something *right*.

The veterinarian arrived minutes later, administering medicines and vitamins and verifying that all mothers and young were well.

"Spencer," Andrew said as they washed up at the pump, "would you take Lydia back to the house? I'll stay to make sure everything's taken care of. I'm sure she's exhausted."

"Of course, but more like she'll be taking me back. I don't think I'm awake enough to stay on that horse. I'm beat."

Andrew chuckled as he dried his hands. "Goldy should be steady enough to keep you seated." He passed Spencer the towel. "Thanks for your help. I know that wasn't expected."

"My visits to Briarwall always were an adventure."

Andrew chuckled again. It was good to see his spirits lighter, after what had happened earlier in the stable.

"I'll see you in the morning," Spencer said.

"I believe it is morning. Today we meet to discuss your big idea. After we get some sleep, of course."

Spencer paused. In all the hubbub, he'd forgotten he'd be presenting his business plan. He nodded. "I'll see you later today, then." He turned.

"Oh, and Spencer?"

"Yes?"

Andrew took in a deep breath and let it go. "Lydia's not allowed to name the animals. Part of the deal we made when we bought the herd. I hadn't the heart to remind her that they're beef cattle, after all. She may need to hear it again."

Spencer winced. "How is that my responsibility?"

"Only if you hear her referring to 'Buttercup' or 'Clover' or some such, let me know."

Spencer rolled his head to the side and groaned, but then

turned and sought out Lydia. He found her at the stall of the last calf, gently murmuring words he could not make out to the little animal at his mother's teat. No, he would not be reminding her of the animals' destinies. Watching her wipe a tear from her cheek made him guess she was aware.

He approached with caution. "Miss Wooding?"

She turned, an apology in her eyes. "I'm afraid I'm a bit weepy."

"It's been a long evening."

"Indeed." She stepped away from the stall and joined him to walk to the horses. "Yet you still insist on calling me 'Miss Wooding.'" She passed him an electric torch and clicked hers on. "Why is that?"

He took the torch and breathed steadily through his nose before answering. "Respect. Propriety."

"Propriety? What is this, 1810? We've been introduced, we've revived an ancient clock together, witnessed the miracle of birth three times over, and saved a baby cow."

He hid a smile.

"What more could you need to feel free to call me Lydia? Friends of Andrew's must consider themselves friends of mine. As rare as it is for Andrew to have friends."

His smile broke free, and he shook his head, but still said nothing.

She sighed heavily and swayed a bit on her feet. "If you will be silent, then I shall have to puzzle it out. Find the key to your clock, if you will."

He coughed to cover a laugh.

She laughed outright. "I *will* find you out. What makes Spencer Hayes tick?"

He felt no obligation to respond. Though amused, he was too

exhausted for honesty. They reached the horses and mounted. Andrew was right about Goldy, the mare assigned to him for his stay. She was sturdy, and Spencer would almost have to try to fall off her broad back.

Lydia seemed to be dragging as well and did not urge her horse any faster than a walk. He hoped she was too tired to pursue her line of thinking.

"So, out of respect and propriety, you will not call me Lydia. Respect for whom? Myself? Because in that case, I grant you permission to respectfully call me Lydia. However, if it is out of respect for Andrew, I would ask why you would defer to my brother on how you, your own person, should address me, over here, not being Andrew."

She was not giving it up, and from the sound of it, would go on for quite some time, perhaps until she fell asleep. Or until he did. He eyed Goldy, wondering if the animal would continue home if Spencer happened to doze off.

"Or, perhaps you don't want the familiarity that calling a person by their first name brings?"

He sat up, and his horse, perhaps too intuitive, immediately halted.

She pulled her horse to a stop and frowned at him. "Is that right, then? You don't wish to be friends?" She put a hand on her hip. "Is it the breeches?"

Shaking his head, he closed his eyes. Given Andrew's earlier reaction to her clothing, Spencer could not ignore that question. "No, Miss Wooding, it is not the breeches. I understand why you would choose to wear them in certain circumstances. I'm quite fond of them myself."

Her brow lifted in his direction.

"Of mine. Of *my* breeches—trousers. Not yours." Apparently his brain had succumbed entirely to exhaustion.

Both her brows rose high.

He started his horse walking again. "Not that there is anything uncomely about your breeches—they fit you very well—I—" He sighed and slumped in the saddle. He was too tired for this. "You look well in any circumstance, is what I'm saying." He rubbed his eyes.

She drew up next to him again. "Thank you, I think."

"It is only that I am in need of certain—boundaries—in order to—" *Protect my heart*, he finished silently. "It is for the best."

She chuckled. "Florrie would say you are protecting yourself from falling madly in love with me."

He froze, except for his ears, which grew rather hot.

Her mouth formed a circle. "Oh bother, I meant to keep that thought inside my head."

He frowned, unaccountably irritated. "You think rather loudly."

"I know it. My thoughts are quite demanding."

"Even in the middle of the night."

"Especially in the middle of the night."

He blew out a sigh of frustration. "Have you ever been in love, Miss Wooding?" Well, he'd meant to keep that thought inside his head.

"Oh sure, scads of times."

That was not the answer he expected. "Really? With whom?"

"Oh, Mr. Darcy, Laurie Lawrence, Mr. Rochester, and the Scarlet Pimpernel. Robin Hood. And Peter Pan, of course—"

He found himself laughing.

"Oh, you meant real people." She smirked.

"Never mind," he said, waving her off. "I'm not sure why I asked." Indeed, he was sorry he asked.

A heavy silence settled between them.

"I once offered someone my heart," she said quietly.

He tried not to be interested. And yet. "What happened?"

"He did not offer me his," she said. "It was a long time ago. We were both young, and I think I mistook the thrill of being noticed for love." She tipped her head toward him. "And he was too much of a gentleman to succumb to my wiles." She waggled her brows, and he chuckled.

"So, in answer to your question, I do not know if I've ever truly been in love. But I hope if it comes, it hits so hard that neither party can deny it. Because otherwise, how do you know?"

He remained quiet for some time, having no answer for her question. Indeed, it was a question he'd asked himself after his own mistake with Catherine Bradshaw.

She covered a yawn. "Since we are too tired to guard our words more carefully, might I ask you a question?"

His pulse leaped as if to remind him to be cautious. "That depends on the question."

"How was it that you and Andrew became friends?"

He heard the amusement in her voice rather than saw it, as they were in the thick of the woods now, and the horses had been given their lead home.

"He hasn't told you?"

"My brother has not told me a great deal of things, Spencer Hayes. I've learned to ask questions if I wish to know things, and to expect an answer to only half of them."

"I see." He wondered if that was part of the change in her from the shy little girl to the sure-eyed young woman. "Well, it's a simple story, really. I was a Colleger—"

"A what?"

"A Colleger. A member of the working class with enough wits about me to pass the entrance exam and get into Eton. My father had built his success and reached the higher echelons of his sphere, but that, as you know, does not make one gentry."

She sighed. "No, it does not."

"The irony is that Eton was built for the education of poor and lower-class boys, did you know?"

"I did not."

"But over the years and the changes in policies, it became more and more difficult for those with fewer resources or connections to get in. I was rather lucky. Not that my family couldn't afford it, mind you. Only that I had no connections. No family history with the school."

"You were a forerunner," she said.

A corner of his mouth lifted. "That's rather a romantic take. I was a twelve-year-old vessel of spit and fire, and I didn't want to be there."

She chuckled, and he liked that she did.

"But I worked hard, kept my nose down. Did my best to 'keep out the oss road' as my father'd say. He was depending on me, and even though I didn't want to be there, I was loyal to my family. But even boys full of spit and fire can endure a bully for only so long. A boy a year older than I—in Andrew's form—had singled me out. I can only guess as to why. Prejudice against Collegers was strong, and I wasn't just scraping by, like they thought I should be. No, I was in the top of my classes and angling for a spot on the cricket team. His team. His position. He was ferocious."

He paused, remembering the fat lip and the swollen eye, how he'd gasped for breath from the pounding his gut had taken, the hours he'd spent rewriting torn pages from his books under his master's watchful eye.

"One day I couldn't take it anymore." He let the rhythm of the horse's gait settle his agitation. So long ago, yet still a blight on his memories.

"What did you do?" Her voice was hushed, and he thought perhaps he'd built up the story too dramatically.

He cleared his throat. "The day before exams, while the bully was in class, I faked a stomachache. I stole to his room and removed all but the most minimal hardware from his furniture. Then I released seven crickets and reversed the lock on his door. Once he'd returned to study, I simply strolled past, locked him inside, and waited for the havoc to begin."

"Did it work?"

His smile grew. "The crickets started up, resulting in him moving a piece of furniture to find one, only to have the furniture collapse at his touch. When it grew to be too much for him, he attempted to recruit help, only to find—"

"He was locked in," she said with a giggle.

"Yes. And I had deposited the key in a nearby potted plant. By the time a locksmith came 'round, the room was in shambles, and the boy had gone mad by all the incessant chirruping. They never did find all of the crickets that evening." He joined in her laughter. "He was a wreck for exams."

"But where does Andrew come in?" she asked.

Spencer sobered, taking a deep breath. "In my limited knowledge of aristocracy, I'd failed to realize the power of the titled. The bully was a lord, from a long line of powerful lords, and, during the impassioned search for a culprit, I was found in possession of the simple tools I'd used to dissemble the furniture. I was faced with immediate expulsion. I'd let my family down. I'd let my father down. As much as I didn't want to be there, I didn't want to be a statistic even more. I'd wanted to beat the odds. And I'd allowed a bully to steer my fate."

She was quiet on her stallion. They were leaving the woods and approaching the open lavender field. The flowers weren't in bloom yet, but the dewy breeze still carried the crisp, powdery smell their way. They paused and lifted their eyes to the stars strewn above them.

"Out of nowhere," he said, "a boy stepped forward. I was called to the headmaster's office, and for the first time, met Andrew Wooding." He shook his head. "A twelve-year-old boy who held himself like a senior."

She huffed in agreement.

"He'd given testimony, and had brought more signed testimonies, of the history of the young lord's bullying, from primary school up. He'd observed enough, had had enough, and with his parents willing to act as my additional sponsors, petitioned for my right to stay in school."

He turned, meeting her wide-eyed gaze. "And the headmaster agreed."

"Andrew did that?" she asked.

He nodded. "The Apollo who beat the lords."

"And what happened to the bully?"

"In an act of spite against the school, his family transferred him to Harrow, and we had the pleasure of trouncing him every year in cricket."

She laughed. "Marvelous."

"Yes," he said, urging Goldy forward again. Lydia followed. "And that is how I became friends with your brother, and how I graduated Eton, then Oxford." Not only graduated. He'd committed himself to be worthy of Andrew's friendship and had finished with highest marks and honors.

"As infuriating as my brother can be," Lydia said, "he does manage to step up when it is crucial."

He thought of Andrew and Lydia's fiery exchange in the stable. And her fight to save the calf. "I believe you also step up when you deem something crucial, Miss Wooding."

She growled. "I'm finding it crucial that you stop calling me that."

He laughed. Perhaps he shouldn't have, but he was tired, and the subject had gotten too deep, and he was ready to climb off his horse and drop onto his own bed. Fortunately, the stable lights appeared, and the horses hurried their pace.

"You know," Lydia said, "I was perturbed that we have a perfectly good motorcar in the garage and yet no good road to the hunter's lodge, or to the tenant houses for that matter, so we are left to literally ride to the rescue." She dismounted and pushed a lock of hair off her face as she handed the reins to a stable boy. "But I'm rather glad we had to ride home, aren't you?" She looked up at Spencer, an exhausted, genuine, hopeful smile on her lips.

He dismounted and patted Goldy in thanks as she was led away. He turned to Lydia, studying her smile and the warmth behind it, pushing down the nervous energy that rose inside him in response. He shook his head. "I have no complaints."

Her grin widened. "Good. Now, walk me back to the house before both of us drop dead on our feet."

His grin pushed through, and he swept his hand toward the house. "After you."

"I think not," she said and took his elbow. "We shall continue together. You need me to hold you up, and I need you to catch me should I fall."

He chuckled. "Are you that unsteady?"

"No, I'm that sleepy. Now quiet. I've no wish to wake the servants."

Mrs. Parks and a kitchen maid were still awake, waiting with a pot of tea, cold ham and cheese, and warm scones. After Lydia and Spencer ate their fill, leaving some for Andrew, and shared the good news with the servants, they quietly made their way upstairs with their electric torches for lamps. When they reached Lydia's door, Spencer paused.

"Lydia," he said, trying out her name on his lips, his voice steadier than he felt.

She lifted her gaze to his, her pleasure at his use of her first name apparent in her expression. Fine. He'd let her have this small triumph. He needed a bigger one.

He hushed his voice. "May I ask your opinion on something?"

Her eyes widened once more. "Of course," she whispered.

He swallowed. "I'm meeting with your brother later today about an investment opportunity. A very good investment opportunity. I want him aboard as much for his sake as my own. Can you give me any tips or warnings as how to best go about it?"

She studied him in the light of her torch. "You may know him as well as I. Be honest. Be yourself. He likes you. He is . . . at ease with you, and that is a rare sight."

He nodded. It wasn't anything revelatory, but the encouragement was welcome.

Lydia reached for her door handle. "I'm sure you'll do well." She leaned forward with a secretive grin. "As long as it isn't anything to do with motorcars." She waggled her brows. "Good night, Spencer."

His words lodged in his throat. He'd been so careful, testing the waters with Andrew, but he'd found nothing to warn him that while Andrew might have healed from his parents' accident more than thirteen years ago, he was still outright against motorcars entirely.

Lydia opened her door and slipped inside, blissfully unaware that she'd upended any amount of confidence he'd gathered thus far.

CHAPTER 8

Spencer paced back and forth in one of the private meeting rooms of the club. True to his word, he'd played a laughable game of tennis—and he would've laughed at himself but for the fact that his nerves were stretched tighter than a racquet string. He'd tried to speak to Andrew before the presentation, but Andrew had cut him off with a hardy slap on the shoulder telling him not to worry, and oh—by the by, he'd invited several interested parties to listen to the proposal and had arranged for a room at the club to lend it added legitimacy.

Spencer had rushed through his post-game toilette in order to be the first to arrive at the room and think while the others finished dressing. His portfolio and notes lay on the table in the center of the room, and he'd run through his practiced speech so often he'd been afraid of losing the fire beneath his words. That was no longer his main concern.

As long as it isn't anything to do with motorcars.

Spencer paused and closed his eyes. He should've guessed. What had he been thinking? He knew the family's history and yet still allowed himself to think enough time had passed and surely

Andrew Wooding could look to the future now. Could see the wisdom in this venture.

And here he was, about to make a grand fool of himself. He could hear his father now: *"Why bother fixin' what don't need mendin'?"* His father had struggled to embrace solid change, no matter Spencer's attempts to make him see reason, but had no qualms with throwing everything he worked for at underhanded schemes.

"What did you send me to school for," he muttered, "if not to learn how the world could look?"

And now Spencer had learned that Andrew, though different from his father, might likely throw this particular facet of the future—and Spencer—out the door of this very club.

The door clicked open behind him, and Andrew walked in, his stride brisk, his expression eager. He was followed by Oscar Burke, the young man with the build of a fighter and the energy of a hunting spaniel. Just after him, Sir Lawrence Piedmont—more of a giraffe with long legs and neck—entered with all the presence of the *ton* but none of the intrigue.

Spencer still found the man bland, and, thankfully, about as good at tennis as himself. He seemed genuinely pleased to renew his acquaintance with Spencer, however, and his apparent wealth buoyed Spencer's hope.

In discussion with Piedmont was an older gentleman, portly and dignified, finely dressed, and completely unknown to Spencer. A footman entered with a tray of crystal decanters and a teapot, set it on a sideboard and removed glasses and teacups from the cupboard below, bowed to the room, and closed the door behind him.

As the men turned to help themselves to refreshment, Spencer pulled Andrew aside once more.

He spoke low so the others couldn't hear. "Andrew, I must

speak to you. I am torn. I feel I cannot leave you out of this, and yet I fear I've misjudged. Perhaps I was blinded by my enthusiasm."

Andrew watched him, his brow drawing low. "You mean to talk me out of this venture before you've presented it? That's awfully sporting of you." He grinned.

"I am not trying to amuse you." Spencer sighed in frustration. "I only mean to—"

"Wooding, shall we get on with this?" The older gentleman spoke pleasantly but firmly. "I've a meeting with my solicitor on the hour."

"Of course. First, Mr. Lucas Janes, allow me to introduce you to Mr. Spencer Hayes. He'll be addressing us in a moment."

Spencer started at the man's name.

"Hayes," Mr. Janes said with a nod. "I believe you've met my Florrie. Said something about a clock."

"Yes, sir. Delightful young lady."

"Well," Mr. Janes said, "she can be."

Spencer nodded, silenced by the risk of saying something upsetting to this wealthy man about his daughter. Mr. Janes took a seat at the table.

Andrew turned back to Spencer, gripping his shoulder and speaking low. "Allow me to decide whether or not you've misjudged. I will consider your warning." He nodded, then turned to the refreshments.

Spencer swallowed. He'd done what he could with these men and potential investors looking on. His belief in his vision had brought him this far. He would move forward. He only hoped it would not cost him a friendship.

Andrew returned, setting a glass of amber liquid on the table near Spencer with a pointed look. Spencer lifted it with a slight salute and took a swallow, then pushed the rest away.

"Gentlemen," Andrew began. "Thank you for accepting my hasty invitation. We're here to consider an opportunity from an old friend whom I hold in high esteem." Andrew tossed him another pointed look. "Mr. Spencer Hayes has a great mind for innovation. He has since we were boys. I urge you to listen and decide for yourselves. Spencer? The time is yours."

Spencer approached the head of the table as Andrew took a seat. He opened his portfolio and took a deep breath. *Look 'em in the eye, boy. You've 'alf won 'em.*

He met each man's gaze, gave a nod, and began.

"Thank you, Andrew. Gentlemen." He cleared his throat, hoping to clear his nerves as well. "I've spent several months in America. In Detroit. Studying the motorcar industry."

He glanced in Andrew's direction, noting a slight tightening of his gaze. Spencer pushed forward.

"I met Mr. Ford himself, albeit briefly. A firm handshake as he made his way to his office." He read the interest in the men's eyes at that. "His ideas are groundbreaking. Currently, it takes a team of four to five men to build a car from axle to hood—a meticulous and time-consuming task."

Mr. Janes nodded, encouraging Spencer on.

"Imagine, instead, a car being assembled from the first frame to the last knob by a hundred machinists who do their assigned part as the cars are slowly carried past on a conveyor belt. Mr. Ford's vision of assembly-line manufacturing will speed up production and affordability to meet an increasing demand of car ownership for the Everyman."

"No doubt," Mr. Janes said. The man was familiar with the subject. That boded well.

"But what attracted my attention," Spencer said, "was the incorporation of standardized parts."

"Standardized parts have been around for centuries," Sir Lawrence said.

Spencer nodded. "True, but the automobile has not. Look at the bicycle. The ordinary man in need of a repair will take his bicycle to a general repair shop, hoping the necessary part is in stock. If it is not, the repairman orders it from the particular manufacturer, waits on the shipment of said part, and then makes the repair." He took a breath and turned to Andrew. "What do you do now, if your Singer should need a part for a repair?"

Andrew folded his hands in front of him. "I suppose we would order the part from the catalog or take the car to Singer Motors for repairs."

Spencer firmly rapped his knuckles on the table. "Exactly. Even if it was the simplest part—a carriage spring, for example—you would shoulder the trouble, time, and cost to order it from a catalog or return it to the manufacturer—in this case, Singer Motors Limited of Warwickshire, a company producing bicycles and motorcycles as well as the automobile—and then you'd wait for the repairs to be done.

"Now, what if you—or your garage man, Warren, was it?—could simply ring up a supply shop here in Albury, or Guilford, where they kept replacement parts for every top make and model car produced in England? They match the part, and you are able to pick it up immediately. Or they could deliver it to you for a fee. Possibly even install the part for you for an additional fee, should you be unable to do so yourself."

He gauged each man's reaction. So far, he had their attention in varying degrees. Andrew remained tense, his eyes on his own fingers as they silently tapped the tabletop.

Spencer continued. "Imagine one of these shops outside every major city in England, easily available to the Everyman. The Everyman who will someday soon be able to afford a motorcar, if Mr. Ford has his way."

"And where do these parts come from?" Mr. Janes asked.

"Purchased in bulk from the auto manufacturers at a discount."

"Why would they sell their parts out?" Oscar Burke asked.

"The same reason they sell them through catalogs. They recognize that they make their money by selling new cars, not fixing minor repairs in cars already sold. Making simple repair parts available to the Everyman encourages the Everyman to feel more at ease investing in their automobiles. Let me ask you, when you make a major purchase, say, a horse, do you not weigh the cost of the upkeep of your investment, decide whether or not the continual maintenance is within your budget?"

His question was met with nods of agreement.

"I assure you, the growing middle class considers these things greatly. They take pride in their self-sufficiency. And knowing the part they need to quickly replace—be it a spark plug or the ignition timer—is down the street, or in the next town over? It's a security that frees up their worries about investing their money in the first place. They will foresee the satisfaction of the money they'll save maintaining their motorcars themselves. Money they will gladly spend at the *motor supply shop*. More specifically, a *Hayes* Motor Supply Shop."

Mr. Janes raised his brows in interest. Sir Lawrence leaned forward in his chair.

Spencer's pulse quickened with hope. He splayed both hands

on the table in front of him and leaned forward. "I have the idea. I have the plans. I even have locations. What I need are investors. Who will help me establish these shops to meet the need when it arises? And it will arise, gentlemen, I assure you. Within a few short years, I predict a motorcar for nearly every middle- and upper-class family." He looked each man square in the eye. "Will you be there with me to greet them?" He pushed away from the table and folded his arms. "Questions?"

An hour later, after many answers and much discussion as each gentleman studied the specifics—most notably the ledgers of necessary capital investment and predicted earnings—Spencer stood at the door of the meeting room and shook hands with each man as he left.

"Interesting, Mr. Hayes," Mr. Janes—who'd forgone his solicitor's meeting to ask more questions—pulled a cigar from his mouth. "Very interesting." He placed a card in Spencer's hand. The man gave no more sign, but Spencer couldn't help but feel a thrill of encouragement.

"That was smashing, Spencer," Oscar said. "Much better than your tennis game."

Spencer smiled, pleased to have presented his idea well. It would do no good to come off as arrogant. "I'll accept the compliment."

"You should. I can't make any promises, but you've given me much to consider. I'll talk to my brothers. If Andrew's in, well, that goes a long way." Oscar slapped Spencer on the arm with a grin and left.

Spencer nodded belatedly though his stomach turned. Andrew had grown quieter throughout the discussion. He'd played it off as allowing his guests to lead the questioning, but Spencer knew his friend.

Sir Lawrence paused at the door, his expression unreadable. He glanced at Andrew, who was standing across the room at the window, then leaned toward Spencer. "I'm in." He handed Spencer his card and nodded. "I might be able to pull a few more investors on board as well."

Spencer kept his features smooth, though he wanted to leap with joy. Instead, he gave a single nod. "I thank you."

"Inform me of when you're ready to move. Not all of us are blinded to the future by fear." With another glance at Andrew, Sir Lawrence tossed his ebony walking stick up and grabbed it midair in a surprising display and left.

Part of Spencer wanted to collapse into a chair and pour himself a celebratory drink. But he shut the door, watching Andrew, who finished his own drink.

Andrew set the glass down on the windowsill and stared at it.

After another moment, Spencer opened his mouth to speak, but Andrew beat him to it.

"You did try to warn me," he said, his tone quiet but on edge.

"Yes. I—"

"You did misjudge me."

"Andrew, I—"

"You brought to light perhaps my greatest weakness. My greatest suffering. And asked me, in front of my friends, to perpetuate an industry in which I have little respect. Even disdain."

Spencer hung his head. "It was thoughtless of me. I'd imagined—"

"You'd imagined I'd overcome my hatred of the means by which my parents died a gruesome and premature death."

That brought Spencer's head up. Still, he had no words. That's exactly what he'd hoped of his friend. And not just for this venture.

Andrew gave a slight bob of his head, staring off. "That would've been the healthy thing to have done, I suppose." He shoved his hands in his trouser pockets. "But I have not. I cannot."

"I understand—"

"*Do* you?" Andrew turned sharply toward Spencer.

Silenced by his friend's raised voice and intense glare, Spencer could only wait him out like a rabbit, unmoving, his shame battling with his persistent sense of rightness. He was not wrong. His aim might need some readjustment, but this vision of his would succeed. It was nothing, though, without money.

And any sense of true friendship he'd gained in life was nothing without Andrew Wooding. Even when that friend bristled like a wolf.

"Andrew," he offered as steadily as he dared, "forgive me."

Andrew blinked, then released a breath, his shoulders sinking. He ran a hand over his face, and Spencer leaned back against the door with relief.

"There is nothing to forgive." Andrew sighed. "The idea is a solid one. Watching you, I was filled with both pride and resentment. But I can't—" He halted. "I'm sorry."

Spencer nodded. "I have a great deal of respect for you, friend. Too much to let this come between us. You were like a brother to me, did you know? I still feel that way, I suppose."

Andrew groaned and rolled his eyes. "Of course you'd say that after I've refused to invest in your future."

"What are brothers for if not to refuse their siblings money?"

Andrew's smile flickered, then it was gone.

Spencer sobered. "I cannot ask you to shirk your principles. They've come at too high a cost."

Clenching his jaw, Andrew nodded. "I thank you."

As the men gathered their coats and hats, Andrew ordered the carriage brought around. "I wish it were different," he said. "Truly. At any rate, please consider extending your stay with us. I don't wish you to think you're unwelcome over this. Besides, from the looks of things, you've some interest to cultivate and connections to strengthen."

Spencer stepped out of the club into the rain. How strong would those connections be when word spread that Andrew Wooding was unwilling to invest in his longtime friend's venture? Still, he nodded. "I'll think on it."

The carriage pulled up, and the men boosted themselves inside.

"Sir Lawrence and Mrs. Piedmont have a standing dinner invitation with us for the last Friday of every month, by the way. They'll be dining at Briarwall tomorrow."

"You wouldn't mind if I took the opportunity to discuss . . . business? Only if it's brought up, of course."

Andrew paused in thought, watching the village roll by in the gray afternoon. "I suppose you could use my study if need be." He faced Spencer. "But who knows? Lydia might have us diving for mermaid treasure under the full moon. Wouldn't want to miss that, would you?"

Spencer frowned. "To miss it would be utterly rude."

Andrew nodded. After a few moments of silence, he added, "Can you imagine Sir Lawrence bobbing in Briarwall Pond shouting, 'I think I've found something'?"

Both men chuckled for some time.

Dinner was a simple affair, owing to Lydia spending her afternoon volunteering with the Ladies Guild of Helpers to Women and Orphans and the later hour of her return. She'd worried about disappointing Andrew and Spencer, but after the events of the previous evening, the men didn't seem to mind. In fact, Andrew seemed grateful for the subdued mood.

"And then," Lydia said, filling the particularly sullen atmosphere as best she could, "Mrs. Chatham came with four baskets of boys' clothes that her sons had outgrown. It was a miracle, and you can't convince me otherwise."

"I wouldn't dream of it," Spencer said.

She smiled.

"Indeed." Andrew finished his soaked orange cake and wiped his face with his napkin. "If I may, I'd like to retire early."

Lydia stiffened. "Are you not feeling well?" She hoped it wasn't something he ate.

"Only tired, and I've some letters to write before I turn in."

Lydia relaxed somewhat. "All right, then."

He and Spencer exchanged looks of understanding. The men had been unusually quiet, and Lydia wondered if there was more to Andrew's retiring than exhaustion.

Andrew stood, nodding his good evening, and left the dining room. He'd left Lydia alone with a gentleman in the house, which she couldn't recall ever happening before. Not that she hadn't ever been alone with a boy—man. She'd been alone with Spencer numerous times now. Just not in the house. For the evening. Due to Andrew.

For a moment, Lydia and Spencer blinked at one another, then refocused on their cake.

With Andrew gone, Lydia searched her mental list of evening entertainment for their guest, crossing off items that would be inappropriate or impossible without the presence of her brother at hand. Even a musical performance for Spencer alone seemed too intimate. She felt herself blush at the idea. The evening had already grown late.

"Will you be joining me for port after dinner, Miss Wooding?"

She started at the question. "What?"

He gestured to the glassware on the table. "Are we to hold to tradition and part ways—you to the sitting room while I drink alone?"

"Is that what you wish?"

"Not at all."

She calmed a girlish thrill that he'd all but admitted he wanted her company. "Then let's not. I've always thought it a silly tradition. Not that I want my own port. I don't care for it at all. I simply don't see why men and women can't enjoy after-dinner conversation together. If a separate conversation needs to be had, then have it when we are not in company for the evening, for heaven's sake. Being sent out of the dining room makes me feel as if I'm a child who is in trouble. And I am certainly not a child."

He watched her, amused. "I quite agree."

"Do you? Will you help me convince my brother of it?"

His gaze intensified, and she noted color rising from his neck to his ears. He cleared his throat and focused on swirling the remaining bit of wine in his dinner glass as the servants cleared the table of the main dishes. At the same time, she realized what she'd asked of him and the various ways in which that convincing might be played out, and she wanted to sink under the table. She glanced around in search of a change of subject as if one would be written on the nearest napkin.

"Oh! How did the investment proposal go?" she asked, overloud and overbright.

He pressed his lips together, his eyes growing round. "Oh that. Yes. Well." He nodded at the footman who offered him port. "It went well." Then he sighed. "And it didn't. I'm not sure how things will proceed without your brother's vested interest."

"Andrew isn't in favor of it?" she asked, surprised. Her brother had seemed to look forward to Spencer's ideas, whatever they would be. "He thinks so highly of you."

He smiled crookedly at her, leaning on his elbows. "Perhaps not as highly as you assumed."

She frowned, truly confused. "Was the idea so outrageous?" The question came out before she realized she might offend Spencer with it.

He seemed to take it in stride. "Do you remember the last bit of advice you gave me this morning before we parted ways?"

Lydia thought back over their conversation in the corridor. It had been so late, and she'd been so tired, and he'd looked so adorably disheveled. He'd asked her opinion on talking to Andrew. "I told you to be honest—and then—" She stopped, her eyes wide. "Oh dear."

"Oh dear."

She leaned forward, looking about her and whispering. "You mean to tell me your proposal concerns *motorcars*?"

He leaned forward and whispered back. "Fully, wholly, and completely."

She slumped back in her chair, biting her lip. Then she pushed herself forward again. "You must know that if I'd had *any* idea, I would've been far less flippant in my answer."

"That doesn't do me any good now, but I thank you all the same."

They still whispered fervently, and with Spencer leaning forward as he was, she could see the chandelier light playing through his clear hazel eyes in the otherwise dim room.

"Was he terribly upset?" She cocked her head to the side. "He didn't seem put out with you. And your bags aren't packed and waiting on the landing. Curious."

The corner of his mouth lifted. "Is that what you would expect, normally?"

Her eyes drifted to that full mouth as she nodded. His accent had been grinding its way out as they spoke, and hearing it did funny things to her insides.

"I cannot even ask him to teach me to drive. I do not tell him how often I ride in Mr. Janes's motorcar. Andrew hasn't taken me for a ride in the Singer, even when he first brought it home. We take the brougham everywhere. I've heard him insist in company, darkly, that automobiles are a flash in the pan. That the horse is more reliable, much steadier, and definitely safer."

Spencer closed his eyes a brief second and exhaled. "Of course." He leaned even closer, bringing his cedar scent with him. "Because of your parents."

She nodded, meeting his soft gaze, his deep voice like a bow across strings. She watched his eyes roam her face, and the room grew very warm, making it difficult to breathe.

"And how do you feel about motorcars, Miss Wooding?"

She glanced to his mouth once more. *"Lydia,"* she whispered.

The click of the door from the servants' hall caused her to jump back, the legs of her chair skipping on the floor, nearly tipping her over.

Spencer, she noted, was once again fully seated, his fists steepled above his elbows on the table, his forehead pressed to them. His shoulders shook.

Lydia suppressed a panicky giggle and hoped her face did not look as warm as it felt.

The footman and two maids began to clear the remaining service, determinedly *not* looking at either diner.

Lydia leaned forward again with another whisper. "Are you *laughing* at me?"

He shook his head in his fists, then nodded and leaned back, letting his laughter escape to the room, his shoulders still shaking with it. He wiped his eyes. "You nearly . . . you nearly . . ." His voice dropped to a whisper, though it was hardly quiet through his laughter. "You nearly fell out of your chair . . ."

Lydia stood, pulling her gloves on and doing a clumsy job of it. Dash these gloves. Dash chairs and servants and—and *men*. "If you'll excuse me, Mr. Hayes." She straightened and strode out the dining room doors, ignoring the scrape of Spencer's chair behind her.

"Lydia," he said, his footsteps gaining.

She had to be four shades of red and did not turn. "Yes, Mr. Hayes?" She kept walking to the foot of the stairs. Was she even allowed to retire and leave her guest to himself? *Dash* being hostess.

Warm fingers wrapped around hers. "Lydia, wait."

She slowed, and he turned her in one measured pull of her hand. Every instinct told her to keep her eyes to the floor, but she was a Wendy girl, and so she lifted her chin and her gaze to meet his. Her heart pounded with embarrassment.

"Forgive me," he said. "I should not have laughed."

She didn't know whether to agree with him or not. If he'd been the one tottering in his chair, she'd have laughed, too. She shouldn't be mortified. She shouldn't be acutely aware that he still held her gloved fingers in his. She shouldn't be feeling as if this were the first time a boy had held her hand.

Maybe that was it, though. Spencer was not a boy.

She swallowed and nodded, slowing her racing pulse. "Apology accepted. I understand it was not malicious."

He frowned. "Indeed, it was not." He blew out a breath as if exasperated with her. "I don't know that I've ever laughed maliciously in my whole life."

"I'm glad to hear it, but considering I've not known you your whole life, I have only your word."

His eyes widened. "Do you believe your brother would defend and befriend anyone who had a malicious bone in their body?"

"No, but that was before."

He balked. "Before what?"

She leaned forward and lowered her voice once more. "Before he knew of your passion for motorcars." She arched a brow.

His gaze narrowed, and a slow smile spread across his lips.

She matched it. She couldn't help it.

His thumb grazed over the back of her hand, and it might as well have been a strike of lightning considering the current it sent through her body. *Dash* lightning.

Spencer stepped back, bowing over her hand with another graze of his thumb. He lifted an intense gaze to hers, his voice unsteady. "Good evening, Lydia."

With that, he climbed the stairs, taking them two at a time toward the top, apparently unable to get away from her quickly enough.

Still, the smile pulled at her lips. She lifted her wrist to her nose and inhaled Edwardian Bouquet, wondering what had just happened.

Because *something* had happened.

CHAPTER 9

Spencer paced the length of his room. He'd opened the window to let in a cool night breeze. His tie and starched collar had been flung on the bed.

How had things become so very *warm* with Lydia just now?

His mother would say he'd gone yampy, and he would've nodded his head and agreed. Right out of his mind, he was. The outcome of the proposal had him hopeful and stomach-sick at the same time. His stay at Briarwall had been extended, but for all the "no hard feelings" expressed between himself and Andrew, an awkward distance prevailed. And he'd just flirted with Andrew's own sister with little reserve.

He'd drunk no more wine than usual with dinner and had barely touched the port. A cack-handed job he was doing of keeping his distance from that kind of temptation.

He didn't mean the wine.

He meant the pretty woman.

He paused in his pacing and ran his hand through his hair.

And how had he handled it? Legging it up the stairs to his room. Like a real gentleman. He moaned and dropped himself onto the wide ledge of the open window, leaning against the casing.

The soft breeze reminded him of the September day he'd boarded the return ship from Boston—the day he'd set eyes on Miss Catherine Bradshaw of New York. He'd already become acquainted with Mr. Bradshaw; the man's interest in the automobile industry was as passionate as his own, and already far more lucrative. They'd discussed Spencer's ideas at length. And here the man was, traveling with his daughter to England for what was—Spencer had been led to believe during the ensuing three weeks—a European holiday. A holiday in which he'd imagined himself part of in a more intimate capacity with Catherine. He'd been so taken with her, and she'd given every indication she'd felt the same about him.

But a holiday it was not. Catherine, upon setting foot once again on dry land with Spencer at her side, had promptly taken her umbrella from his hand, thanked him for his companionship with a kiss on the cheek, expressed that it was indeed good practice in acquainting herself with an Englishman, and turned to meet her intended—Lord Amesbury of Cambridgeshire. An earl who needed an American heiress to save his vast estates in exchange for the status of a British title for her.

The flicker of remorse he'd seen in her eyes had done little to halt the humiliation soaking through him as readily as the rain. Mr. Bradshaw hadn't even nodded in his direction or shaken his hand. He simply left, taking not only Spencer's dignity but his ideas as well.

Though Spencer had assured himself that Mr. Bradshaw meant to continue his business endeavors in America alone, the man had been intrigued by Spencer's audacious hint that branches in both England and America would be a worthwhile pursuit.

If only Spencer hadn't been so eager. So trusting. So deuced romantic.

He'd regrouped, walled up his broken heart, shored up his pride, and gone to work knowing he could still take his idea to the one man he could trust most in this world.

The one man who had the best reason not to want anything to do with motorcars: Mr. Andrew Wooding of Surrey, who had an unexpectedly lovely sister whose eyes lit up at the word "motorcar."

A soft knock on his door pulled him from his thoughts. He stood, part of him imagining it was Andrew, changing his mind about investing after a long think. He quieted that hope and crossed to the room.

He did not find Andrew at his door, but Lydia.

"What are you—?"

She immediately stepped back and pressed a finger to her own lips.

Spencer exhaled, exasperated, and averted his gaze from her lips. He leaned heavily against the doorframe. "Are we whispering again?" he asked, ignoring the way his heart pounded. Blast if she didn't smell delicious. Like fruit and woods, but also something uniquely *her*.

She nodded. "I'd like to hear your proposal," she whispered, glancing down the corridor toward her brother's room.

"What, right *now*?"

"Well, yes, but no. First thing tomorrow morning. At the temple. Can you manage it?"

"Why do you want to hear my proposal?"

She rolled her eyes. Now *she* was exasperated? "Because I want to hear it. Perhaps I can help."

"You?"

"No, Nibs. *Yes*, me. Can you manage it?"

He hesitated. Meeting secretly with Andrew's little sister, no matter how innocent, was no way to move forward from all the thoughts he'd just put himself through.

She stepped toward him, and he instinctively stepped back, a little too sharply. The action made her pause. She shook her head. "I feel like part of this is my fault. If I'd only listened more carefully to your concern this morning, I could've helped you better prepare."

"I don't think anything I could've said today would've swayed Andrew."

"Perhaps you're right, but I have an idea. Please?"

Spencer pinched the bridge of his nose, then nodded. "Alrigh," he growled. He winced at his rolled *r* and dropped *t*, the Brummie in him coming out as it did when he was agitated. He took a breath. "But do you have a lady's maid? A chaperone you trust?"

She frowned but nodded.

"Bring 'er, then."

She nodded once more and turned to go. He moved to close his door, placing a barrier between him and her captivating scent, when she turned back.

"I'm nearly twenty-one," she said, frighteningly above a whisper. "It's important you understand that."

He opened his mouth to respond with heaven-knew-what, but before he could get a word out, she hurried away down the corridor.

He stood rooted to the spot, unsure what to make of that information, and chiding himself that he'd been a full year off in guessing her age.

Not that it mattered.

The house creaked above his head, and he retreated into his room and shut the door. Her fragrance, however, followed him in.

"Blast it." The girl would be the death of him.

The following morning, Spencer approached the temple, hurrying his stride. He'd had a restless night and slept later than he meant to. He'd no idea when he'd finally drifted off, but when he'd jolted awake with a slight headache, the sun was already on the rise. He'd splashed himself with cold water, tidied up as best he could, and headed straight outdoors. It was still early for a country household. He only hoped he hadn't kept Lydia waiting long.

He approached the temple and ran up the steps. "Lydia?" he called, wincing as the echo aggravated his headache.

"Ahem."

He skidded to a halt and found himself under the scrutiny of a woman he did not recognize. She wore a servant's uniform and sat on a stone bench, mending in her hands. He suddenly remembered he'd required Lydia to have a chaperone. "F-Forgive me," he stuttered. "I did not see you there. Er—Miss Wooding, is she here?"

The woman narrowed her gaze, her disapproval obvious. "Down the back stairs at the pond."

"Thank you." He moved to go, noting the woman was gathering up her things and would likely follow him. Well, good. This needed to be on the up-and-up.

He walked through the temple, passing the rows of columns, his steps echoing on the stone. He kept his eye on the rear entrance—a sort of walk-through annex. The opening framed the provincial scene of the pond, its bulrushes, and the misted woods surrounding it. As he drew nearer, he noticed a rhythmic plopping and ensuing ripple effect of stones being tossed into the water.

He exited the temple and found Lydia at the edge of the water in a white, billowy blouse, a loose necktie, and her breeches again.

A high-buttoned vest seemed to hold her all together and specifically made for her curves.

He slipped his hands into his pockets, leaned against a column at the top of the steps, and watched her select a few stones from the narrow shore and throw them one by one into the pond. A few waves of hair had slipped from the loose knot at the back of her neck, but she'd tied a wide, yellow ribbon around it all and, like the vest, it seemed to be holding everything together well enough. Indeed, watching her eased his concern for rushing, while at the same time making him utterly aware of each heartbeat in his chest.

Just before she threw the next rock, he cleared his throat.

She yipped as the rock slipped from her windup, flipped up high, and landed with a *kerplunk* in the shallows next to her. She turned.

"Your form could use a little work," he drolled.

She set her hands at her waist, her shoulders thrown back. "Who are you to criticize my form?"

He swallowed, attempting to maintain a collected demeanor, especially as he realized he'd meant it as less a criticism and more wishful thinking on his part. "I take it back. Obvious lapse in judgment. By all means, toss your rocks."

"Why does that sound impertinent?"

"Because you're a cheeky girl?"

She laughed, brushing a curl out of her eyes. "I am not. It's that accent of yours."

"My accent?" Had he let it slip again?

"You hide it, but I like it."

He sighed, almost a growl. "I liked you better when you were hiding from me behind pillars."

She laughed. "Do I scare you?"

"Outta my boots, ye fair wench."

She laughed more, and he found himself chuckling. Help him, he was in trouble over this key-hunting, chair-tipping, cow-loving, rock-throwing enchantress.

She walked toward him, watching him, and he tore his gaze away, suddenly in a frantic search for the chaperone. "Where did—"

"You asked that I bring her. You didn't say she had to stay."

He straightened up from the pillar. "Lydia, I don't think—"

"Settle down, Spencer. I had an idea, and it would be impossible for Mary to come along." She motioned beyond him to the far corner of the temple. Two bicycles leaned against the steps. "I thought we could go for a ride. See the old grounds? Mary hasn't learned to ride. Apparently washing and mending transport her to another world altogether, and she has no need of wheels. I'm quoting her, of course."

"Of course." He dropped his head, shaking it, both relieved and frustrated. "A ride sounds lovely."

"See? There it is."

"What?"

"You say 'lovely' as if you were saying 'drove-lay.'"

He blinked at her. "And you like that?"

She nodded. Shrugged.

He descended the stairs and headed for the bicycles. "Well, you'd be the first person outside Brum to say so. You know as well as I that most of England would rather listen to a Cockney than a Brummie. And Cockney makes their eyes twitch."

She followed. "Is that why you hide it?"

He pulled up the first bicycle for her and waited until she had it in hand. He pulled up the second, which had a small hamper belted to the rack over the back tire. "I hide it because my father paid a tutor to teach me how to hide it. He didn't want me to have to fight as hard as he did, you see." He threw a leg over the bike and mirrored her pose, one foot on a pedal.

"Fight for what?"

He threw her a brief, sharp look. "Respect."

She opened her mouth to argue.

"You're a smart woman," he said, cutting her off. "Surely you see the reasoning behind his choice."

After a moment, she relented with a nod. "And behind yours."

He shrugged. "My father might be gone, but I'll use what he sacrificed to give me."

"Language is a beautiful gift, in all its forms."

A grin pulled at his lips. "An idealist, you are."

"No. I just believe people shouldn't be pigeonholed for being born into circumstances they had no control over."

"Like in the choking squalor of Birmingham?"

"Yes. Or having been born a woman." She leveled her gaze, as if challenging him. Then she shifted her weight on the pedal and took off on the bicycle. "Follow me," she called over her shoulder.

He imagined it would become more and more difficult *not* to follow her. Anywhere.

After some minutes on a path winding around the pond where small fish jumped at morning insects, they approached the woods.

"I thought you wanted to hear my proposal," he called ahead to Lydia.

"I shall," she said, turning her head slightly. "In a moment."

He fought a grin, considering how such an innocuous answer could be so intriguing. They crossed into the shaded portion of the path where the canopy of trees muted sound and light dappled through from the east. Birdsong and treetops rustling in the breeze met the crunch of their bicycle tires over fallen pine needles and twigs. All was quiet, cool, and sheltered.

They rode down into a gulley, over a plank bridge spanning the small creek that fed the pond, and then up a gradual climb snaking its way slowly up the treed hill.

Spencer remembered this trail from his and Andrew's riding lessons. The path had been pounded smooth and compact and served the bikes fairly well. He watched Lydia rise to her feet on the pedals, using the downward momentum of her weight to get her bicycle up the last portion of the hill. He shook his head, wishing her figure did not draw his attention so easily.

She cycled well, proving her skill as they came to a severe dip and she remained standing, allowing the bike to take the brunt of the obstacle while she floated through it. She laughed with delight, and he smiled more at her enjoyment than his own.

She paused at the top of the rise, and he drew up alongside her, somewhat out of breath. She, too, breathed deeply, her hand at her waist.

She pointed. "There."

He followed her direction. The other side of this hill had fewer trees, and they could see farmland spread out in the vale below. But Lydia pointed to the right where the path forked, and instead of going down the hill, they rode along the ridge a short distance to a clearing of felled logs circling a ring of stones—a fire ring. Here Lydia stopped. The vantage point afforded views of both sides of the hill for miles, and the morning sun skimmed across the fields, hills, and estates.

"Beautiful," he said.

"Picnic Hill. We used to come here—my parents, Andrew, and me. We would have a picnic, of course. One of my very few memories of my parents. Did you ever come here, during your visits with Andrew?"

He shook his head. "Only to ride horseback, and we stayed on the other path."

She nodded, still looking over the vista. "I've come here often since my parents died."

"Alone?" he asked.

She smirked up at him. "Andrew has kept a tight leash on me outside of Briarwall, but within its boundaries, I've more freedom to roam than most girls, I suppose. I'm thankful for that."

He nodded, looking at the natural beauty about them. "I can see why you'd be grateful."

They set the bicycles against the trunk of a large oak, and Lydia set to work gathering kindling. "Help me get the fire going. I'm assuming you didn't eat breakfast."

"You assume correctly." It had been too early yet when he'd left the house. He found a pile of cut wood under the boughs of an old pine and collected a few of the dryer logs.

"Well, we shan't be hungry for long. I raided the pantry and larder." She deposited her kindling next to the fire ring and brushed her hands. "I'll leave you to this, and I'll get the food."

"As you wish," he said, watching her stride to the bicycles. At times she reminded him of Andrew with that innate confidence and natural command. He removed his coat and rolled up his sleeves. "Do you chop the wood yourself, as well?" he asked, grinning, ready to hear her claim command of that chore.

She threw him a glance. "Warren sends someone up here to keep me stocked. I did not ask him to, and he doesn't tell me, but I know he does it."

"That is very kind."

"It is. He could easily go to Andrew and inform on me. But he does not. And for that, I count him a dear friend."

"I'll not go to Andrew, either," he said, brow lifted. "Perhaps you'll count me as a dear friend, too."

She grinned. "Perhaps. But Warren has known me since I was a babe."

"And I have known you since you were not much older than that."

She paused, as if she'd forgotten that fact, and a flush touched her cheeks. "Well." She turned her back to him and pulled a paper-wrapped parcel from the hamper. "I'll take that into consideration."

He smiled to himself and returned to his assignment.

After the fire had settled, they speared sausages with whittled sticks and roasted them over the flames. Slices of bread, tomatoes, and boiled eggs from the kitchen completed their meal. They washed it down with a thermos of coffee, chatting easily about Briarwall and growing up with Andrew.

As they finished, Lydia brushed the crumbs from her hands and scooted to the edge of her log bench. "Now, it's time to show me what you've got."

His brow rose. "Pardon me?"

"Your presentation. I'm all ears."

He doubted that very much. However, he straightened his posture, then stood.

Her eyes widened, following his height. "You're going to stand?"

"Do you wish me to sit?"

She blinked. "I suppose whichever way you think will win me over."

He paused, looking over the area, then made his choice. He sat down, but this time he sat next to Lydia so they shared the log bench. He leaned forward, resting his elbows on his knees, and met her curious gaze.

"How's this?" he asked.

She grinned. "We shall see."

He grinned in return. He was breaking every rule with this girl. But she had a way of keeping things light and harmless. *Harmless*, he repeated to himself. Like knocking on his door in the dark of night. He took a deep breath. "Very well. I'll begin."

He told her about Michigan and Detroit. About Mr. Ford and assembly lines and standardized parts. But instead of waiting until the end to ask her questions, she peppered him throughout. Was Detroit like Birmingham? How many people owned motorcars in America? Did he prefer a side or foot break, a steering wheel or lever, an open or enclosed cab? What did he think of the newer petrol cars? What did he think of women drivers?

"Women drivers?" he repeated.

"Yes. I wish to drive." Her leg bounced, and her fingers gripped the edge of the log. She pursed her lips and looked away. "Andrew won't hear it."

"You asked him? And he refused?"

She folded her arms. "Did you know that Florrie's father will allow her to learn to drive, but she claims she has no need to learn since they have a driver?" She threw her hands up. "Can you believe that?"

He widened his eyes and shook his head at her passionate outrage. "Unfathomable."

"Absolutely. And my friend Violet Whittemore can drive, but then, so does her mother. Sometimes we take her Rover for a spin."

"Can't Miss Whittemore teach you?"

"She's not allowed to let anyone else behind the wheel. One of the family rules. She dares not break it. I don't blame her. If I could drive, I would keep every rule for the privilege."

"Every rule?"

She looked at him sideways. "Every *reasonable* rule. Andrew can be rather unreasonable at times."

"True. For what it's worth, I find women drivers an inevitable part of the future of the industry. Women shop, visit, teach, conduct meetings, midwife, farm, create, and so on. The use of the motorcar to aid their endeavors makes perfect sense."

"Oh, I like you, Spencer Hayes."

He darted a look her way as she sat up straight, her complexion turning rosy.

"I mean—I—like what you think about motorcars and women. That's all," she said.

He nodded. "I'm guessing you don't get to talk about the subject often with your brother."

She deflated. "I can't press him. He still aches, you see. Of course, you see. You witnessed his reaction to your proposal."

"What about Warren? Could he talk Andrew into teaching you?"

"Neither of us know how to go about it, really."

"I see." Warren likely wouldn't jeopardize his position by telling his employer how to handle his own sister.

They sat silent for a moment. A breeze blew, and he stole a glance as it played with Lydia's errant curls. She tucked one behind her ear and gazed about.

"Andrew never comes here," she said quietly.

"Is that why we're here now? To discuss such a sensitive subject as the motorcar?" He might've teased her, but he kept his tone serious.

She nodded. After another moment, she straightened, folding her hands in her lap. "I've interrupted your proposal. Please, do continue."

He nodded, intrigued by her fluctuation between frustrated girl and self-assured woman. He had no idea how she intended to remedy the situation with Andrew, but if she wished to talk motorcars with someone, by Jove, he'd talk.

She listened intently to the rest of it, asking surprisingly astute questions about investment, capital, and shares.

After a particularly intelligent question about reinvestment and chain shops, she gave him a look and said, "I don't just read novels, Mr. Hayes."

He chuckled. "Forgive me."

"It so happens that what my brother lacks in discussing automobiles he makes up for in spades when it comes to discussing business."

"*That* does not surprise me. What does surprise me is that you entertain a similar interest."

Her smile widened. "All a girl needs to fly is a little fairy dust." She held her fingers aloft in a sprinkling motion.

He recognized the reference from James Barrie's play. "The fairy dust being . . . ?"

"Knowledge, Mr. Hayes. Knowledge. I've become an excellent listener." She leaned into him, her brown eyes soft, her scent welcoming. "I turn twenty-one next month," she said quietly.

He found himself leaning in as well. "You mentioned that." He should pull away, and soon, but the caress of her voice was far too enticing.

"I come into my independence. I should very much like to invest in your motor supply shop."

He arched a brow, an attempt to hide his ricocheting heart. "I believe that to be very wise. Thank you." He would not shirk her. He would use whatever trifle she wanted to pledge and be sure of her return. He knew her interest in his proposal would not make up for Andrew's lack, but whatever disappointment he felt about that dissipated at her nearness and the heady scent of her perfume. He swallowed, his gaze drawn to her lush mouth. "I shall be very judicious with your sum."

"I'm counting on it." She blinked slowly, a slight tremor in her breath. "I think twenty thousand pounds will be sure to draw more investors."

"Of course," he whispered, the space between them slowly disappearing. Her eyes closed, her chin lifted—

Twenty thousand—

He jumped up and teetered toward the smoldering fire in front of the log.

"Spencer!" She hopped up and reached for his arms, grasping his wrists to pull him away from the fire and directly into her arms, his momentum pushing her back and over the log bench as he tumbled helplessly after.

"Oof."

"Lydia—" He pulled himself to his elbows and twisted to see her face. "Lydia, are you alright?" He took her face in his hands and tapped her cheek. "Lydia?"

Her eyes fluttered open, and she found his gaze. Her shoulders began to shake. She gasped, laughing. "Did we just fall over a log?"

He watched her, baffled and bewitched by his need to protect her, by the utter nearness of her. He was afraid to touch her yet needed to be assured she was unharmed.

She looked around, taking in their awkward position in the winter detritus and new growth of spring grass, one of her legs bent over the log and him sprawled across her midsection. "Really, Mr. Hayes, if this is how you react to your investors, perhaps you should put up a little sign: 'Prone to step in fire when excited; may tumble over low furnishings.'" She turned back to him, her eyes alight. "You're not burned, are you?"

He shook his head. No, he was fighting a different kind of fire altogether.

She stilled.

Likely because his fingers remained cradling her face, his traitorous thumb stroking the silky corner of her smile. Or because he was not laughing. Indeed, he could hardly breathe.

"Lydia—" Her name came out breathy. He swallowed and tried again. "I cannot allow you to invest your entire inheritance in this endeavor."

She blinked at him. "I agree. You have no say in what I do or don't do with my money."

Her words broke the spell he'd been under. He sat up, pushing his hand through his hair. "That is not what I meant, and you know it—"

She sat up as well. "Let me put your mind at ease. Twenty thousand pounds is not even half of my inheritance. It is, however, the amount Andrew and I agreed upon to invest. And I'm choosing to invest it in motor supply shops. *Your* motor supply shops."

Twenty thousand pounds was *not even half* of her inheritance? He stood, brushing off his trousers. "I doubt Andrew had that in mind when advising you."

She peered up at him, shielding her eyes from the morning sun. "Well, fortunately for you, I don't care what Andrew thinks."

"That will certainly convince *him* to invest."

"Convincing him to invest isn't the goal. He will never invest. Not in this."

He turned away, his mind and body still fighting over the desire to either throttle her or kiss her. "Then what is the goal?"

She stood, picking at the debris on her blouse. He peeked at her and huffed at the sight of grass and leaves in her hair. She couldn't very well return to the house in his company looking like that.

"Here, let me help." He stepped forward and began pulling nature from her tresses.

"Thank you," she said.

He felt her gaze on him but couldn't look her in the eyes.

"Spencer."

"What?"

"Please look at me."

"No."

She put her hands on her hips. "Why not?"

Because to look at her was to want her more. He didn't answer, only continued to pull leaves from her hair, the act itself far too intimate for his own good.

Her hands wrapped around his wrists, and she pulled his fists in front of her. "Listen to me, clock boy."

He frowned at her, bemused.

She sighed. "The goal is to tie the Wooding name to the investments. To instill the confidence that our name provides in other potential investors. Do you think I don't know how that would make a difference? That you are our guest—that my brother is an old friend—will influence our friends and acquaintances to place their trust in you."

He lowered his chin, meeting her hopeful gaze. "And what will Andrew say, Lydia, when your friends and acquaintances ask him about his investment, and he, being a man of integrity, tells them he could not bring himself to invest? That it is not his investment, but yours? That he disapproves?"

She shrugged, poorly covering her wavering confidence. "It will make no difference. It is Wooding money."

He wished that were true. He sighed and raised his wrist, kissing her hand still wrapped there, inhaling her scent.

She pulled in a soft breath of surprise but did not relinquish her grip.

"It is a very sweet thing you wish to do," he said. "But perhaps you should discuss it with your brother before you do anything more."

He felt her hand stiffen and then she pulled away. "Because I'm a woman."

He bobbed his head. "Honestly? Yes. I will not insult your intelligence with pandering."

She huffed. "Oh, well, thank you for that." The brightness had left her eyes, but she had not dimmed. Indeed, she smoldered, brazenly holding his gaze. "But I think the pandering made an appearance at the word *sweet*."

He swallowed hard. "Lydia, please don't turn this into something it's not." His voice had taken on the tone of begging, and he winced. "I'm astonished at your offer. I only wish for you to be certain—"

"And I cannot be certain without a man's permission." She turned and stomped to the bicycles, hefting hers upright. "Well, right now I'm so very uncertain I can remain and clean up this misguided picnic. Whatever shall I do?" She positioned herself on the bike and shot him a look, her eyes wide. "I hope I can manage to make it down this treacherous hill with my frail womanly form. If only there were a real man about to ask for direction. Ah well."

He stood, silent, humiliated by her brilliant performance.

She placed her foot on the pedal and blew a stray lock of hair from her eyes. "I have a new sign for you, Mr. Hayes." She swept her fingers in the air before her as if reading. "'Lacks the courage to take money from anyone in a skirt—though claims women are an inevitable part of the motorcar industry.'" With that, she lurched the bicycle forward, down the path, and away.

He stepped forward, his own hypocrisy feeling like lead in his feet. "You're not wearing a skirt," he called lamely and to no avail. "Lydia!"

When there was no response, he threw his hands out, letting them flop down at his sides. He took in the remnants of their picnic with a deep sigh, then set to work clearing things away.

This. *This* was why he'd vowed never again to mix the volatile emotion of romance with business. It became a powder keg in a pile of dead leaves near a crackling fire.

Spencer looked down the path where Lydia had ridden away, whisps of her hair fluttering behind her, her blouse billowing. He closed his eyes, and his insides tightened.

Her skin might very well have been the softest thing he'd ever touched, the loveliest thing he'd ever smelled.

Done for was a severe understatement.

CHAPTER 10

After returning to the house, Lydia ordered a tray of drinking chocolate to her room then immediately regretted it as her stomach had knotted itself in a fine twist. She changed clothes, and Fallon wordlessly brushed the remaining leaves from her hair before rolling it into the latest pompadour, smoothing the curls at her temples and the nape of her neck around her fingers to soften the look further.

Lydia watched herself in the mirror, wondering not for the first time what her parents might think of her. She knew so little of them. What would they think of her picnic on the hill? Of the way her heart had hammered as she'd offered Spencer her investment, how it had leaped at his weight and his touch, and how it had flared in anger as she'd been spurned—been made to feel like such a child after such an adult . . . *everything*.

She lowered her gaze, not knowing if they'd be ashamed or proud.

"There you are, miss. Pretty as a picture."

She nodded. "Thank you, Fallon."

"Is there anything else I can do for you, miss?"

Lydia hesitated. Fallon had been a new upstairs maid when

Lydia's parents had died, then filled in as Lydia's lady's maid when she left the nursery at age thirteen. Fallon had done so well with it, Andrew hired her for the position. Fifteen years older than Lydia to the month, the woman was quiet and confident, exhibited good taste, and had proven trustworthy when Lydia's world took the odd swipe at her adolescent hopes and dreams.

The woman waited patiently. Often, Lydia felt Fallon was more a gentlewoman than she could ever hope to be, but it wasn't an intimidating or discouraging thought. Indeed, Lydia often leaned on the woman's steadiness to fortify her own. She knew herself well enough to own that steadiness was not one of her strongest traits.

Lydia straightened. "You remember my parents, Fallon."

"Some, miss."

"I only wondered . . . Had you ever observed my father—what I mean to ask is . . . Was my father a very progressive man? Or more entrenched in tradition?"

Fallon tipped her head. "In what aspect, miss?"

"Specifically, in the way he viewed my mother. Or . . . women in general."

A gleam lit the maid's eye as if she had expected that direction. "'Twould be inappropriate to share an opinion of that, miss. But factually speaking, Mr. Wooding showed Mrs. Wooding every respect and often deferred to her when it came to matters outside the household. Anyone who observed them together knew he held your mother's opinion in high esteem."

"What kind of matters?"

"Oh, matters of the property and the livery, for example. Or politics. If you don't mind my saying so, I was pleasantly shocked when I first observed them sharing the daily papers every morning, discussing happenings and articles as though they were great colleagues and not husband and wife." She lowered her gaze. "At least, no husband and wife I'd ever witnessed."

Lydia drew in a breath of pleasure at the image of her parents engaged in lively conversation. "Did they ever speak of money?"

Fallon's eyes widened, and she took a half-step back. "'Tis not my place, miss."

Lydia flushed. "Of course. Forgive me."

Fallon dipped a small curtsy. "Not at all, miss."

"Thank you, Fallon. That will be all."

Fallon turned to leave, but before she reached the door, she turned back. "I said it wasn't my place to share my opinion, but I will say . . . they'd be right pleased with you, miss. I know that as I know my own self."

A warmth bloomed within Lydia, and she welcomed that hope. "Thank you, Fallon."

The woman nodded. "If you're wanting to know more of your parents, might I suggest you ask Mr. Hayes? I know he thought highly of them, and they of him."

Lydia did not miss the maid's attempt to hide the gleam in her gray eyes. "That will be all, Fallon."

Suppressing a grin, Fallon curtsied.

Her chocolate arrived just as Fallon left, and Lydia no longer regretted the request. She took a cup to the window seat overlooking the lawn stretching before the temple. A lone figure slowly walked a bicycle toward the house, a basket strapped to the back. Lydia's flush renewed. Her anger kindled, but not near to what it had been. What had he said that had been so wrong? Indeed, he had been right about everything, and that, she realized, was what had angered her most.

Investing that sum of money in the motor supply shops

without Andrew's blessing would upset him greatly, and potentially make matters worse—and extremely awkward—for Spencer, let alone Lydia. Andrew might even see it as a betrayal, though he'd never say so.

. . . discussing happenings and articles as though they were great colleagues . . .

Lydia had wished that exact thing for her and Spencer today on the hill, but didn't she wish that, too, for her and Andrew?

Spencer disappeared from view as he headed toward the kitchen to return the basket.

If only he hadn't made her feel like a child. She did not want to give up on her idea, but the thought of approaching him again over the subject upended her nerves. She closed her eyes and took a long swallow of the chocolate, letting it warm her. Cook always added sugar and cream just the way she liked it. Her shoulders settled.

She'd send word downstairs that upon Violet's arrival that afternoon she was to be sent directly to Lydia's room while Violet's clothes for dinner should be sent to the second guest room. For now, Lydia need only to hide in her room for the remainder of the morning until her lingering humiliation subsided. Besides, she'd need to fortify herself against the Piedmonts' impending company at dinner.

She sighed and picked up the miniature of her young mother from the small table beside her, searching for a connection to the blonde, blue-eyed beauty in her high Victorian ringlets and lilac ruffled neckline.

Had *she* struggled so with her guests at Briarwall? Lydia glanced at her door then back to the portrait. "Mother," she whispered, "I am trying, but hostessing guests is *not* for the faint of heart."

Aside from a brief visit from Mrs. Parks to review the menu for the remainder of the week and the delivery of the post, the morning passed without incident. Lydia was deep into *The Hound of the Baskervilles* when the secret knock sounded on her door. She tossed the book aside and leaped to open it.

Violet startled as Lydia grabbed her arm, pulled her into the room, and closed the door behind her. She turned and pressed her back against it, her hand still gripping the door handle.

"Lydia," Violet said, pressing her hand to her chest. An amber and onyx bumblebee nestled above a flounce on her blouse. Her gaze suddenly narrowed. "What has happened?"

Lydia took her hand and led her to the window seat. "You must tell me what to do."

Her friend's eyes widened as they sat, then she leaned forward, pressing a hand to Lydia's forehead. "Are you feeling well?" She took both of Lydia's wrists and looked her in the eyes. "You just suggested I tell you what to do."

"Oh, stop that." She pushed Violet's hands away and folded her arms across her middle as Violet grinned. "It so happens I am *not* feeling well. I've been hiding in here since this morning, and I still haven't worked out how to show my face again to certain members of this household."

"What happened?"

Lydia put a hand over her eyes and groaned. "I had such high hopes. I was to do this grand thing, and it all just went—" She sighed. "It fell like a soufflé." She slapped her hand on the seat cushion between them.

"Was it something with Andrew? Florrie said he was most patronizing when she was here last."

"If only." Lydia gazed out the window. "With Andrew I know what to expect, and I put up my shield in advance. He has the added benefit of being my brother, and so I must love him and he me. But with Spencer—" She swallowed. "*Mr. Hayes*, I mean. With him I expected—I don't know what I expected—something different, I suppose. He seems such a forward-thinking man. But now, after I made the offer to invest in his proposal, and it seemed as though he might even—but then he nearly stepped in the fire and we fell over the log and—" Her cheeks warmed. "It turns out I'm not as powerful as I think I am, and it was absolutely humiliating." She let her head fall against the window with a thunk.

Violet's wide eyes did nothing to ease Lydia's concern. "I wish to help you sort through this, but before I can, you must answer some questions."

"Yes. Anything. I imagine I'm not making much sense."

"Not a dot." Violet studied her. "Have you fallen in love with Mr. Hayes?"

An unladylike guffaw fell from her mouth. She stood. "No! Absolutely not! How on earth did you get that impression?" She began to pace in front of the fireplace, unable to remain still. "Being in *love* is not so *agitating* as this certainly is." She pressed a hand to her thumping heart, attempting to calm it. "Am I right?" she added.

"Indeed." Violet remained placidly observant. "How a person could associate one feeling with the other is unfathomable."

Lydia narrowed her gaze at Violet, who barely hid a smile.

"This is no laughing matter, Vi. I am mortified."

Violet sobered. "Forgive me. I'm trying to understand. What was this offer you made to him?"

Lydia stopped pacing, then sat back down next to Violet. She explained the bicycle ride, the picnic, Spencer's proposal, and her offer. Then, with her hand back over her eyes, she shared the resulting fall and exchange that led to her leaving Spencer on the hill with nary a glance backward and fury coursing through her from head to toe. The retelling left her flushed and breathless again, and she stood again to pace out her frustration.

"Well," Violet said, "obviously, you're both in an uncomfortable spot. Perhaps Mr. Hayes needs some time to consider your offer."

"Yes, and I need to discuss it with Andrew, but Violet, that does nothing to give me any courage to leave this room and play hostess tonight. How does one recover from such a foible? He is our guest, and despite my foolish assumptions of him, I still need to perform my duties and see that he is comfortable in our home. Yet all the while, I want to snort and paw at the ground, ready to charge at him. Perhaps that would knock some sense into the man."

"It would knock something into him, to be sure."

Lydia knelt at her friend's knees and took her hands. "What do I do?"

Violet thought a moment, her lips pursed, her pale green eyes unfocused. "Have you changed your mind about your investment offer?"

"No. I believe his plan a brilliant and sensible one." Lydia considered her reasons for her decision. "I want to be a part of it. I want to be part of the future of the motorcar industry. I don't want to watch from the sidelines." She frowned.

"Andrew remembers everything about our parents' accident. About the brakes giving out down Box Hill, and the bluff at the turn. He wasn't there, of course, but I believe he imagines it as if he had been. His pain remains sharp, and he is still unable to speak of it. My knowledge of the accident comes from questioning Warren and Mrs. Parks.

"Perhaps if Andrew had shared it with me when I was younger, I would feel more as he does. But while I feel the loss of my parents, the loss is disconnected to blame. Just as I wouldn't blame the whole orchard for one bad apple, neither will I blame all of the motorcar industry for a faulty pair of brakes. Arnold Motorcarriage accepted their part in the accident and settled an appropriate amount for our loss. For a future without our parents. And who knows, but that my small part will go toward safer cars? A well-maintained car is a safer car." She took a deep breath and blew it out with a nod. "Yes. That is precisely how I'll approach Andrew with it. I want to invest in a future of safer cars."

"That is perfectly noble of you. And Mr. Hayes?"

Her shoulders slumped again. "I have no idea."

Violet took her hand and drew her gaze. "How *do* you feel about him, Lydia? How would you have answered that question before this morning's incident?"

Lydia lifted her brow. "I admire him. He is interesting. I had hoped we were becoming . . . friends. I suppose that was exciting to me because none of Andrew's other friends treat me as an equal."

"And then this morning, Mr. Hayes made you feel less than that."

"Yes."

"How disappointing."

Disappointed. Yes, that certainly described how Lydia had felt on the hill.

"I suppose we all disappoint people at times," Violet said.

She shrugged. "I'm surprised Andrew doesn't introduce me as 'My little sister, Disappointment Wooding.'" She huffed a laugh.

Violet smiled compassionately. "I suppose it's too much of a mouthful," she said. "And not nearly as pretty."

Lydia nodded, gazing outside once more.

Violet leaned back against the window. "Isn't it a good thing we're given chances to prove ourselves better?"

The truth stung, but as it settled into her soul, Lydia sensed a rekindled determination—something more familiar to her than this unnerving humiliation. She nodded. "I must give Mr. Hayes time and space. He'll not forget my offer soon."

Violet's lips quirked. "Indeed, he won't."

"In the meantime, I'll speak to Andrew. I don't need his permission, but I see the wisdom in confiding in him. I found the courage to approach a veritable stranger with my idea. I can summon the courage to take it to my brother. Correct?"

"Correct."

"If only Andrew didn't think of me as a girl still in my plaits and pinafores."

"I wish I could argue that, but you've hit the nail on the head." She tipped her head to the side. "Perhaps we should do what we can to change that."

"What do you mean?" Lydia asked. "I dress like a woman—usually. I speak—mostly—like a gentlewoman. I have learned the duties of a woman, while seeking to expand my abilities and interests. What more can I do?"

"What will Andrew expect of you tonight?"

"The usual. To be welcoming to our guests. To escort the ladies to and fro and direct the evening's entertainment."

"Will that entertainment include a hunt for a clock key?"

Lydia bristled and opened her mouth to defend the way things had unfolded the other evening, but Violet put up her hand.

"I'm only making a point from Andrew's perception. I'm wildly jealous that Florrie had all the fun. But what do you think *Andrew* will be expecting tonight?"

Lydia frowned. "He likely expects more of the same. Looking for buried treasure, perhaps. Or a secret passage leading to the temple."

Violet grinned. "Wouldn't that be scrumptious?"

"Yes, and it would save me from a sopping wet return after a rainstorm."

"Indeed. But what if for the next while, as you ready yourself to approach Andrew with your wish to invest in Mr. Hayes's shops, you show him the woman you are."

"The woman I am, or the woman my brother wishes me to be? Because I don't think I can change who I am in an attempt to manipulate him into gaining his blessing."

"No, and I wouldn't ask you to do that. I'm simply suggesting you set aside the more fanciful—and delightful, I might add—inclinations of your nature and recall all that you've been taught as you manage this home. While I agree it's a shame you need to show your own brother that you are an intelligent, trustworthy *woman* soon to be of her own means, it wouldn't hurt your cause to display those particular feathers to gain his ear."

Lydia sighed. "I suppose he'd be more apt to hear me out."

"And not dismiss the idea without a decent discussion."

"And this begins tonight?"

Violet shrugged. "Let it begin now. Stop hiding in here, and let's go about some of your responsibilities before Sir Lawrence arrives. Show Andrew that *Wooding competency* he's always bragging about."

Lydia straightened. "I do need to attend to the tea cabinet and review the wines with Ralston for dinner. Could you help me assemble the charity baskets for tomorrow? And I'm sure the flowers could use some freshening."

"Yes, those are all perfectly responsible—"

"—and boring—"

"—duties to attend to. Though, will it startle Mrs. Parks to finally find you in the tea cabinet?"

Lydia smiled. "It might. She'll think I'm displeased with her performance."

"She'll more likely clap her hands with joy."

"And I don't need to pay any particular attention to Mr. Hayes?"

Violet shook her head. "Mutual apologies must be expressed at some point, but give it a rest unless he approaches you. Likely you are both feeling similar discomfort from this morning and need space. If he is anything like the man you originally deemed him to be, he is reviewing the things he said to you with regret."

Lydia felt her cheeks warm and nodded. "Will you help me?"

"Of course." Violet's gaze swept over her face, a glint in her eye. "And you must do something about that blush if you are not falling in love with him."

"*That* is not helpful, Vi."

"Agree to disagree," Violet muttered to the room. "You smell divine, by the way."

"Likewise."

Lydia had to admit that carrying out her responsibilities had garnered Andrew's attention in a positive light, and it had taken her mind—somewhat—off Spencer's presence in the house, though he did not make an appearance and Andrew did not mention him nor did she ask.

After Mrs. Parks recovered from her initial shock to find Lydia in the tea cabinet, she quickly expressed her delight and gave Lydia a lesson in choosing teas and maintaining the cabinet. Freshening the flowers about the house proved quite relaxing, and by the time Lydia and Violet had finished practicing a musical piece in "the Wendy League" room, Lydia suggested taking a rest before dressing for dinner.

"It is only for a moment," she implored Violet.

"And what happens every time you lie down before dinner?"

Violet knew very well what happened. "I fall asleep and am late for dinner."

"So, what are you going to do?"

"Lie down but not fall asleep?"

"No, we are going to the drawing room to play a game of chess, and I will allow you to rest your eyes whilst I beat you soundly. Then we both shall go up to dress for dinner. You will have your rest while still appearing to be an attentive and intelligent woman."

"Not if I nod off at dinner and awaken in my soup."

"I won't let that happen."

Lydia narrowed her gaze.

"You asked me to tell you what to do," Violet challenged.

Lydia sighed deeply. "Thank you for taking on the task with such . . . enthusiasm."

Violet bowed her head. "I am your humble servant."

"Oh, please."

Violet laughed.

They entered the drawing room, and Lydia stopped short, grabbing Violet by the arm.

Spencer stood at the fireplace, one hand on the mantel, staring at the freshly built-up flames. It appeared as if he'd just come in from outdoors, as he still wore a long duster and his hair looked mussed by the wind. A tweed cap was bunched in his hand, likely in need of a good reshaping when released from his grip. It seemed he hadn't heard them enter.

"Is that him?" Violet whispered.

Lydia nodded, her dratted pulse skipping.

"If he's a bird-watcher, I'm my Great-Uncle Beauregard."

Lydia choked on a laugh.

Spencer looked up then and immediately schooled his bright expression as if remembering something miserable. Like this morning, for example.

It was a long moment before Lydia remembered she was the one to make introductions. She squared her shoulders. "Mr. Hayes. I hope we're not disturbing you."

He faced them, his hands behind his back. "I was just warming myself before removing to my room. The day turned chilly after such a promising sunrise."

She paused at his observation, wondering if the reference meant more than talk of the weather. "Yes, well, Mr. Hayes, this is a dear friend of mine, Miss Whittemore."

"Another dear friend?" he said. He turned to Violet with a bow.

"Yes, and you must call me Violet. I've heard too much about you to stand on ceremony."

"*Violet*," Lydia said. "Hush."

"I didn't say they were good things." Violet grinned in reply.

Spencer, thankfully, seemed to fight his own smile. "Very well. Call me Spencer." He flicked a glance at Lydia, which she ignored.

"And what feat did you accomplish to earn Lydia's *dear* friendship? I seem to have failed miserably."

Violet answered as if asked the question daily. "I found her as a lost little lamb roaming the woods bordering our estates, dried her tears, and returned her home, where we shared brambleberry pie and a glass of milk. I was seven, she was four, and she's been following me about ever since."

"How fortunate," he said, glancing between them. "For both of you. Though I imagine she's done a fair amount of leading since then."

Violet scrutinized him, smiling. "Indeed. And what about you, Spencer? How is it you are esteemed as a 'chum' of Austere Andrew?"

His brow rose. "*Austere Andrew*?" He chuckled. "I've not heard that one. It suits."

"What others have you heard?" Violet asked.

Lydia listened intently while trying not to look as if she cared at all.

"Oh, let's see. Andrew the Great. His Royal Andrew. And finally—and likely the one he detested most—Apollo." Again, he glanced at Lydia, knowing she knew the story behind that nickname.

Violet frowned. "As in—?"

"The Greek god, yes."

Violet lifted her chin. "Handsome, athletic, knowledgeable—"

Lydia raised an eyebrow at the ease with which her friend drew similarities between Andrew and the god.

"And a tragedy in matters of the heart."

All three of them turned sharply at Andrew's bold response. A twinge of guilt pulled Lydia a half-step back at being caught discussing her brother, though she'd said nothing. Spencer and Violet, however, stood tall and unrepentant.

"Though I understand your loathing of the nickname," Violet said to Andrew, "I can see how you came to have it."

"Can you?" Andrew said. He maintained his easy stride to join them, but his expression was stoic. "Please, do not enlighten me further."

Violet grinned and bowed in acquiescence. "*Mr.* Wooding."

Lydia shook her head. Violet had addressed Andrew by his given name until he'd returned from his final year at Eton. Ever since then, she addressed him as formally as Andrew had become.

He bowed in return. "Miss Whittemore. You look lovely."

"Thank you. And Lydia looks lovely as well, don't you think?"

Lydia blushed as both men turned their gaze upon her. She made a mental note not to ask Violet for help again. Still, she pulled her shoulders back and lowered her eyes.

"Lydia, you look very fine," Andrew said with a bow.

"Fine?" Violet countered. "Why, she is a woman of beauty, depth, and heart. Wouldn't you agree, Spencer?"

Lydia grabbed for Violet's hand and gave it a shake behind their skirts as the tips of Spencer's ears turned pink. What happened to giving the man space? Violet kept her gaze on the gentlemen.

Spencer cleared his throat and, with a glance at Andrew, bowed his head to Lydia. "Indeed, no one could question that you are a force for womankind, Lydia." He lifted his searching gaze to meet hers.

Was he referring to her anger on the hill? Or had Spencer considered her words about being treated as a simple female? Under his intent gaze, she felt the heat of their earlier connection reignite, but just as quickly, he pulled his attention away, and she was cold again.

Violet squeezed her hand, and Lydia took a deep breath to steady herself.

He addressed Andrew. "Thank you for allowing me to take the motorcar. I needed to clear my head, and the drive was exhilarating."

Spencer had gone for a drive? In *their* motorcar? An unfounded sense of being left out tugged the corners of her mouth downward.

"I'm glad to hear it," Andrew said. "But I'll thank you to refrain from feeding anymore tales of 'Andrew the Great' to these two." He motioned to the ladies. "I fear you've given them ammunition, which they will use at the most inopportune moment, mark my words."

"I beg your pardon," Violet countered. "You can be sure our moments are always perfectly opportune."

Andrew studied her a moment, then leaned toward Spencer. "Fearsome creatures, are they not?" he asked, a glint in his eye.

Spencer glanced at Lydia once more. "Terrifying."

Lydia attempted to look serene and womanly.

Violet narrowed her gaze. "Then perhaps now would be a good time to challenge you to a chess match. Andrew, what say you? When was the last time we played?" She was already walking to the small table they often used for the game.

"I forget," Andrew said, following Violet.

She laughed. "That is because you lost."

"Then I'm due for a win."

"We shall see."

Their banter faded to the other side of the room as Lydia's stomach tightened. This was not the plan. She grew increasingly aware of Spencer standing near her. *Dash* Violet for abandoning the plan in such a way that instead of giving Spencer time and space, Lydia was now obliged to be attentive to him, and only him.

She clasped her hands in front of her, and Spencer watched the tips of his shoes.

She cleared her throat and bounced on the balls of her feet.

"About this morning—" they both said together.

They both paused and glanced about the room, Spencer squeezing his poor hat between his hands.

"I wish to—" they both attempted again.

This time Spencer huffed out a laugh, and Lydia pressed her cool hand to her warm neck.

"Please," he said, "continue."

She could have argued with him, but perhaps it was better to say her piece first. "I apologize for losing my temper. I ought not to have abandoned you on the hill. A gracious host would've never done such things."

"A gracious gentleman would've never spoken to a friend—let alone a potential investor—the way I spoke to you."

His words softened her. "I'd hoped we were friends." She wasn't ready to address the other matter—the "potential investor" part of their relationship.

"That is my hope still, Lydia."

She lifted her head and met his hesitant, hopeful expression.

She nodded slowly. "You only wish me to be careful of my inheritance, am I correct?"

He sighed in relief as he answered. "Yes. Entirely."

She peeked over at Andrew. He and Violet were focused on their game. She lowered her voice. "I intend to speak to my brother about it. Not for permission, but to explain my plan and hope he understands my intent." She turned back, surprised to find that Spencer had leaned closer to hear her better; the mingled scent of sunshine on skin, spring wind, and cedar proved intoxicating.

He watched her carefully. "I think that a splendid idea."

She nodded and looked away, taking in a deep breath. She could do this. She wasn't hiding. She was behaving as any educated woman of sense and feeling should. "So, you took the Singer for a spin?"

"Yes. It did me good to . . . get away for a bit. To be honest, a quiet drive does more to settle my nerves than nearly anything else."

"I can imagine how a drive in the countryside would be a welcome reprieve from—well—a breakfast gone horribly wrong, for example. I should try it sometime."

"Not horribly wrong," he said softly.

"No?" she asked.

"No."

"Utterly wrong?"

He smiled.

"*Painfully* wrong?"

He paused, frowning. "I'm horribly and utterly sorry I caused you any pain."

She thought to argue, but instead let him continue.

"I'll have more care of my words from now on. You deserve no less."

The verity of his statement seeped through her like hot tea. "Thank you, Spencer."

His smile returned and brought out hers. The air between them warmed as the burning logs in the fireplace hissed and popped, and the desire to be closer nearly made Lydia take that step to him. He would take both her hands and bring them to his chest, and then he would tell her he would take her money and make her a part of the future of motorcars.

But instead, she stayed rooted where she stood.

Spencer blinked rapidly with a shake of his head. "It's getting quite warm in here," he said, more to himself than her.

"You're still wearing your duster."

He cleared his throat. "Yes, of course."

He stepped away, removing his coat and setting it and his hat on a nearby chair.

"Where did you go?" she asked. "In the car, I mean."

He shrugged. "I headed east, following the River Tillingbourne. I turned down a narrow road canopied in trees, but after a time I stopped and had words with some cows who would not be moved. So I turned around and gradually made my way back here."

"Sounds wonderful."

"I suppose it was."

"Next time will you take me with you?" she asked.

He blinked in surprise. He glanced to Andrew, who held Violet's knight in his hand as he frowned at the chessboard.

She lowered her voice. "Will you take me with you and teach me how to drive?"

He turned toward the window, running a hand through his mussed hair. He settled both hands on his hips.

She drew beside him and casually picked up a book from a nearby table. "I won't tell Andrew," she said, thumbing absently through the pages.

"That doesn't help me feel better about it."

"I'm a quick study. I've been driving in my head for practically a year now. Florrie's driver answers all my questions. Surely you can see the practicality of it. Someday I hope to have my own car. And really, you must agree that any investors in your shops should be familiar with the workings of a motorcar. At the *least,* how to drive one."

"It will pain you to know I'm not that stringent in the qualifications of my investors, other than that they have money to invest and have come by it legally."

"That does pain me, seeing as you recently turned *me* down as an investor."

He ducked. "I did *not* turn you down."

She paused, looking up at him with rounded eyes. "I'm holding you to that," she said, before he could retract his words.

He looked away and muttered something she didn't make out. Something Brummie, no doubt.

She tugged on his sleeve, and he turned, scowling down at her as she blinked up at him. "Please," she whispered, "teach me to drive."

"Is my sister bothering you, Spencer?" Andrew called from his chair.

Violet, not taking her eyes off the chessboard, answered. "No more than you're bothering me. Oh, but look. *Check.*"

That drew Andrew's attention back to the board.

Lydia swallowed and stepped away, a rush of embarrassment flooding through her. "*Am* I bothering you?"

Spencer huffed as he stared out the window, shaking his head. "You are not bothersome, Lydia. You are . . ."

She peeked up at him, finding her courage. "Agitating?"

He stared down at her, his brow forward. "Yes."

Her pulse flitted like a hummingbird among flowers. "But . . . in a startlingly pleasant sort of way?"

His chest rose and fell as he searched her face. "You are the most pleasantly agitating woman I've ever met."

A smile pulled at the corner of her mouth, and he matched it handsomely. "Do you wish me to stop agitating you?" she asked.

He dropped his gaze to her lips. "I—"

A whoop of victory sounded from the chess table, and Spencer jumped back, his eyes darting to Andrew. The man sat crumpled in his chair, watching dully as Violet held aloft his king.

"Well played, my good sir," she proclaimed. "But not well enough. Would you care for a rematch? Perhaps this evening after dinner? We mustn't allow so much time to pass between games. You've become rusty."

"I have not become rusty. You are an excellent opponent, and you shall get your rematch. However, my wounded ego requires days for recovery after such a pounding, so this evening we shall listen to music. You shall play."

"Indeed? And what will *you* be doing to entertain us?" Violet asked.

Lydia pressed her lips together to stop her laugh. Nobody had ever asked Andrew to perform anything. But then, nobody was as competitive as Violet.

"I shall sit on my chair," he said sternly, "fold my arms, and listen intently to your playing all the while reviewing my chess strategy so next time you won't so much as lay a finger to my rook."

Spencer chuckled as Lydia struggled to contain a giggle.

Violet merely cocked an eyebrow and leaned forward. "Challenge accepted."

Spencer leaned into Lydia. "Those two are . . . cozy."

"Cozy like porcupines." She watched Violet and Andrew trade

a few more jabs, then she shook her head. "They've always been this way."

"I noticed a similar relationship between your brother and Miss Janes, as well."

"Florrie and Violet have been pseudo members of this household since we were small children. Andrew is like an older brother. A stuffy, pushy older brother whom they get to stand up to for my benefit. I suppose through the years they've lost their awe of him."

Andrew was escorting Violet to join them at the window, and Lydia took a moment to consider. They *would* make a handsome couple. But she couldn't see past the fact that Andrew had driven her friends to rolling their eyes, stomping their feet, and muttering curses in Lydia's behalf.

"Come, Lydia," Violet said. "Let's leave these men to lick their wounds and ready ourselves for dinner."

Spencer lifted his chin. "*I'm* not wounded."

"Oh," she said, looking pointedly between Lydia and Spencer. "I'm happy to hear it. In that case, would you lend some of that chipper spirit to Andrew? He lost his at about the same time he lost his second knight."

Andrew pulled himself up to his full height, his audible sigh nearly a growl.

Spencer gave her a determined nod. "I'll do my best. We'll see you ladies at dinner."

Lydia could barely wait until they'd left the room before taking Violet's arm. "What on earth? What happened to the plan? Giving Spencer space, remember?"

Violet didn't even pause as the pair climbed the stairs. "It's *Spencer* again, is it?"

"Violet—"

"Were you able to clear the air with him?"

"Yes, but—"

"Wasn't that the most important thing?"

"Well, yes, but—"

"I saw an opportunity and switched strategies. Much like the way I trounced your brother." She paused on the landing and faced Lydia. "I apologize for doing so without any warning to you. You handled it beautifully, though, if that's any comfort."

"It took me a few moments to get my bearings, but I don't think I'll have a problem mustering the courage to approach him with my investment when it is time to do so again."

"No trouble at all," Violet murmured, "from what I observed." Before Lydia could take in the full meaning of her words, Violet tugged her hand. "He should get down on his knees and thank the stars he has you in his corner. I know I do. As a matter of fact, I'm going to speak to Mother about my own investment in these motor supply shops."

"Oh, Vi, that's a wonderful idea!"

"I agree." They resumed the walk to their rooms. "Now, to put on our feathers. Let's see if we can't get Sir Lawrence to spit out his drink from shock or—heaven forbid—laughter at the dining table."

Lydia smiled, but then slowed her steps. "No. If I'm to show Andrew I'm a grown woman, I should refrain from such frivolity, especially when we have guests. I'm afraid I must make the Piedmonts quite comfortable this evening."

"You're right, of course."

"You, though, are free to enjoy yourself in your usual charming manner."

Violet sighed. "I will do all in my power to support you in your cause."

"So you've said before, only to abandon me."

"That wasn't abandonment. As I said, it was redirection."

"Suppose next time you'll give me a signal?"

"Certainly. I'll squawk like a peacock."

Lydia's giggle burst forth as she reached her door and pushed through it.

"See?" she heard Violet say as she continued to the next room where her valise had been stowed with her dinner things. "I'm helping already."

CHAPTER 11

"What were you speaking of at such length with my sister?"

The ladies had barely left the room when Andrew lobbed the question in Spencer's direction.

Spencer froze. *Motorcars. Secretly teaching Lydia to drive. Meeting secretly. To drive motorcars* . . . He searched his brain. Surely they must have spoken of some safe subject. "I apologized. For my behavior earlier today. I was dismissive of an idea she had, which resulted in hurt feelings in need of mending."

Andrew watched him with acute interest. "I see. And are the hurt feelings mended?"

Spencer nodded. "I believe so, yes. She has a very keen mind, your sister. Her idea was a good one, and I should have listened instead of treating her like a child." *As I've seen you do*, he added silently.

Andrew's gaze narrowed. "May I ask what the idea was?"

Spencer swallowed hard while attempting to look as if he were an open book. "I believe she will come to you with it herself soon. She was merely practicing with me."

"Practicing? To come to me with an idea?"

Spencer grinned. "Is it so hard to believe you are an intimidating figure? After all, it's not every day that men are compared to—"

"Don't say it."

"—Greek gods."

Instead of the expected chuckle, Andrew frowned. "Am I really so unapproachable? Even to my sister?"

"I didn't say you were unapproachable. Miss Whittemore doesn't seem to have any trouble approaching you, wouldn't you agree?"

Andrew eyed him. "What is that supposed to mean?"

Spencer lifted his hands in defense. "Nothing. Only that watching you two is like watching an old married couple."

"In what way?"

He puffed out his cheeks as he exhaled. "Well, you seem very comfortable with one another."

"I've been responsible for the safety and reputation of Lydia's friends as they've come into our home over the years. Miss Whittemore, Miss Janes, and Miss Burke—"

"Miss Burke? As in Oscar Burke?"

"Yes, his younger sister. His only sister out of six siblings. I'm sure you'll meet her at some point. The four girls are nearly inseparable. It's been a godsend, really. I don't know what Lydia would do without her friends."

"She's had you."

Andrew gave him a knowing look and lowered his voice. "No, she has not. Not the way she's had those girls."

"Women."

Andrew blinked. "What?"

Spencer steeled himself. "I've observed that your sister and her friends are far past being girls and are, as we say in Birmingham with the utmost regard, *women.*"

Andrew huffed. Then sobered, blinking. Then he huffed again.

Spencer slapped him on the shoulder. "Don't worry yourself. I'm sure it would've dawned on you in twenty, thirty years. See? I've saved you some time. Anyhow, we should change for dinner. No doubt Sir Lawrence will arrive soon, and I'm famished. What say we beat the ladies back down here, hm?" With a nod, Spencer made to escape the room, leaving Andrew staring out the window.

"Spencer."

He turned back. "Yes?"

Andrew had turned his head away from the window only enough to give Spencer his profile. He spoke quietly, but with command. "I'm all too aware that my sister is growing up. All the same, I thank you for the reminder."

Spencer eyed him with suspicion but found his friend sincere. "It was nothing."

Andrew turned back to the window, and Spencer barely heard his response. "It is not nothing."

An hour later, Spencer stood alone in the drawing room, having arrived before the others. His focus warred between anticipating the opportunity to discuss Sir Lawrence's investment and seeing Lydia again. It was a war he did not wish for. He hadn't expected her to be so forthcoming about their exchange that morning, nor so adorably nervous. And when she'd suggested he take her for a drive—*teach* her how to drive—well . . . His silent answer hadn't been, *"Certainly not."* It had been, *"How soon?"*

He had to slow this down. He had to stop whatever it was that was growing between them.

But when the ladies entered the drawing room, his breath halted at first glance.

Lydia had always looked lovely in her gowns, always the picture of fashion with sheer fabrics draped over silk, lace tucked into her waist, and a wardrobe indicative of her wealth and status. But this evening she was more radiant than ever, her cheeks and lips rosy. Her dress was a deep blue, barely held together at her shoulders, her skin creamy above her long gloves and low neckline. A single silk vine of pink- and red-ribbon roses descended over her bodice, caressed her slender waist, and flowed down to the floor. No one, not even Andrew, could mistake her for anything but a beautiful woman coming into her own.

Everything about her reminded him of a summer stroll in a midnight garden.

She lifted her gaze to meet his, arresting all other thoughts but one: *Danger. Very. Pleasant. Danger.*

The corner of her mouth lifted as if she could hear his thoughts, but a commotion outside the door turned her head. It was only then that he took notice of Violet's presence. She was lovely in her gown of green silk, but his heart did not stutter at the sight of her. As he wavered between stepping forward or retreating, the door opened. The butler formally announced the arrivals.

"Sir Lawrence and Mrs. Piedmont."

To Spencer's surprise, Andrew entered with a decidedly plump, much older woman draped in yellow silk on his arm. Sir Lawrence entered just after and, upon spying Lydia, made a bee-line for her. He took her hand, kissed it, and did not release it.

Indeed, he held it as he spoke softly, eventually eliciting a smile from her, his own placid countenance brightening.

Spencer noted Andrew kept an eye on the exchange, a look of expectation in his expression even as he held a steady conversation with the older woman.

He followed Andrew's gaze to Lydia once more. Indeed, she smiled politely, modestly averted her gaze, laughed discreetly. His nails dug into his palms from his hands curling into fists.

Andrew had mentioned that the Piedmonts had come for dinner every month for more than a year. Spencer had wrongly assumed that *Mrs.* Piedmont was Sir Lawrence's *wife.* But of course, she would be addressed as Lady Piedmont if that were true. Obviously, she was the man's mother.

And Sir Lawrence was drawing Lydia's hand around his arm, situating her closer to his side. She did not look up, but kept her eyes on the carpet, her cheeks burning even brighter. Sapphires sparkled at her ears, matching the subtle shimmer of her gown.

Andrew's cryptic words came back to him. *I'm all too aware that my sister is growing up.*

Spencer had made a huge mistake.

Lydia Wooding is an heiress. The observation struck him for the first time since he'd set foot in Briarwall.

And Piedmont is for Lydia.

His stomach lurched with a mix of anger and humiliation. He'd let it happen. Again.

"Spencer," Andrew called, jerking him out of his own particular circle of Dante's Inferno. Andrew motioned him forward.

Spencer forced his feet to carry him in that direction.

"Sir Lawrence you know already," Andrew was saying.

Sir Lawrence nodded. "Good to see you again, Hayes. Looking forward to continuing our discussion from the other day."

Spencer nodded, present enough to lift his eyebrows in some sort of expression of agreement. He felt Lydia's gaze but didn't dare meet it.

"May I introduce Mrs. Piedmont?" Andrew said. "A dear friend of my mother's."

Spencer bowed. "Pleasure, madame."

The woman gave him a nod. "My son has told me much of your motor supply shop idea," she said. "I find it quite intriguing, though I do admit any suggestion of the middle class possessing motorcars is hard to swallow."

"What a snobbish thing to say, Mother. Why, Doctor Russel owns a Sunbeam, and he's as middle class as they come." Sir Lawrence turned to Spencer. "Present company accounted for, of course. Tell me you own a motorcar, Hayes."

From the corner of his eye, he saw Lydia's jaw drop open. Andrew shifted uncomfortably at his side, but Mrs. Piedmont and Sir Lawrence simply waited for his answer, as if they'd asked him whether or not he summered in France or if he'd ever dined with the prince.

Spencer gathered his wits. This was business. It was what he'd been built for. "I do, in fact," he said, widening his stance. "A two-point-six-liter Wolseley-Siddeley phaeton."

He chose to ignore Lydia's small gasp of admiration, as much as it bolstered his pride in his own horseless carriage.

Sir Lawrence nodded, clearly impressed. "A solid vehicle."

"Agreed." He'd worked hard for that car, right up until the day Hayes Livery and Carriage became Johnson Livery and Carriage. Any revenue from the sale of his father's company and the manor house on Westfield Road went to paying off the debt collectors and securing a future for his mother and sister. It had barely been enough.

But he couldn't sell investors on the shop idea if he himself did not own a motorcar. It lent him legitimacy he did not have otherwise, no matter how much expertise he claimed.

Much, it occurred to him, in the same way Lydia felt that knowing how to drive a car would lend her legitimacy as an investor.

Sir Lawrence turned to his mother. "Her Majesty owns a Wolseley, Mother."

"Oh my." Mrs. Piedmont snapped open a fan and created a breeze for herself. "Are you quite enamored?"

Spencer couldn't help the tug of a smile at his lips. His car was an older, bare-bones model compared to the queen's, but it did shine. "Quite, madame." He leaned forward and lowered his voice. "It's yellow." He winked.

Mrs. Piedmont giggled and swatted his arm with her fan. She clutched at her ample chest, threatening to wrinkle the many flowers sewn on the gown's bodice. "You are a charmer."

"You didn't tell me you had your own car," Lydia said.

"You did not ask," he answered, still not daring to meet her gaze.

Sir Lawrence glanced between them, then cleared his throat. "Andrew said you came by locomotive."

"I did indeed. Next to my passion for motorcars is a lifelong fascination with the railway. I find that traveling a stretch on the rails every now and again keeps me inspired."

Sir Lawrence tipped his head. "You and I have much in common, Hayes."

Spencer's gaze automatically slid over to Lydia on the man's arm, her steady look questioning, then back to Sir Lawrence. Spencer loosened his clenched jaw. "Well, let's make that work to our mutual benefit, shall we?"

He may have made a fool of himself—or at least he had come very close to it—with Lydia Wooding, but he would not lose Sir Lawrence's interest over it. He needed the man's money, his name, and his influence.

Violet interjected. "I do find the railway trip romantic, don't you, Mrs. Piedmont? Sharing a car with strangers all surging along the rails toward shared destinies."

"I prefer a private cabin," she said.

Violet leaned forward. "That, too, can be romantic?"

Mrs. Piedmont snapped open her fan, but nodded her agreement. "I suppose."

Spencer's mouth quirked again. "Lydia tells me you have a Rover, Violet." He noted Sir Lawrence stiffen at his use of Christian names. "How do you like it?"

"I adore it."

"She's named it Edwin," Lydia offered, "after her first love."

His brow rose. "The relationship must have ended amicably, then?"

"Not at all. He pushed me into a puddle of mud, and I threw as much of the muck as I could at him until our nannies separated us and I was promptly returned to the nursery." She sighed. "I never knew what became of him, the darling."

Spencer chuckled as Andrew ran a long-suffering hand over his own face.

Violet continued. "I can say, 'I'm taking my love for a drive in the country, Mama,' and the dear woman has a moment of apoplexy every time before she realizes what I mean."

"Poor soul," Mrs. Piedmont said, tsking.

"You'd think," said Sir Lawrence, "that Mrs. Whittemore would have little qualm with you driving any man about, as involved as she is in the suffrage."

"Oh dear." Mrs. Piedmont opened her fan again and flapped it like a wing of a pheasant, clearly uncomfortable with the turn of topic.

"Now, now, Sir Lawrence," Violet said with an air of compassion. "We all know that mamas everywhere can be staunch in their causes, but when it comes to their children, they may have a different line of thinking altogether."

"Rightfully so," Mrs. Piedmont said, pulling herself taller—if one could call five feet *taller*.

"At least your mother allows you to drive a car," Lydia muttered to Violet.

"*Your* mother wears too much starch in his collars," Violet murmured in return.

Spencer bit his cheek, and Lydia stifled a snort.

"What was that?" Andrew said.

Lydia brightened. "Nothing. Mrs. Piedmont, I believe you like the chicken and oysters. Cook has prepared it for tonight's main course."

And with that, Lydia deftly brought the conversation back to ease and comfort for everyone. Spencer couldn't help noticing the pride in Sir Lawrence's eye as he watched Lydia converse with his mother, nor the way he'd patted her hand in gratitude.

He swallowed tightly, having lost his appetite for dinner. Nevertheless, a few moments later, he found himself escorting Violet into the dining room.

"She doesn't suspect, you know."

"I beg your pardon?" He spoke low, matching her whisper.

"She doesn't know of Andrew's intentions for her and Sir Lawrence."

He clenched his teeth and exhaled, not wanting to speak of this, but unable to ignore her. "But *you* know," he observed.

"We—my friends and I—have only just begun to suspect. But his attentions tonight . . ." She watched him sidelong. "She has no idea. I thought you should know."

"Why?" he asked, knowing full well why, but he was curious to hear what Violet would say.

She paused as they entered the dining room and, as the others found their seats, she faced him.

He blanched under her scrutiny, pulling at his collar.

"Because, Spencer, I do not wish you to believe she plays games when it comes to people. She may follow us girls on our little dares, and she pays her guests their due attention"—he followed the flick of her gaze to see Lydia smiling up at Sir Lawrence as he pushed in her chair for her—"but she is genuine."

He turned back to her. "Genuine," he repeated.

She nodded. "Surely you learned this after the great *clock key hunt*?"

He had. He'd been dazzled by it. "Well," he said, clearing his throat. "How fortunate for Sir Lawrence, then."

Her brows lowered in confusion. "I was mistaken about you."

He held out his hand toward her chair, eager to be done with this conversation. "How so?"

"I was under the impression that you don't play games, either."

"Indeed," he said, causing her to pause. "I cannot even afford to consider the invitation."

She scrutinized him further. "Some would argue that love does not invite. It commands."

"Love?" he asked, a bit too loudly. All eyes turned on him, and he blanched.

Violet glanced between him and the other diners, and, ironically, his gaze was forced to Lydia's, whose eyes were wide.

Violet smiled and addressed the room. "We were speaking of foreign delicacies. Mr. Hayes is shocked that I claim a love for haggis."

Sir Lawrence made a baffled face. "As am I. *Haggis*?"

The room erupted in a debate over haggis, and before Spencer could take in what had transpired, he'd seated Miss Whittemore, taken his own chair, and dared another glance at Lydia.

She had moved her gaze from Violet, who was entirely too focused on the conversation at hand, and transferred it to him, searching and steady. He should have been able to breathe with the redirection of subject, but he could not seem to get enough air into his lungs with Lydia's dark eyes boring into his. She was lovely, compelling, and, yes, fearsome.

Love.

He'd known her all but a week. Yet just that morning he'd claimed to have known her most of her life. It *felt* as if he'd known her that long, and yet, every moment with her was new.

But then, he'd felt that way about Catherine Bradshaw. Hadn't he?

No. If he allowed himself to think on it, his weeks with Catherine dulled in comparison to the last several days with Lydia.

He frowned as the first course was served, remembering the excuse he'd used with Andrew, that Lydia had been "practicing" with him. Was that what he was? Practice for every woman who managed to turn his head before she attached herself to some titled buffoon who wouldn't see past her dowry? What was this, 1810?

"Florrie told me you were a natural conversationalist."

"Hm?" He looked up to find Violet watching him. "I beg your pardon. I'm not much for dinner company tonight, I'm afraid."

"We shall see about that. Do you sing?"

"What?"

"Do you sing? Play an instrument?"

"Er, I sing, a little, but not—"

Violet began to laugh loudly, throwing her head back and shaking it to and fro. "Oh really, Mr. Hayes, you are too droll."

"What are you on about over there?" Sir Lawrence asked.

Violet leaned forward. "Mr. Hayes has made the most entertaining suggestion."

Andrew frowned. "He has?"

She turned. "Tell them, Spencer." She waited a moment as Spencer, no doubt, became a quick shade of red, his mouth opening and shutting like a fish on the dock. "You are too modest," she said, throwing him back into the water after she'd yanked him out. "I'll tell them." She turned to her audience as he waited to hear his idea. "We were discussing the music tonight, and he suggested we turn our entertainment into a musical match of sorts."

"*He* suggested this, did he?" Andrew said, his eyebrow cocked.

"Well, perhaps I helped a little," she said quite modestly, considering Spencer had no idea what she was talking about. "Wouldn't it be fun to draw names, and whomever you are partnered with is your performance partner, musical or otherwise, for the evening? I happen to know that there is not a person in this room without a musical talent or ear."

At this, Mrs. Piedmont smiled bashfully, once again crushing her flowers.

Violet continued as Spencer watched in awe of her audacity. "I told Mr. Hayes so, and he thought such a game would suit this unique gathering perfectly. What say you?"

Andrew cleared his throat. "I cannot claim any musical talent—"

Spencer opened his mouth to argue, but Andrew continued.

"—*but* I would gladly turn pages or whatever needed to be done on my partner's behalf—if that is what you wish, *Spencer*? And Violet, of course?" The mirth in his eye told Spencer he'd read the woman well.

"What fun," Lydia said, drawing Spencer's eye. "I wish it, too." She nodded encouragingly at Spencer, as if he needed reinforcement for his brilliancy.

After the topic veered off and the others were once more occupied, Spencer leaned over. "You, Miss Whittemore, are a liar."

"I'm a strategist. And that"—she nodded toward Lydia—"is the liveliest I've seen her all evening."

He couldn't disagree, watching Lydia beam in his direction in anticipation of what was to come. Afraid to question Violet further, he gave her liberty to look smug. He could've been mistaken, but the Piedmonts' presence had a subduing effect on Lydia, as if being her true self became an afterthought she only remembered with particular prodding.

He glanced at Andrew. Did her own brother not see it?

In the drawing room after dinner, Violet decided to pair one woman and one man, as that seemed a more even distribution of talent.

"Only the men's names are in the dish," Lydia said, taking the lead after consulting quietly with Violet. "Each woman here shall draw a name, then remove to a corner with her chosen partner to decide how you'll perform together, followed by a brief practice."

Spencer caught a glimmer of the excitement Lydia had shared the other night with the clock. Because Violet had suggested this game—or *Spencer* had—Andrew could not censure Lydia for bringing something high-spirited to the evening yet again. Spencer felt a mixture of relief for her, something near burning jealousy for Sir Lawrence, and both hope and dread that he would be partnered with—

"Mr. Hayes," Lydia said with delight. After all, she had no idea Sir Lawrence was courting her, and she and Spencer had said their apologies earlier for what had transpired that morning. She smiled brightly at him, but he could barely return it. He could not give her hope for anything more than friendship.

Mrs. Piedmont drew Andrew's name, leaving Sir Lawrence to perform with Violet.

Violet caught Spencer's attention and nodded toward the piano, where Lydia sat, running her fingers lightly over the keys. He sighed with forbearance.

He could not give Lydia hope, but he could be *kind*. He moved his feet in her direction. *Friendly.* He approached the piano. In no way did he have to entertain thoughts of a romantic nature concerning Lydia Wooding. As if to fortify himself, he looked in Sir Lawrence's direction, but the man's attention was all on Violet and a servant who was delivering what looked to be a violin case.

"Violet told me you sing," Lydia said.

Blast.

He took a steadying breath and drew up to the piano. He shook his head. "I'd no idea what she was up to when I told her that."

Her mouth drew to the side. "That sounds like her." Her brow rose, and she cleared her throat. "Will you sing a duet with me, Spencer?" she asked.

He glanced at the piano. "You play and sing?"

She shook her head. "I *plink* and sing. I was a horrid piano student with a slight crush on my vocal instructor. So naturally, I languished in one instrument and advanced in the other. My poor heart broke when Mr. Atwood married, but at least I could sing my melancholy." She sighed dramatically, a spark of humor in her eye. "Thirteen is such a hard age."

He could not help the smile that came so easily when she was like this. Absolutely charming in her self-deprecation. He looked to the floor. "Indeed, it is. And yes, I will sing with you. But I'm not by any means proficient. The only instruction I've had was the boys choir at Eton. At the time I was a high tenor. Unfortunately—or fortunately, depending on how you look at it—I'm now somewhere in the deeper middle range, my only practice being church on Sundays and perhaps as I shower."

She grinned, dropping her eyes to several sheets of music before her. "Perhaps we could arrange for a downpour for our duet."

Her pink cheeks and the way she'd said "our duet" brought on his own blush, realizing he'd been far too candid in mentioning himself in the shower. *Church.* He should have ended it with church. In church he was . . . well . . . clothed. "I'm sure the acoustics in here will do more for us than singing in the rain." He gulped, wishing to move on.

Her eyes widened. "Oh, but the acoustics at the temple are wonderful, even in a downpour. I sing there sometimes, just to make use of them."

"A goddess to behold, I'm sure."

The way Lydia glanced down at the suggestion, a beguiling

smile on her lips—he pushed a hand through his hair, undoing any smart styling he'd managed for dinner. What a lummox he was. His father would say he'd gone soft in the 'ead.

With a forced exhalation, he veered the subject. "What will we be singing, then?"

She shuffled through the music sheets. "I like this one."

He took the song she handed him and recognized it immediately. "'In the Shade of the Old Apple Tree,'" he said. "An American song?"

"An immensely popular American song," she said, holding out her hand. "Florrie has a Victor Talking Machine, and this is one of my favorite songs to play."

"It's quite sentimental, is it not?"

She arched a brow in his direction. "It is positively sentimental."

He gave her back the music, and she placed it on the piano. He stepped behind her as she began to play out the melody, humming to find the notes.

"In other lands I've wandered since we parted," he sang softly behind her, staring intensely at the paper, urging his nerves away.

She paused and looked at him over her shoulder.

He only nodded to the page, and she quickly resumed her playing. "I seek the garden fair beside the stream."

She drew in a breath and took a turn. "I tread each well-known pathway heavy-hearted. For all I see recalls the old, sweet dream." Her voice was a sweet, full alto, her vibrato gentle as a lullaby.

He caught himself staring and joined her. "No more on earth your loving smile will cheer me. No more on earth your dear face I shall see. Yet memories of the past are ever near me. They linger 'round the dear old apple tree."

She stopped playing and looked up at him.

He glanced at her. "Are we not going to sing the chorus?"

"You, sir, have a charming voice."

"I have a serviceable voice. You, on the other hand, sing like your talented mother. I am struck by it."

Her eyes brightened. "Truly?"

"Has no one told you that before?"

She shook her head. Had Andrew never mentioned the likeness?

"Then I suppose you shall have to believe me."

She smiled widely. "I suppose I shall."

"She often called on me to sing with her." He chuckled at the memory. "I think she did so to make me blush."

"I believe she did so because you are pleasant to sing with."

"My dear woman, you've sung a mere four measures with me."

"A testament to how good you are. I have an ear for this sort of thing, you know."

He took a deep breath, watching his shoes. "Then I suppose I shall have to believe you."

"I suppose you shall."

He shook his head, suppressing a grin. Blast this woman. "Now then, if you wish me to persevere in this endeavor, you shall stop with your pretty words and get on with this rehearsal."

"You are the one who started with the pretty words."

He opened his mouth, but a crooked smile was all he could manage as words failed him. Her brown-eyed gaze lingered on his.

"Ahem."

They turned to find both Andrew and Mrs. Piedmont watching them stiffly.

"We are in need of the piano, Lydia," Andrew said, eyeing Spencer. "I assumed you could finish your piece without it."

"Indeed," Lydia said, standing from the bench as she collected their music. "We shall adjourn to the morning room."

"By yourselves?" Mrs. Piedmont said loudly enough to draw Sir Lawrence's attention from the opposite side of the room. "Really, the impropriety of it. Mr. Wooding, surely—"

"Fallon will accompany us, of course," Lydia offered brightly.

Out of the corner of his eye, Spencer noted Ralston ringing the bell immediately, no doubt to summon the lady's maid.

Lydia met Andrew's hard stare with an unwavering grin and held it.

Andrew flicked another look at Spencer, and Spencer shrugged. The presence of the lady's maid provided all the required propriety necessary, and to be honest, Spencer was relieved that Lydia had offered the solution herself.

"We shall do the same," Violet said, approaching the group with a violin in one hand, a bow in the other, and Sir Lawrence on her heels. He looked paradoxically interested and bored. She gave Ralston another nod, and he responded in kind.

"Not in the morning room, of course," Violet continued. "Perhaps the study? We wouldn't want my strings to disrupt either of your practicing, now, would we? Come, Sir Lawrence. Let us loosen up our cords."

With a questioning glance between Lydia and Spencer, Sir Lawrence followed Miss Whittemore as Mrs. Piedmont watched wide-eyed and silent.

Lydia gestured to the piano. "It is all yours, Mrs. Piedmont, as it should be. I cannot wait to hear what an accomplished pianist such as yourself will play."

The woman's face softened mildly. "Thank you, Miss Wooding. Perhaps Miss Whittemore is right. A violin can be a very disturbing instrument when not played to perfection. Forgive me for making assumptions."

"Not at all. You are only being watchful of the young people." Lydia curtsied and strode out of the drawing room. She paused at the doorway, where her maid had just arrived—thankfully not the grim-faced woman from the temple—and turned. "Are you coming, Mr. Hayes, or do I have to sing this duet all by myself?"

Spencer started out of his stupor and followed her, not daring a glance backward at Andrew. He didn't need to. He could feel his friend's glare burning holes into his back.

CHAPTER 12

With Spencer following a few steps behind her, Lydia pushed open the door to the morning room where she usually met with the Wendy League and kept going to one of the windows on the far wall. She released the latch and pushed the pane open, breathing in the cool evening air, willing the lazy patter of raindrops to calm her . . . her *agitation*.

Oh, if only Peter Pan would show up, sprinkle her with pixie dust and fly her away to Neverland. She caught her reflection in the second dark windowpane: her gown, her curves, her hair, even the flush of her lips—they all spoke of growing up. And the roiling feelings inside her as Spencer had sung low and mellow behind her at the piano—those beckoned a growing up as well. The glimmer of the sapphires at her ears drew her gaze, and then Spencer's reflection appeared behind her, watching her intently.

"Shall we start from the beginning?" he asked.

She turned. "Yes. I was so focused on the piano keys I didn't give the lyrics my best effort." What was she to do with all of this *energy*?

"Very well." He held up the music, and she joined him, gripping one side of the songbook as he kept hold of the other. He angled himself to accommodate her nearness. "This is quite like fixing the clock," he said with a frown.

"The anticipation?"

"The proximity."

A shiver caressed her spine, and she swallowed. "Ah. Yes. That, too. Shall we? I liked how you started before, and then I had a turn."

"And then we joined together," he said, his eyes focused on the music, his voice low and soft. "Here." He touched the sheet.

She dared a glance at him, wondering if he knew how enticing that sounded. "Yes." She gently cleared her throat, and they both stood a little taller. She recalled the beginning note and gave it to him with a hum.

He began. When she'd been seated at the piano, his voice had floated above her, surprising her, coaxing a smile to her lips. It was not a refined singing voice like Sir Lawrence's trained vocals, but certainly clear and true. Now, as she stood so close to him, the timbre of his baritone moved through her as a tangible thing, the sound of his breathing matching her own.

She startled when it was her turn, and he smiled at the ground as she began. She carried her part through, strangely eager to hear their voices combine, to have him recall the sound of her mother, to tie his memories with her own lack of them.

She was not disappointed. Even Fallon paused in her stitchery and watched them, a faraway look of pleasure in her eyes. At the gentle touch of his hand cupping her elbow, Lydia dared a look at Spencer. He was already watching her, his voice softening as his gaze dropped to her mouth, their words mirroring one another.

They finished the verse and paused. Neither of them spoke, and Lydia felt as if she'd run up Picnic Hill and back, though they hadn't even completed the song. The air between them seemed to push and pull with an indecisive force, bewildering and powerful.

Lydia swallowed. "Fallon? Can you fetch us some water? Already my throat is dry."

Fallon blinked, as if waking from a dream. "Yes, miss. That was lovely, miss. Mr. Hayes." With a curtsy, she left.

Bless Fallon.

At the gentle click of her exit, Lydia turned to face Spencer, who was bringing his gaze from the closed door back to her.

"Lydia, I don't think—" he started.

"We cheated," she said, pulling in a deep breath of cool air from the still-open window.

He dropped her elbow. "What?"

"Violet and I. She wrote your name and folded it a certain way. I chose first, knowing that particular fold had your name attached to it." Her heart pounded with the confession. "I chose you. Deliberately."

He hesitated, likely believing her mad. "Why?" he asked.

Surely, he knew why. She huffed a laugh. "Because word of your excellent singing voice has made its rounds about Surrey, and I'm determined to outshine the others."

At his baffled expression, she threw her eyes heavenward and took a step to him, ran both trembling hands up his lapels and around his collar, and dared bring herself inches from his face, her eyes on his full lips. "I don't give a brass farthing about the others," she whispered with a slight tremble.

"You don't?" he whispered back, visibly swallowing.

She shook her head. Bravely, she leaned forward so the tip of her nose brushed his, and his eyes closed.

"Lydia . . ."

He hadn't returned her embrace. But she wasn't wrong. She couldn't be. He seemed as breathless as she.

"What about Sir Lawrence?"

She frowned. "Sir Lawrence? He is old and dull and predictable, and why are you even asking about him?"

"I—"

"I want you to kiss me," she said quickly, half-shocked, half-spurred by her own brevity. "Kiss me now, or I'll lose my mind."

He pushed out a quick breath. "You're already halfway there if you think I want t—"

Lydia stopped his mouth with her own, having had just enough experience to give her confidence. And oh, his lips were as soft and cushioned as she'd imagined them to be. He resisted for a moment, as she thought he might.

But then his hands slowly circled her waist, and then he tightened his arms around her back, his fingers grazing her bare shoulder blades. She sighed, and he growled low, moving his lips across hers and over her neck, then back to her mouth. Tingles raced through her body. He tasted even sweeter than he smelled, his freshly-shaven skin brushing over hers as they exchanged kiss after kiss until she became dizzy with the power of it.

The morning room, Briarwall—all of Surrey—faded beneath the vibrant light of Spencer Hale kissing Lydia Wooding.

"This," she whispered, smiling, "this is what I want."

He breathed hard against her grin and pulled back, his brow furrowed. "Lydia—dazzling Lydia, we shouldn't—"

"I know," she whispered. "We haven't much time."

His lips captured hers again, but too quickly the potent kiss slowed, gentled, his hands caressing her back and neck, sending shivers through her limbs.

A knock sounded at the door, and in one smooth movement, Spencer stepped away, a stricken look on his face. He turned, covering his mouth with his hand, picked up the sheet of music, and paced across the room just as Fallon stepped inside with a tray.

She set a water pitcher and two glasses on the sideboard, then discreetly reclaimed her chair, pulling some stitching from her apron pocket.

Lydia stepped toward the pitcher and poured herself a glass, her hands shaking. After finishing off the entire glassful, she filled her lungs with air. "Thank you, Fallon."

Her maid only nodded, not looking up from her embroidery.

"Shall we run through it again?" Lydia asked without looking behind her. Her pulse still raced, and she suppressed a warm shudder as she waited for Spencer to respond. She'd guessed correctly. He wanted her. He had kissed her as she'd never been kissed before. His desire had been in every touch, every embrace. Careful and yet reckless. She'd felt utterly vulnerable and yet secure in his arms.

"I think we've practiced enough," he said.

She frowned and turned to read his expression, because his tone had reminded her of Andrew's when he reprimanded her. But surely Spencer wasn't angry; she must be mistaken. Yet, his back was to her, his arms folded tightly across his chest, the music still gripped in one hand. He stared at an ancient painting of Briarwall hanging on the wall.

The security she'd relished moments before teetered. "Surely you jest."

He huffed out a breath. "Not everything is in jest, Miss Wooding. I'm sure the performance will be adequate. Take care not to place too much importance on it."

She lifted her chin, her pride hit. "Why are you speaking to me as if I were a child?" She dared a glance at Fallon, who watched Spencer with a look of confusion. She caught Lydia's eye and straightened.

"Perhaps I shall see if the others are ready, miss." Without waiting for an answer, Fallon hurried from the room, throwing Lydia a look of caution as she did. She left the door open.

Lydia crossed the room and shut it soundly. Then turned. "Spencer?" Her heart thudded painfully. "What has just happened?" she whispered. "I thought . . . I thought—"

"What did you think?" he asked. He turned and walked casually to the center of the room, where he dropped the music on the table. "That you could lure me closer with your feminine charms until I'm senseless to resist? That you could toy with my heart with your own beguiling inexperience, and I would relent? Bow down? Worship you? Even knowing you were meant for—?" He shut his mouth and frowned, avoiding her eyes.

She closed her fingers into fists, fighting to overcome her confusion and inadequacy, because he was right. She was inexperienced. And perhaps she'd been entirely wrong about his feelings for her.

"That I was meant for what? I'm not toying with anyone. I believed—I believed you felt as I do—did. Oh, I don't know." She paced toward him. "Violet hinted that love and agitation were linked, and I couldn't see how, but—"

"*Love?*" he said, his eyes widening. He shook his head, as if she'd suggested she'd seen a pirate ship floating above the house. His posture softened. "Lydia," he whispered. It was the tone she'd hoped to hear from him earlier but was incongruous with the drop of his shoulders and look of pity in his shadowed eyes. "Do not mistake this attraction between us for love. Do not throw that into the mix of all that I'm juggling during my *very brief* stay here."

Lydia flinched. "I've not thrown anything."

"I beg your pardon. You very recently threw yourself at me."

She squared her shoulders. "And what of you? Did you not throw yourself right back?" She angrily swatted away a tear.

The door opened behind her with a knock. "Miss? The others asked for ten more minutes."

Spencer's hand went to his head, and he turned away.

Lydia nodded at Fallon. Ten minutes to gather her wits. She began to pace and paused. She walked swiftly to Fallon, wringing her hands. "Will you ask Reed to clip some of the branches of blossoms from the kitchen orchard and put them in vases for our song? It will be the perfect thing, don't you think?"

Fallon hesitated, but conceded. "Indeed, miss."

"Thank you." Lydia turned to Spencer as the door shut gently with a click.

They both stood before one another, looking anywhere but at each other.

"You don't want me," she said. "Not . . . in that way."

He huffed out a breath, pity on his face. "I can't."

She lifted her arms, only to let them fall to her side, her face flaming. "So, we just sing, then?" she said, feeling flat and defeated.

He sighed. "Lydia, you are beautiful, smart, evocative—"

"Go on," she choked out, painfully amused that he could compliment her while rejecting her.

He stepped forward and brushed away another of her tears. "Andrew would kill me for making you cry." He pulled out a handkerchief and handed it to her.

"If I don't first." She took his offering and dabbed her eyes.

The corner of his mouth lifted. "How am I ever to resist you?"

"Don't." She wanted to take it back as soon as she said it. And she hated that she was desperate enough to mean it.

He stepped away but took her hand and kissed it. "I must." He winced as if pained. "And you must trust that I have my reasons. I wish you will know what love is one day. But it cannot be with me."

Lydia wanted to shout. To shake him and ask, "Why not? Were you not just here? Did you not feel the earth shift beneath us during that kiss?"

But the insecure little girl in her guessed that he had not, and she simply nodded. "So. We just sing, then."

He nodded. "We just sing."

Lydia sat stiff in her drawing room chair, doing her best to appear unruffled, wishing the musicale was over and she was upstairs in bed, buried under her covers. She hoped she did not look like the unraveled mess of yarn she felt like on the inside. The last thing she needed were questions over the state of her well-being. If only she could spin herself into a tidy ball and roll right out of the room.

Unaware of what had transpired in the morning room, Violet stood poised and elegant at the front of the drawing room. "Sir Lawrence and I will be performing a classic poem that has recently been set to music by the late composer Miss Ellen Wright. I've always held Miss Wright in high esteem, and upon her death, I took it upon myself to learn as many of her songs as I could. I am still learning." Violet stepped aside, holding her violin as though it were an extension of her arms. She did not raise it yet, and Sir Lawrence stepped forward, clearing his throat.

"The poem is entitled 'She Walks in Beauty' by Lord Byron." His mother gasped, and he lifted a handkerchief to his neck, as if he'd anticipated his mother's shock and was already perspiring. His gaze flickered to Lydia's. "This is for you, dear L—ladies. Here. In this room tonight."

Lydia pressed her lips together, finding relief that she was not alone in her discomfort that evening. Indeed, Sir Lawrence looked a bit piqued. She recognized Violet's subtle smirk as she raised her violin to her chin, the bow poised and ready. Despite the turmoil of Lydia's own feelings, she could not help her pride in her friend's self-assurance.

As Lydia settled further into her chair, her skirts brushed against Spencer's leg, and she quickly adjusted so that even her clothing would be clear of him. Her humiliation was too fresh, too sharp, to ease back into a friendship with him, as they'd quietly agreed to before coming down. She was not quite sure, after their kiss, how she could even accomplish that feat. Her face warmed at the memory—and at the following mortification. She'd experienced stolen kisses before, but nothing in the realm of what had taken place in the morning room. Perhaps she was more of a child than she'd wanted to believe.

With a jolt, she realized Violet was already playing a steady, sweet melody as Sir Lawrence's bass vibrato was filling the room, and that his entire focus as he sang the words of Lord Byron's love letter was solely on *her*. She glanced to her right and left to see if anyone else noticed the attention she was receiving from the man.

Andrew seemed to quickly redirect his gaze away from her as Violet began the second verse. It was a variation of the first, with lilting lifts and falls over Sir Lawrence's sure melody. Lydia might have enjoyed the rendition if not for his intense stare and mottling purple of his cheeks, the light sheen of perspiration on his upper lip. Could he not see he was making a scene?

She burrowed deeper into her chair and dared a glance at Spencer. He was frowning, his chest rising and falling, his eyes trained on Violet's violin. She glanced at Mrs. Piedmont, who fanned herself and could not look prouder. Indeed, she peered knowingly at Lydia with a haughty lift of her brow. In a blink, the woman's focus was back on her son.

"One shade the more, one ray the less, had half impaired the nameless grrace which waves in every rrrraven trress . . ."

Oh, dear heavens, he was trilling his Rs.

Andrew's lips were now pursed, and he looked uncomfortably at the floor.

Lydia closed her eyes. She knew the poem well enough to know it was almost done.

"—the smiles that win, the tints that glow—"

Indeed, she was surely glowing now. Bright and hot.

"—but tell of days in goodness spent, a mind at peace with all below, a heart whose love is innocent!"

The four members of the immediate audience and members of the staff who'd been invited to view the performance from the back broke into varying shades of applause.

Lydia kept her eyes glued to Violet and clapped ferociously as her friend curtsied. She averted every notion to look at Sir Lawrence, though she saw him bow low from the corner of her eye, then a flash from his white kerchief as he wiped his neck and face. She felt his intense gaze upon her, but she could not bring herself to return it.

He'd always been a sedate sort of man. Sure of himself, but not in any memorable way. A mediocre person that had earned Andrew's loyalty by way of the elder Mr. Piedmont's overseeing the care of her family. But suddenly she wondered how far Andrew's loyalty reached, and if she was entangled in that loyalty. If she somehow had become a part of Sir Lawrence's suddenly unnerving aspirations.

Violet sat in the empty chair next to her after setting her instrument in its case and arranging her skirts.

On Lydia's other side, Spencer leaned forward, his elbows on his knees, his hands clasped together. His head was bowed, and his knee bounced.

"What do you know?" she murmured.

A jerk of his head told her he'd heard her, and his head lowered once more.

Lydia turned to Violet, whose eyes were wide and questioning. "About what?" she asked.

"Who chose your song?" Lydia asked quietly.

Violet shrugged. "I wrote up a list, and Sir Lawrence insisted upon that one. I was quite surprised, but I wasn't going to argue." She read Lydia's expression and sobered. "What happened?"

Of course, from Violet's perspective and focus, she'd missed Sir Lawrence's embarrassing display.

"Nothing," Lydia said, forcing a smile. "You played beautifully. I'm sure your lady composer would be very proud."

Violet's smile returned, gentled by the compliment. "Thank you." She leaned closer and dropped her voice. "Though I will say I was surprised with all the trilling and flourish Sir Lawrence added to his performance. He was quite timid during rehearsal."

"It was very . . . stirring," Lydia said, swallowing hard. "Don't you think so, Spencer?"

She knew he'd been listening to their conversation.

He nodded, not looking at her. "That's one word for it." He lifted his gaze to Violet and straightened in his chair. "What a marvelous surprise to hear you play, Violet."

"What, because I'm a woman?" she asked good-naturedly. Though more women had been taking up the instrument in the past decade or so, a female violinist was still rare.

"Not at all. I've never heard the violin performed in person before, by man or woman. I hope it's not my last opportunity to do so."

"Thank you," Violet said, her gratitude genuine as it always was when it came to her beloved violin. "I'm pleased to have provided a more intimate introduction to the instrument."

A clearing of a throat drew their attention to the piano, where stood Mrs. Piedmont. Andrew waited to the side of the piano bench.

She pulled herself to her full height. "I shall be performing 'Flight of the Bumblebee,' or '*Polyot shmelya*,' by Russian composer Nikolai Rimsky-Korsakov. The song was written for his opera, *The Tale of Tsar Saltan*, in which a magical swan turns a prince into a bumblebee so he might visit his imprisoned father." She pressed her hand to her breast. "What a vivid imagination Mr. Korsakov had, to be sure." She turned to Andrew. "Mr. Wooding will be turning pages for me, which is no easy task for this particular piece." She bowed her head to Andrew, and then to her audience, and regally took her seat at the piano.

After a steadying breath, the woman began, her fingers immediately climbing the keys, nimbly building on the bee's furious flight of fancy. Indeed, in her yellow gown, the silk of her billowing sleeves shivering with movement, the woman portrayed the image quite effectively.

Andrew, Lydia noted, turned the pages as Mrs. Piedmont flew through them without need of her signaling nod. He simply knew when to turn the page because he could read music. A pang of sadness pulled at Lydia's heart. It could be him at the keys. Or the violin, or the cello, or probably a lute if they had one lying around. She'd been told he was brilliantly gifted on strings of any sort, but he'd not played since their parents had died.

She'd asked him once, why he never played anymore. And would he play for her? He'd simply shaken his head over his ledger, and said, "I've no time for that, now."

All at once, the bumblebee's frenzied flight ended, and amidst the bows and applause, Lydia's nerves decided it was time for a flight of their own. The servants brought in vases of clipped apple tree branches covered in blossoms and set them on the side tables and floor. Their scent filled the room, and Lydia closed her eyes, taking a moment.

When the pause after Mrs. Piedmont and Andrew had taken their seats became too long, Spencer pushed himself up and offered Lydia his hand with a bow. She stared at it, then placed her gloved fingers in his and allowed him to support her as she rose.

She swallowed as her head neared his. "We didn't practice," she whispered, as if only just realizing it.

"I've no doubt you'll be splendid," he said.

"Yes, but what about you?" she said, and he broke into an achingly beautiful smile.

He chuckled, shaking his head. "I'll try to keep up."

They turned to face their audience, and Lydia froze. She

couldn't possibly do this after what had taken place in the morning room. "Say something," she whispered to Spencer.

Spencer straightened. "We'll be singing a song called 'In the Shade of the Old Apple Tree,' written by some lonely bloke who misses his darling." He glanced at the piano. "Er . . . unaccompanied, because our talent only goes so far."

"Brilliant," she muttered under the chuckles in the room.

"Not at all. Ready?" He held up the music for both of them to see.

She reached back and played the opening three notes on the piano so they could find their pitch. Then, with a nod, they were off.

Spencer began as he had in their first attempt, singing of the reminders of an old love. As his voice cleared and strengthened, Lydia was spurred to match it. She took her turn with the verses about never seeing that love again on earth. Their voices combined for the last bit, leading straight into the second verse they hadn't yet practiced. Spencer nodded her way, so Lydia led, determined to look everywhere but at Sir Lawrence.

"The oriole with joy was sweetly singing. The little brook was babbling forth its tune. The village bells at noon were gaily ringing. The world seemed brighter than a harvest moon." She looked to Spencer, who met her gaze and took his turn.

"For there, within my arms, I gently pressed you, and blushing red, you slowly turned away. I can't forget the way I once caressed you . . ." He faltered and swallowed, then glanced at the page and took it up again, looking out to their audience. "I can't forget that happy bygone day."

With a deep breath against her flittering heartbeat, she joined him for the chorus of the song as it changed from four-four time to a three-quarter waltz.

"In the shade of the old apple tree, when the love in your eyes I could see. When the voice that I heard, like the song of a bird, seemed to whisper sweet music to me.

"I could hear the dull buzz of the bee"—Spencer gestured to Mrs. Piedmont, who seemed delighted to be acknowledged—"in the blossoms as you said to me . . ." He turned back to Lydia and lifted her hand, his eyebrows raised.

She took the part, willing her voice unaffected and sweet. "With a heart that is true, I'll be waiting for you . . ."

Spencer turned and gestured for everyone to join in singing the last line, and Lydia lifted her hands in accord.

". . . in the shade of the old ap-ple treeeee."

Resounding applause and laughter reached her ears even as she painted on a smile, ignoring Andrew's intense scrutiny of both her and Spencer as her brother absently clapped his hands. She felt tears rise up in her eyes, but she swallowed them down past the rock in her throat and lifted her chin.

Spencer was right. She had no idea what love was, or what she was thinking believing she had any power over it. The Wendy League girls were playing with fire. All of them.

And fire burned.

CHAPTER 13

Spencer glanced out the window. He'd rather stomp about in the downpour than remain in company for the rest of the evening, but there he stood, not gazing at Lydia. Not remembering the velvety softness of her skin, or how her lips had searched for more of him to claim, or how intoxicated he felt when she'd pulled him to her. He clenched his jaw. The need for a stomp in the rain was becoming imperative.

After the musicale, Mrs. Piedmont suggested a game of whist—she apparently loved the game—but Sir Lawrence invited Spencer to join him in the study to talk business. "After all, that leaves a nice four for the game whilst we discuss ventures. Wooding, you don't mind, do you?"

Andrew shook his head. "By all means, take yourselves to the study. I'll remain as rooster among these lovely hens."

"I would like to go," Lydia said.

But before Andrew could answer, Sir Lawrence said, "Do not trouble your head about such things, my dear. I assure you, you would find our discourse dull indeed."

"If you believe that," Violet muttered, "you do not know her a fig."

"Spencer?" Lydia asked, struggling to look at him squarely. "You wouldn't mind, would you?"

Spencer looked between Lydia and the other men, feeling trapped. But he affected the composure he knew was required. "It would be best to honor Sir Lawrence's request of a private business discussion, don't you think?"

"But—"

"Lydia," Andrew said, his tone stopping her argument. "Be my partner in whist, would you? I think we can take Mrs. Piedmont and Violet together, hm?"

"Yes, Miss Wooding," Mrs. Piedmont cried from the game table. "You must give us your best effort. I do love a challenge. Let Sir Lawrence and Mr. Hayes have their talk of shops. It's nothing to concern yourself about."

The woman smiled prettily, but Spencer could feel the waves of indignation coming from where Lydia stood.

Andrew held his sister's elbow gently, coaxing as one would a wild horse. Then her dark eyes met Spencer's, a dare to speak up for her.

Help him, her eyes were captivating.

"I shall make you a deal, Lydia," he said.

"Yes?" She seemed to be searching his face for any sign of what he could not give her.

Andrew let up on her elbow, taking interest in Spencer's next words.

"As I have things to discuss with this gentleman, so do you with your brother, correct?" He pointedly threw a look in Andrew's direction.

She followed it and gave a nod in understanding. "Correct."

"Then let us allow one another our discussions in their due course and all will be considered."

Her lips pursed in a pleased, if impatient, smile. "Agreed."

His stomach hardened at the sudden thought of being in business with either of them if she became Lady Piedmont. He nodded tightly, controlling his tone of voice. "Good. I'd like to give Sir Lawrence my full attention right now, if that would be acceptable to both of my hosts?"

Lydia straightened. "Of course. Though I'll maintain that I would not find your discourse *dull*." She glanced at Sir Lawrence. "But it is your discourse to have, and I will attend to my other guests. Good evening, gentlemen."

"Good evening, Miss Wooding," both gentlemen murmured.

Andrew nodded a thank you to Spencer, curiosity lighting his eyes.

Spencer turned, reminding himself of his sole reason for being in Surrey at all. "To the study, Sir Lawrence, before we're pulled into the fierce battle I have no doubt this particular game will become."

"Now where do you think he got that idea, Andrew?" Violet asked from the table.

"I've no idea," Andrew replied. "We are the epitome of acquiescence and apathy. I hope you win."

"As I do you."

"Take care, you two," Spencer heard Lydia say, "or we're liable to be struck by lightning from all this *apathy*."

The mouth on that woman. Spencer warmed uncomfortably, suspecting he'd be remembering kissing that mouth for a very long time. Regret that their first kiss must also be their last already weighed heavy in his chest.

In the study, Sir Lawrence stood before the fireplace while Spencer poured each of them a drink. He paused near a large potted fig tree. Frederick the Griffin had been placed on a pedestal, no doubt awaiting his plaque. What spontaneous fun that had been. He'd let his guard down so easily. Too easily.

"Tell me something," Sir Lawrence said. "What did you mean by that deal you struck with Miss Wooding just now?"

Spencer released a breath. He had no qualms with being honest about it. "Miss Wooding has offered to invest in the motor supply shops and promised to discuss it with Andrew before moving forward."

Sir Lawrence huffed. "Andrew will never approve." He took the offered drink.

"She is not seeking his approval," Spencer said. "Merely letting him know of her intentions."

"He will not release the funds."

"It is my understanding that the funds are her own. Or will be shortly."

"Ah." Sir Lawrence waved his hand as if shooing a fly. "A needless endeavor, then."

Spencer chuckled. "I beg your pardon, but as the party seeking investors, no matter the sum, I take exception to the word 'needless.'"

"Superfluous, then."

Spencer frowned. "How so?"

"You see . . ." Sir Lawrence took to perusing the bookshelves. "In the near future, mine and Miss Wooding's fortunes will combine."

Spencer's jaw clenched.

Sir Lawrence turned to him, his drink sloshing in the glass.

"So, my investment will be her investment, and hers mine and so forth."

The man waited to be asked further details. Spencer could see it in the lift of his brow and chin. It was perhaps the most expressive he'd ever seen the man.

He took a breath and nodded. "Does Miss Wooding know of this . . . merger?"

Sir Lawrence's smug look faltered but he recovered it. "It has been some time in the making."

Spencer fought to keep his own expression as neutral as a cat's. "But you've declared yourself? About your monetary takeover, I mean?"

"Well," the man said, his gaze narrowing. "Not yet. But it is understood."

"Is it?" Spencer nodded. "Splendid. In my interactions with Miss Wooding during my stay here, I must say she's given no hint she has an understanding with anyone."

"Well, that is because it is an understanding between me and Mr. Wooding."

Spencer's brows rose. "I see." Actually, he couldn't. No matter that he could have no interest in Lydia, he couldn't for the life of him see how Andrew would select this wooden plank of a man for his vivacious sister. "So, it stands that Lydia herself has no idea of an understanding."

Sir Lawrence pulled out his white handkerchief and dabbed at his forehead. "It does not signify. *Andrew* is aware of my intentions for Miss Wooding."

"Your intentions to take over her finances?" Spencer bit back a smile and folded his arms. "Would this be an advisory position? Or more like piracy?"

Sir Lawrence's features became as stone. "I am not a barbarian, Mr. Hayes. Miss Wooding's finances are her own."

Spencer nodded, putting his hands in his pockets. "I must have misunderstood when you said yours and Miss Wooding's finances are to combine." He put his hand up to stop Sir Lawrence's next argument. Provoking the man was counterproductive, to say the least. He bowed his head. "Forgive me, sir. There is something about this house that provokes one to banter. Especially over things of little importance. Don't you agree?" He turned away to inspect a globe of the earth. Birmingham was such a small speck.

"Indeed," Sir Lawrence said cautiously. "Mother has expressed something similar after our evenings here. I often leave with a mild headache."

"And yet you keep coming back," Spencer muttered to himself. He turned, brightening his expression. "I don't know about you, but I'd like to discuss motorcars and how to keep them running. Much better than a headache. What say you?"

Sir Lawrence inhaled deeply and let it out, his gaze direct. "That would be most welcome." His features smoothed over with a pleasant look. "I've spoken with some associates of mine. A select few with deep pockets. They want in."

Spencer's pulse quickened though he kept his expression neutral. "That is good news. I believe I can be candid with you. Is their interest tied to the Wooding name?"

Sir Lawrence frowned. "If you are asking if they will only invest if Andrew Wooding invests, then no. If anything, their interest is tied to mine. They trust my good judgment. However, Mr. Hayes, I'm sure I don't have to tell you that this opportunity stands on its own merit. Anyone with a sense for these things will see it. I'd wager even Mr. Wooding sees it. He just can't get past the sentimental notion that a car killed his parents."

Spencer narrowed his gaze at the flippant tone but kept his voice calm. "They *were* in a car accident. The brakes gave out. It was entirely out of their hands. I do not fault Andrew for remaining wary."

Sir Lawrence eyed the griffin clock with disinterest and turned. "You are more generous than I. Everybody knows the elder Mr. Wooding could not resist pushing his vehicle to its highest speeds. There was not a hay wagon or bicycler he did not pass with a tap of his horn. Story after story came out after the accident of townsfolk nearly or absolutely run off the road by the Wooding motorcar. Gads, man, did you ever lay eyes on the thing?"

Spencer had. On his second trip to Briarwall, Mr. Wooding had eagerly shown Spencer his Arnold Benz. At the time, it was a wonder. A posh, open carriage with a raised bench seat for two, a central steering wheel, and not much more. Nothing in front, where horses might have been hitched were it not a self-locomotive, and a rear-facing seat in back. Andrew's father had been giddy with excitement, and Spencer had been caught up in his spirit of possibilities.

It felt traitorous not to defend Mr. Wooding. But Spencer had been taken for a jaunt, and though the contraption only reached fifteen miles per hour that day—roads were not built yet for the likes of a motorcar, and a number of pedestrians, sheep, and wagons were evaded with little more than a honk—Mr. Wooding rarely slowed down, not even for oncoming vehicles.

Could the fatal accident have been brought about by Mr. Wooding's own recklessness? It certainly would add a layer as to why Andrew was so cautious, so deliberate in turning away from all things automotive—

And why he would forbid Lydia from driving. Lydia, who was so much like her father in temperament.

Spencer closed his eyes and exhaled.

"You can see how it is as I say, can you not?" Sir Lawrence asked.

Spencer nodded, not wanting to discuss it further. He fought the urge to leave the room, to clench his fists, to pace the temple until he felt calm. Instead, he shrugged. "We will never know the truth of the tragedy, only that it caused great grief to their children and all who knew and loved them."

Sir Lawrence pursed his lips. "It has been my observation that Miss Wooding has not dwelt on the matter, nor does she seem possessed of any excessive feeling toward it as her brother does. I quite admire her for it and sense her to be a . . . kindred spirit, if you will."

Spencer stared at the man, not knowing whether to bark out a laugh at the absurdity of such a statement or earnestly ask if he'd mistaken Lydia for someone else of his acquaintance. The empty suit of armor in the gallery, for instance.

But no, the man was quite serious. "Hm," was Spencer's benign response. He took a moment to walk toward the desk, collecting himself and any "excessive feelings" he had. He rounded the desk and stood beside Andrew's chair. "Shall we discuss the matter of my shops?" Spencer suddenly felt possessive of Hayes Motor Supply. Indeed, the more he came to know Sir Lawrence, the more the idea of doing business with him soured. But there was the matter of the man's money. And his influence.

"But of course. I seem to have led us off topic."

Several times, thought Spencer.

Sir Lawrence sat in the chair opposite the desk and pulled a folded stack of paperwork from his dinner jacket. "I have here pledges to the sum of one hundred fifty thousand pounds."

Spencer sat down hard in his chair, swallowing loudly. "That's a start," he said, an unusual rasp to his voice.

Sir Lawrence dropped his chin and squared his gaze at Spencer. "A very good start."

Over the next two days, Lydia avoided Spencer, which was easy to do as she was sure he was avoiding her also. Church couldn't be helped, but Andrew sat between them like a castle wall—so straight was his posture and definite their separation. At least, it felt that way.

However, after service, Sir Lawrence encountered no such obstacle and directly made his way to where she waited in the sunshine while Andrew lingered in the church with Spencer, making introductions.

As Sir Lawrence strode toward her, two young gentlemen of her acquaintance passed by, and she looked to them, hoping that they might stop and converse, but they merely touched their hats and nodded to her before continuing on.

"Miss Wooding, you are looking fine today." Sir Lawrence took her hand and pressed a kiss to her glove, a new gesture in his greetings.

Her hand stiffened, and she wondered if he noticed. She wished he did. "Thank you, Sir Lawrence. Many young ladies are looking fine today. Is that not what Sundays are for? To promenade after church and be admired?" Her sarcasm seemed to be lost on Sir Lawrence.

"Indeed. But you are particularly fine today."

"I am particularly fine today, as opposed to other days? Or I am particularly fine, compared to the other ladies?"

He paused, his smile—if one could call it that—drooping. "Eh, that is to say, I am drawn to your particular . . . fineness."

"How kind of you to say," she said, extricating her hand. How was it his touch was so off-putting and Spencer's was so . . . not? Her thoughts flew to the memory of Spencer's lips pressed to hers, his hands encircling her waist. A pleasant shudder coursed through her spine, and it took focus to suppress it.

" . . . if I do say so."

She blinked, swallowing hard. "Pardon?"

"Come, come, Miss Wooding. Let's not pretend that a pair of fine horses, when properly matched, do not turn heads with admiration and, dare I say, envy?"

Lydia stared, clearly having missed this turn of subject. "No," she said, scrambling for a response. "Fine horses. Who would pretend such a thing?"

"Yes. Exactly." He bowed again. Then he leaned closer, speaking in a whisper. "Though, I admit no person can match the beauty your blush brings to your visage."

"There you are, Lydia."

Lydia spun in relief to find Ruby Burke approaching, her parasol shading her delicate features and gentle green eyes from the sun despite the olive satin toque she wore over her deep-brown curls.

"Ruby, how wonderful to see you!" Lydia's joy was not feigned. She could use the support of a Wendy League girl at the moment.

She turned. "Sir Lawrence, will you excuse me? I have need to talk to my friend."

He nodded to both ladies. "Miss Wooding. Miss Burke. Good day to you."

Lydia threaded her arm through Ruby's and all but pulled her toward the cemetery. "I'm very glad to see you."

"So I gathered. I have it on good authority that you would appreciate my interruption." Ruby nodded back toward the road, where Violet gave a small wave before getting into her car with her mother.

"Yes, well, I'm grateful. And flummoxed."

"By Sir Lawrence?"

"Certainly. He is suddenly . . ."

"Interested?" Ruby offered.

"Too close," she corrected. "He keeps kissing my hand. And he's begun whispering to me. What is that all about?"

"Do you truly need me to explain it to you?" Ruby stopped and looked at her, kindness and patience in her gaze.

Lydia sighed. "No. Only perhaps you can explain to me why he has decided that, after years of regular association with my family, he is suddenly . . ."

"Interested," Ruby repeated.

"I suppose."

She shook her head. "I can only speculate. We are not girls anymore. *Any* man would be ridiculous not to take notice of you, whether he is a family friend or a new acquaintance . . . or even a *renewed* acquaintance?" She lifted her dark brows.

Lydia groaned. "What did Violet tell you?"

"Only that Spencer Hayes may be in love with you."

Lydia frowned. "That is not funny."

"It wasn't meant to be. She also said you may be in love with him."

Lydia's cheeks flamed, and her breathing became difficult. "Well, she's mistaken."

Ruby pulled her closer to her side and resumed walking. "Violet is the most reliable observer of all of us."

"Aside from you," Lydia said.

"I am too shy."

Lydia shook her head. "You are quiet. Often that makes you the best of us. You see things we miss in our exuberance. Yet I know you to be more confident and wiser than I feel most of the time."

"That is quite a feat, considering I am in the middle of six brothers of varying heights and energies, and I constantly feel as though I somehow stepped on the wrong boat and it is too late to return to port. I assure you, it is no confidence booster to hear your parents boast of their sons and mention you as an afterthought. *Oh, and this is our Ruby. Heaven knows what the Lord was thinking sending us a girl in the middle of all of this bedlam.*"

Lydia frowned. The Wendy League received regular anecdotes of Ruby's life with her brothers, but they were usually laced with long-suffering humor. She'd heard Mr. and Mrs. Burke refer to their daughter in such a way at gatherings, though.

"I'm sorry you're made to feel distinctive in such a way. Your brothers adore you, Ruby. I've seen it. Even when we're wielding our feminine minds in their direction."

She smiled at the ground. "Well, I can't argue that."

"Knowing how protective my *one* brother is of me, I can only imagine how it might be to have *six*." Lydia made a face.

Ruby looked up and grinned. "The poor boy who comes courting Miss Ruby Burke . . ."

"Will be the luckiest man on earth—if he survives it."

The girls laughed, their heads close together. Lydia had been friends longest with Violet and had embarked on the most adventures with Florrie, but with Ruby, she knew she was in gentle hands, and sometimes that was what she needed most.

"So," Ruby said as they reached a willow and paused. "What will you do about Mr. Hayes?"

Lydia sobered, remembering the way things had turned the night of the musicale. "I do not know that there is anything to be done. He—that is, I believed—" She folded her arms and paced, then stopped. "Why does it feel as though felicity landed right in my lap, and just as I had the courage to embrace it, it turned to sand." She reached out and pressed her hand to the willow trunk. "Have you ever tried to embrace sand?"

"I imagine it's a little frustrating."

"Yes, and difficult to scrub away. It gets everywhere, and days later you're still—you're still—"

"Agitated?"

Lydia groaned and slapped her forehead. "There's that word again."

"What word?"

"*Agitate.* Violet hinted at its connection to love."

"Did she?"

"And I was stupid enough to believe that I agitated Spencer as well."

Ruby suppressed a giggle and pinched her lips closed at Lydia's sharp look. She sighed. "Forgive me. You've painted a very intriguing picture, that's all. Are you sure Mr. Hayes is not . . . agitated?"

Lydia pulled at a willow branch. "I'm not sure of anything!" She hushed herself immediately.

"How can I help?" Ruby asked, her green eyes sincere.

Lydia glanced about and saw Andrew drawing closer, likely coming for her. She took Ruby's arm again and began walking away from her brother. "Come home with me. You have vastly more experience with the male species than I do. Is your mother still in need of you?"

Ruby shook her head. "My aunt returns to Suffolk this afternoon."

"Excellent. Then your mother can spare you, and I daresay you need a change of scenery."

"That I do."

"Then come. You can quietly observe and see what can be done."

"You wish me to spy."

"No. I wish you to help me figure out why a man who 'may be in love' would fight so hard to stay away from it."

"As I said, you wish me to spy."

Lydia caught the gleam in her friend's eye. "Fine. I wish you to spy."

"I'm no expert."

"Have any of your brothers been in love?"

Ruby shrugged. "Some have claimed to be."

"And you live with these men?"

"Incessantly."

"Then you are more expert than I."

Ruby grew quiet, then asked, "Has Andrew never been in love?"

Lydia frowned at the ground. "If he has, do you think he would admit it?"

"Mm, you have a point."

Lydia stopped, as they'd circled the yard and were back at the gate. "Please come. My persistent desire to never grow up is at war with my suspicion that I already have, and I'm left wondering what to fight for."

"Take care. You will be kidnapped to Neverland and forget all about us."

Lydia shook her head. "Never."

Ruby squeezed her hand. "If anyone understands needing a respite after spending a week with Great-Aunt Margaret, it is Mama."

CHAPTER 14

"What do you mean he *kissed* you?" Ruby asked, glancing about as if gossiping eavesdroppers might appear at any moment.

After a midday meal, they'd laid out a blanket on the gentle slope of lawn overlooking the lavender field. Wands of soft green waved in the breeze, reaching up to the aqua sky from silver mounds. Dark clouds loomed in the distance, but that did nothing to dampen the ambience. In a month or so, the field would be a dance of purple with the hum of bees to accompany the birdsong.

Lydia kept her eyes on the stem of lavender she'd plucked. She rolled it between her fingers, knowing the scent would linger. "*I* kissed him, really. But then he kissed me back." Heavens, how he had kissed her back. She shivered in delight at the memory, despite the sun warming her gown. "And then he stopped and said it couldn't happen because I was meant for—I don't know, *something*. He wouldn't say. And then Fallon came in, and I cannot figure out what he meant unless Andrew told him he intended to send me to a convent or the like. And we're not even Catholic." She leaned back on her elbows. "Though I doubt that would stop my brother."

"The Catholics might take pause," Ruby said with a tiny smile.

"Amen."

"In any case, have you considered that it's not some*thing* Spencer was referring to, but some*one*? You did say Sir Lawrence's behavior was rather forward lately. Might Spencer have observed that during his stay here?"

Lydia nodded slowly as she reviewed the events from Friday. The timing of their interactions. The point at which Spencer's ease with her shifted. "Blast. You may be right. But what would that matter? I've certainly not shown any preference for Sir Lawrence."

"I might be right, or I might not. After all, I haven't met Mr. Hayes yet." She looked toward the house.

"Yes, my brother's usual punctuality is mysteriously absent this afternoon." Lydia glanced at Ruby to find her chewing her lip, overly focused on a smooth stone she turned over and over in her hands. "What is it?"

That seemed to snap Ruby out of her reverie. "Well, Mrs. Piedmont was a friend of your mother's, correct?"

"Yes. When Mama and Papa were married, she was the first to welcome my mother to the neighborhood."

"And she has a son only a few years older than you—"

"He is at least twelve years older than I."

"Yes, but that hardly mattered to scheming mothers of the nineteenth century."

"Oh laws. Surely you're not suggesting—"

"I only wonder if it might have been discussed between friends, and now Andrew, as your guardian—"

Lydia abruptly stood, feeling hollow. "Blast it all to Hades in a skirt. It cannot be!" The air in her lungs turned to stone. "I—I won't allow it."

Ruby blinked up at her, shading her eyes with her parasol.

"You said Sir Lawrence is likely to make a significant investment in the motor supply shops?"

She glanced from Ruby to the house and back again. "Oh, Ruby." She put her hand to her stomach, feeling sick. "No wonder Spencer acted as he did. Sir Lawrence, the wealthy investor, has his *misguided* sights set on *me*, the woman who threw herself at the entrepreneur. And my brother"—she huffed—"endorses it—the wealthy match, not me throwing myself at his friends. Heaven forbid Andrew ever finds out about *that*." She closed her eyes and groaned at the mess of things. "How could Andrew *do* this to me?" She screwed up her face. "Sir *Lawrence*?"

"We don't know anything for certain," Ruby offered.

"Is anything ever for certain?"

Ruby remained quiet.

Lydia didn't know who to be angrier with: Andrew for being antiquated, Sir Lawrence for being a pompous fop, or Spencer for putting money before love. Or what could be love, if given the chance.

Or was she more angry with herself for being selfish with Spencer's precarious dreams?

"But I don't *want* Sir Lawrence!" She cringed at the whine in her voice. "With or without Spencer."

"Does Andrew know that?" Ruby asked.

Her simmering anger rose to a boil inside her. Would it even matter if Andrew knew how she felt? "I'm so tired of being treated like I don't know what I want."

"What *do* you want?"

Lydia threw her arms out at her sides. "I want to feel comfortable in my own skin. I want to learn to drive a car and participate in that exciting industry. I want to learn so many things beyond how to host a tea. I want to have a *say*. I want to kiss a man without it ruining me, and I want to fall in love without it ruining a man's future." Her voice quivered, and she swallowed against it. "And I want pigs to fly, apparently." She breathed heavily from her speech.

"Well, at least you know what you want." Ruby smiled up at her, and Lydia was reminded once again how fairylike her friend was.

She growled. "You are infuriatingly disarming; do you know that?"

Ruby lifted a shoulder. "I've learned to be as a matter of survival." She patted the space next to her on the blanket.

Lydia took another deep breath and sat down, pulling her arms around her knees. "The next time I'm around Andrew I'm going to give him a piece of my mind."

"Are you certain?"

"Yes. I don't give a fig about Sir Lawrence even if our mothers were friends. Who does Andrew think he is?"

"Your brother," Ruby said. She nodded toward the house. "And here he comes."

Lydia looked up to see Andrew and Spencer strolling toward them, hands in pockets. Hero raced in circles around them. Her gaze lingered on Spencer, on his shoulders and jawline, the tone of his skin, the shape of his nose and lips. His curious eyes were bright as he took in his surroundings.

"Have any of your brothers tried to tie you to anyone?" she asked Ruby.

She shook her head. "They can't even manage to tie *themselves* to anyone." She threw a meaningful look at Lydia.

Lydia huffed. Neither could Andrew. Her anger calmed, and resolve grew in its place.

Ruby tilted her head, watching the men. "I don't know. I could very well imagine Mr. Hayes a bird-watcher. With a poor-boy cap, a pair of binoculars, and a sketchbook."

Lydia nodded in absolute agreement. "His sleeves rolled up and a pencil between his teeth."

They both sighed.

Hero bounded up first, greeting the girls with a sniff and a wagging tail. He received hellos and pats in return.

The gentlemen approached and removed their hats. "Good afternoon, ladies," Andrew said. "Miss Burke, I'd like to introduce my friend Spencer Hayes. Spencer? This is Miss Ruby Burke. I'd push for formality, but you know as well as I that by the end of the day we'll all be on a first-name basis." He said this in resignation, and Lydia stuck her tongue out at him. He ignored her.

Spencer bowed. "Pleasure to meet you, Miss Burke. I've met your brothers. Three of them, anyhow."

Ruby cast a weary glance at Lydia. "I hope you don't hold that against me, Mr. Hayes."

He chuckled. "Indeed not. If anything, you've earned my respect even knowing nothing more about you."

"A perk that comes with having such siblings, then." She scratched Hero's chin and lifted her eyes to Spencer. "Do you have any brothers or sisters?"

Spencer's expression gentled. "A sister. I do what I can to earn her compassion from others."

She laughed. "A dutiful brother, then."

Spencer chuckled again. Was that a blush?

"If only some brothers knew how much duty to be full of," Lydia mused. She caught all three discerning gazes and smiled innocently. "Generally speaking, of course."

Andrew cleared his throat. "What have you ladies been

discussing in such an idyllic setting? Tennyson? Plato? How Mr. Hanover's donkey's persistent escapes from its pen correlates with the phases of the moon?"

"Bird-watching," Lydia said. "We've decided it a romantic sport, haven't we, Ruby?"

Ruby nodded, her cheeks reddening. "Oh, er, quite. H-have either of you ever been?"

Both gentlemen shook their heads.

Spencer gestured back to the house. "Unless you count the robin building a nest in the walnut tree outside my room."

"Has she started already, then?" Lydia asked. "I should like to have a look. Every year, I put out old ribbons and embroidery floss, and the nest is a festive delight for May Day."

Ruby leaned toward her. "Remember the year when we each snipped a lock of our hair and set it on the shrubbery beneath her tree?"

"She made a nest of our hair," Lydia said, smiling up at the gentlemen. "We were so pleased."

"A most lovely gift," Andrew said, looking between them both.

Lydia paused. "Was that a compliment?"

He narrowed his gaze. "Contrary to popular opinion, I do appreciate a thing of beauty, and I am able to express that appreciation when it strikes me."

She rose to her knees and clapped her hands. "Oh, do give us an example."

Andrew's ears turned pink.

Ruby reached over and rested her hand upon Lydia's arm. "Come now, Lydia, it's inconsiderate to put a gentleman on the spot."

"Is it inconsiderate to put a *brother* on the spot?"

A slow smile spread across her lips. "By all means, do continue."

Lydia beamed at Andrew. "Go on, then."

He drew himself up. "Very well. Miss Burke." He cleared his throat. "*Ruby.* The last time you played the harp for us I was transformed. Indeed, it was a thing of beauty, and I did not express it then. I do so now." He made a small bow in her direction.

Ruby stared up at him, then found her voice. "Why, thank you, Andrew. I'm delighted. And . . . shocked."

"Then perhaps I don't express my appreciation as often as I think I do."

"I believe sincerity trumps frequency, sir."

Andrew nodded in gratitude. "Then count me as sincere."

Lydia looked between the two of them, then caught Andrew's eye. "And me?" she asked, full of cheek. She batted her lashes. "I'll settle for frequency."

Spencer turned aside, his hand over his mouth, hiding his amusement.

Andrew drew in a deep breath and let it go slowly.

She waited, eyes wide.

He squared himself to her. "You, my sister, have more heart than I could ever hope to discipline, more strength than I can fathom, and you sing"—he swallowed hard—"like Mother."

Lydia blinked, and her fingers touched the watch pin on her blouse. The others said nothing as Andrew let her search his gaze—something she realized he seldom allowed.

He lowered his chin. "How was that for frequency?"

She only nodded. Ruby took her hand and whispered, "I believe he covered both that time."

Lydia turned and brushed at her eye. When she turned back,

Andrew had paced a few steps away, and Spencer watched her with a look that said both come closer and stay away. Her heart thudded with hope. She suppressed it with effort. Curse Violet with her love and agitation. Lydia didn't like it. Didn't want it. And she did, help her.

Ruby gently cleared her throat and spoke softly. "Perhaps now would be a good time for you to *give Andrew a piece of your mind*, as I think you put it." Before Lydia could respond, she stood, and Spencer stepped forward to assist her.

"Mr. Hayes," Ruby said, dusting off her skirt, "would you perhaps accompany me on a walk along the pond? I'm thinking of painting a landscape and could use some help finding the perfect perspective."

"Do you paint?" he asked, glancing toward Lydia.

Lydia watched her friend be as bold with a new acquaintance as she'd ever witnessed.

Ruby tipped her head in apology and hushed her words. "Not at all, but a walk would give our friends some time to finish their conversation in private, don't you agree?"

He pursed his lips. "It so happens I'm very good at finding perfect perspectives for imaginary paintings."

Lydia watched them go, Hero remaining at her side. Her dratted heart leaped when Spencer glanced back at her over his shoulder. She made herself smile. He nodded, then gave Ruby his full attention.

She found Andrew strolling along a row of lavender, head bent, hands shoved in his pockets. Very un-Andrew.

"The field is maturing beautifully," she said as she reached him. The lavender was only three years old, but each mound now measured at least two feet across and produced perfectly compact flower heads for drying, making oil, and selling in bunches. Mrs. Parks was especially proud of the lavender and chamomile tea the small estate made and sold at local markets alongside their rose and rosehip teas, as the recipe was her own.

"Yes," he said. "It was a good idea." He looked at her. "I've never given you credit for it."

She tilted her head. "I do not need a plaque with my name."

"No. But I'm sure a thank you would be appreciated."

"I'll not argue that."

He nodded, meeting her gaze. "Thank you, Lydia. The lavender fields not only diversify the estate's income but add a lovely aesthetic that will only increase as time goes on."

"You're quite welcome." They walked a few steps together. "A plaque, unneeded as it is, *would* be a nice gesture, though." She eyed him sideways and caught his suppressed grin.

"We shall see," he said.

They walked along the row for some moments in silence except for the nearby birdsong.

"Did you mean what you said?" she asked. "Back there?"

"Every word," he said without hesitation. "True, I am continually baffled by the way you flout social expectations. But you do it with such a genuine and deliberate air—sometimes I'm quite jealous."

She balked. "Of me? I don't believe you. You are all that is honorable and upright. Most times I feel like I am a burden to you rather than—"

He took her hand, a rare gesture. "Don't say that. Don't even think it. You are my family, Lydia. Do you understand? You are who I have left to care for, to be an anchor for. You, above all else, give my life purpose. And though I might've made a bungle of it, I've given my best effort for you. You are no burden." He looked about him as if trying to find words. "You breathe life into this place when I often feel I cannot find air."

She frowned up at him as she processed what he was saying. "Are you so unhappy, Andrew?"

He sighed and dropped her hand. "It does not matter what I am."

"That is certainly not true."

"What matters is that you are happy and well cared for."

"I am happy," she said, and his furrowed brow relaxed. "Except for a few small matters."

His brow creased again. "Small?"

"Huge, actually." She steadied her breath. "You've acknowledged the lavender field was a good idea—a good investment."

"Yes?"

She resumed walking, and he stayed with her. She ran her hands along the tops of the fragrant stems. "I'd like to discuss the investment portion of my inheritance. I've another idea that I believe to be sound. I've all but made up my mind, but I'd like to include you in my decision, out of respect and because I know you to be discerning."

He watched the ground as they walked, his shoulders taut with tension. "What is it?"

She stopped and faced him. "I wish to invest twenty thousand pounds in Spencer's motor supply shops."

He immediately stiffened, but before he could protest, she continued, keeping her voice as calm as she could. "I hope to specify that my investment go toward *quality* car parts and training so that they're installed *correctly*. I want to have a hand in improving motorcar safety. In this way, perhaps more accidents can be prevented." She watched him weigh her words a moment, then, encouraged, added, "I also want to give Spencer our family name as solid investors to add validity to his efforts."

At that, his expression clouded. He turned away from her, his hand tapping against his leg. "I cannot allow you to do that," he said.

She wanted to scoff and tell him he had no business *allowing* her to do anything, but she'd learned that would do no good. "Which part can you not allow?" she asked. "Because, Andrew, I would like to be part of this venture. It is solid. Despite the pain of losing Mother and Father to an accident and your disdain for the entire automotive industry, I believe you see it as a good idea as well. You've spoken too highly of Spencer's uncanny foresight and ingenuity. And you've taught me too well of business for me to allow this opportunity to pass by."

"So, it's my fault, then?"

Relieved to hear a fraction of humor in his tone, she shrugged. "Isn't everything?"

He bit back a smile, and she counted it a triumph. But then he sobered.

"You may do as you see fit with your investment money, Lydia. But be careful about attaching our name to Spencer's venture. It may not do the good you expect."

She frowned. "What do you mean?"

He dropped his head. "I was reminded recently that you are no longer a child."

Her eyes widened. "By someone other than me?"

He narrowed his eyes at her, and she winked.

He took a breath. "And while that concept is one my stubborn mind is still grappling with, it is time you knew something I've sheltered you from. If you are to pursue this venture, then you must understand."

A cold breeze touched her skin, and she shivered. "What is it?"

He pinched the bridge of his nose the way he did when he was fighting a headache. Then he let it go and set his hands at his hips. "It is highly rumored, and entirely possible, that Father was largely at fault for the car accident."

She stared at him.

He looked out over the lavender rows, his jaw clenching and unclenching.

"But . . . but they found the brake prematurely worn down," she said. "It gave out entirely though the vehicle was fairly new. What could Father have done to prevent it?"

"Father was known for his reckless driving. Out of concern for us, his orphans, the locals kept things hushed during the inquiry. We owe the people of this town much."

"Andrew," she said, her composure fading. "What were they covering up? What did Father do?"

"Father's vehicle was designed to go fifteen to twenty miles per hour at its top speed. The suspicion is that he took the car to the top of Box Hill so he could see how fast the thing could go when given a good enough pull of gravity. That hill has a nice long, steep stretch before the turn at the bluff. A car that heavy would reach beyond those speeds quickly without any brake applied."

"But what would cause the brakes to give out if they were in perfect working order?" she asked, scrambling to make sense of this new information. "Surely Father would've applied the brake with enough distance before the bluff. Mama was with him, for heaven's sake!"

Andrew rested his warm hands on her suddenly cold arms,

and she welcomed the anchor. A brisk wind had picked up, and the sunlight dimmed. The air smelled of rain.

When he looked at her next, it was with compassion. "Father had made the run down that hill several times, had bragged about it at the club, before taking Mother."

She swallowed hard. "Enough times to wear down the brake?"

He nodded, giving her arms a gentle squeeze.

Mama. Papa. The lump in her throat hardened. "Andrew," she whispered, her eyes filling with tears, "how could you bear it?"

He drew her to him, and for the second time in a week, she was in his embrace. She heard the spartan patter of scattered raindrops on the lavender bushes.

"It is a rumor. There was never any proof. The logistics of the accident showed the brake gave way prematurely, and the wear was attributed to an attempt to stop the vehicle during its long descent. We will never know the facts. But knowing Father, it makes sense. He was impulsive and daring and pushed his limits. He was—"

"Like me." She pushed away from him, fighting the sobs building inside her. "That's why you won't teach me to drive. Why you don't trust me to make decisions for myself, for my future."

"Lydia, I just gave you my trust with your inheritance. I only need you to understand why you—"

"Have you arranged a marriage between Sir Lawrence and myself?"

He froze, his blue eyes wide.

Her voice shook, but she did not shrink. "Judging from the way your cheeks have mottled purple, I will take that as a yes." She felt her nostrils flare.

Andrew began shaking his head. "I needed to consider your future, to make sure you were provided for. Mother had mentioned that she and Mrs. Piedmont had mused over the connection, and with your reputation—"

"My what?" she asked, jolted from her fury.

He seemed to realize he was digging himself deeper and backed away, his hands held out in front of him as if she were a tiger ready to pounce, which was not far off the mark.

He spoke softly, almost a whisper. "It's just that you are known to be brash, Lydia. Lovely, but brash. Outspoken. And wild."

"*Wild?* What, like a boar?" Her hands clenched into fists. "I know of no such reputation. I am more relaxed with my friends, yes, but in the company of society, I conduct myself with respect to all those women who've taught me how to do so. Mrs. Parks. Fallon. Mrs. Janes and Mrs. Whittemore. Nanny, bless her soul, and Miss Forrester, who should have been *sainted* as my governess.

"Do I put on airs or present myself as something I am not? A simpering, delicate blossom needing to be staked to a man lest the gentlest wind tear me?" *Blast* her tears. She wiped her face. "No. I do not know where you've heard this summation of my reputation, but I do not accept it. And neither should you. Did you even argue or defend me? Before you rolled over and sold me off as a lost cause? I do *not* accept this understanding you've made with Sir Lawrence. He is not for me." She straightened. "And if you believe he is, then you do not know me at all. I'd sooner marry a *tree*. They smell better and . . . and speak to my *soul*."

She turned to leave and halted. At the end of the lavender row stood Spencer with Ruby, both of them wide-eyed and still. How much had they heard?

Her emotions could not be contained much longer, especially with the way Spencer was looking at her. No wonder he didn't want her. She was *brash* and *wild*. Her lungs ached with every breath. She glanced at Ruby, unable to bear the sympathy on her face.

She picked up her skirts and ran as the sky broke open with a gentle rain.

"Lydia," Andrew called after her.

"No!" was all she could manage before the tears spilled over. With each stride, her shoulders shook with weeping. "Leave me alone," she whimpered, proving herself to be a delicate blossom after all.

CHAPTER 15

"Oh dear." Ruby grabbed Spencer's arm as Lydia ran away from them, the collie bounding after her. She faced him beneath her parasol. "You go after her. I'll handle Andrew." She looked at the man down the row, his shoulders slumped, his hand in his hair. "I've a feeling this will take more than a few quips to mend."

Spencer glanced toward Andrew, but she squeezed his arm. "Do you really think he'd listen to you right now?" she said. "Go to Lydia. They both need to get out of this rain, and I believe neither have the wits to do it on their own."

He nodded and pushed himself after the woman who'd just been told her future was not her own because she had the courage to be herself. What had Andrew been thinking? Allowing rumors of that nature to cage his own sister, all in the name of assuring that somebody *settled* for her?

He paused at the edge of the pond, searching for a sign of Lydia, wanting to shout her name, but not wanting to alert the help or push her further into hiding. The pediment of the northern end of the temple caught his eye, and he set his course in that direction through the trees.

He heard her before he saw her.

"Gah!" she cried. A big *kerplunk* followed. She sniffled, breathing hard. Then it repeated, a large *kerplunk* echoed by smaller *plinks* of raindrops hitting the water.

He emerged from the trees to find the small beach at the rear of the temple where they'd met for their ill-fated bicycle ride. His pounding heart wasn't doing him any favors. Hearing her deny any connection, romantic or otherwise, to Sir Lawrence had knocked something loose inside him. *She* had knocked something loose inside him.

She threw another rock and then clenched both fists at her sides, arms stiff, pacing a few steps, breathing deeply as if trying to collect herself in the rain. The collie sheltered under the temple cornice, watching her every move.

Not wanting to startle her, Spencer cleared his throat.

Hero barked and left his post to welcome him.

Lydia turned his way and stiffened, then spun and climbed the steps to the temple and out of his sight.

He looked back toward the lavender fields as if Miss Burke were there to push him on, then glanced up at the heavy-laden sky, blinking in the rain. On their walk, Ruby had said point-blank that she knew he was in love with Lydia, and somehow, he'd ended up confessing about Catherine and that he wouldn't be made a fool again.

Her response? "You were simply *trusting* with the American. You're being a *fool* with Lydia."

How could a woman he'd met only an hour ago have summed up everything so precisely? Lydia's friends all had their quirks, but Miss Burke's powers of observation were the most unnerving by far.

He still hadn't decided—or admitted—how correct she was.

He headed to the temple. At least Lydia would be out of the

rain. He climbed the steps and brushed water off his shoulders and arms as he looked around. Hero shook himself, keeping close to Spencer's leg.

"Lydia?" He stepped farther inside. "At least let me give you my coat."

"No. I don't need your pity."

He glanced around, the faint echo making it hard to pinpoint where she was. He stepped into the main body of the temple, flanked by both inner and outer rows of columns. Iris, sword fern, and cypress edged either side of the temple among the newly greening rose bushes and creeping ivy. The rain increased, judging by the sound on the surrounding foliage.

"It isn't pity," he said. "It's knowledge that I have both a coat and a cardigan, and you've only the lovely but likely damp dress you're wearing."

"Don't talk flattery to me, Spencer Hayes."

He spied a flutter of pink-and-white stripes—like a candy stick—behind the fourth column on the left. He stepped carefully that way.

"Believe me, you will know when I talk flattery to you."

Hero went before him and circled around the column, tail wagging.

"Go, Hero," he heard Lydia whisper. "Go over there."

The dog sat, panting.

"Hero, I said go. Go fetch a stick."

"I believe—"

She gasped and spun around at the sound of Spencer's words directly behind her.

"—you need to throw a stick in order for him to fetch it."

She collected herself quickly. "Perhaps I should throw *you* a stick. What are you doing?"

Spencer had removed his coat as she spoke and reached around to place it over her shoulders. "I'm giving you my coat. You're shivering."

"I am not."

He pulled the front lapels together at her collarbone. "You are." Her damp hair was curling at her temples, her dark lashes glistening.

She stepped back but was stopped by the pillar behind her.

"Lydia." He sighed. "I heard what Andrew said. Please, let me help you."

"Like you helped me with the song?"

The set of her chin told him the question was either a set-down or a challenge. He went with the former. "You kissed *me*, remember?"

"Yes, and I suppose I just imagined the fervor of your response. I am, after all, outspoken and brash and so wild it's a wonder I manage to walk upright and use a spoon." She brushed away a stray lock of hair and pulled herself up straight. "I understand now why you pulled away from me that night and made it clear you would not have me. I wonder if all of Surrey knows of Andrew's and Sir Lawrence's benevolent plans for the poor, uncouth Wooding orphan girl? Not to mention what getting entangled with Sir Lawrence's supposed intended would mean to his likely sizeable investment in a new venture." Her brows furrowed. "But what I can't understand is, if you already knew, why did you respond to me, to the kiss, the way you did? Before you pulled away, I mean?"

Violet was right. Lydia didn't play games. Spencer's breath

grew labored under the honesty she hurled at him. He shook his head as she waited for his answer. "You are so . . . so—"

"Undisciplined? Brutish? Too—"

He growled and closed the distance between them even as she reached for him, lifting her flushed mouth to his. He tasted salt from her tears mixed with rainwater. He pulled her closer, wrapping her up in his arms. He wanted to shield her from all that would make her cry or make her doubt.

Her quickened breath matched his as he pressed her against the pillar, cradling her with his arms and hands, feeling every touch of her fingers sliding over his chest and around his waist like tendrils of flame.

"You," he said between touches to her lips, "are so . . . full of *fire*."

She drew in a shaky breath as he ran his mouth along her neck.

"And you draw me to you like Icarus to the sun." He felt her shiver as he whispered in her ear.

She pulled away enough to meet his gaze, searching. "That didn't end well," she countered, a small crease between her brows.

He shook his head, watching her carefully, feeling the press of her hand over his pounding heart.

"Are you afraid?" she asked. "Of me?"

A chuckle escaped him. He kissed her forehead, closing his eyes and lingering, breathing her scent. "You, Lydia Wooding, are wonderfully and fearfully made." He captured her gaze with his. "I would be a fool not to be afraid."

She lowered her eyes.

"And," he added, his voice rough, "I'd be a fool not to consider how bleak and cold my life would be without your heat."

Lydia lifted her chin. At that moment, lightning flashed in the distance, followed immediately by a roll of thunder. She broke into a smile, and he matched it, both of them laughing. The rain had increased significantly, developing into a modest storm while they had been otherwise occupied.

He sobered at the depth of his feelings for her and pushed away the questions of his future, her future. Right now, they were hidden from the demands of the world, and she was warm and soft in his arms. He surrendered to his heart and poured that vulnerability into kissing Lydia senseless. Though it might have been the other way around.

"Hayes."

Their lips parted at the very threatening male voice behind him. They searched one another's faces, sharing a moment of breathless panic before Spencer swallowed. Slowly, they released their intimate embrace, and Spencer turned, trying to convey confidence. He kept Lydia's hand in his.

"Hello, Andrew," Lydia said, not sounding confident at all.

CHAPTER 16

Andrew glowered. Lydia had never seen her brother so menacing. So . . . threatening. She could quite easily imagine steam rolling off him with the rainwater puddling on the stone floor at his feet.

"I ought to knock you senseless," he rumbled, his brows low.

She blinked, then looked between her brother and the man standing next to her. He was speaking to Spencer as if he'd come face-to-face with his greatest enemy.

"I ought to thrash you within an inch of your life."

Spencer raised his free hand in front of them both. "Andrew, this is not what you think it is."

Andrew's lip curled. "Lydia, away from him. Now."

She shook her head. "No, Andrew, listen—"

"Now!"

She jumped.

Spencer's hand shifted to her elbow, and he pulled her behind him a step. "Don't you think you've caused enough of her tears today?"

"And what do you think this will do to her? Hm?" Andrew stepped toward them. "How long have you been wooing her money,

Hayes? Is this your scheme? Meet the men in the clubs and the women in shadowed corners?"

She dared a glance at Spencer, who looked as if he'd just been slapped.

"You can't be serious," he said quietly.

"You already have Piedmont's money. Better get your hands on Lydia's, too, while you can."

"Andrew! Spencer is your friend."

"Is he?" He tore his glare from Spencer and met her gaze. "I've just been on the telephone while you've been out here doing—"

"Kissing. It's called kissing, brother, you should try it sometime."

Andrew ignored her. "I received a call from a Mr. Burnett." He turned to Spencer, who had gone very still. "I was actually considering buying into your shops, even before Lydia told me of her plans. A silent partner of sorts. What are older siblings for, after all, if not to lend support from afar."

Lydia frowned, confused.

"Naturally, I had my solicitor look into your standings as a basic precaution, expecting nothing but the records of an honest man steering his future from the seeds his father had planted."

"Andrew, it's *not* how it looks." Spencer's voice held an edge to it.

"Isn't it?" Andrew stepped forward again.

Hero whined and lowered himself to the floor next to Lydia.

"Imagine my shock, then," he continued, "learning your father stole thousands of dollars and then lost it in an illegal investment scam."

Lydia drew in a sharp breath.

"It was a bakery," Spencer whispered.

"Do you defend him?"

He swallowed and shook his head. "No. I was going to tell you when the time was right."

"And when was that? After the funds had transferred to your accounts?"

"I haven't accepted any funds yet."

"Yet."

"Excuse me," Lydia said, her voice a squeak. "Did you say a bakery?"

Andrew nodded. "A chain of bakeries. Bread and Biscuits— sound familiar?"

It wasn't a unique name.

"William Hayes and Charlie Floyd opened up a chain of bakeries for the lower and middle class, all in the name of providing affordable food in larger amounts for the *Everyman*. Only, they took the investors' money, pocketed half, and made the baked goods with plaster, chalk, and alum. Sound familiar now?"

She looked at Spencer. It was a very similar business plan to his motorcar shop except for the dastardly parts. "Is that true?"

He kept his shoulders and gaze squared to Andrew. "My father said he didn't know about the fillers. He said that Floyd crossed him."

"Do you believe him?"

He breathed, his jaw tight.

"People nearly died, Hayes. *Children* nearly died."

Lydia gasped, stepping away to face Spencer. She had to hear it from him. "Tell me what happened."

Slowly, he shifted his gaze to Lydia's. He still held her arm, gently, and made no move to let go. It felt precarious . . . a tether as fragile as a spiderweb.

She saw him swallow, and he opened his mouth. "In my last year at Oxford, I went home with an idea to modernize the carriage business. To transition to motorcar taxis. Father wouldn't hear of it. Too much overhead, too much of a gamble, too much time to retrain all his employees." He flickered a look at Andrew. "He saw motorcars as a flash in the pan. Horses were his business."

Looking out at the rain, he shook his head. "Not wanting to give up, I shared another idea, about getting investors for a motor supply chain. He brushed that aside as well. We argued. I didn't understand. What had he sent me to school for? To come home and work the family business into the grave? I was disappointed, but I returned to school, unable to ignore that my future might not be with my father's business."

She frowned. "He used your idea, anyway, didn't he? For the bakery?"

Spencer nodded, resentment evident on his face.

"And how'd that go for him?" Andrew asked.

She whipped her head around. "Andrew. Show some respect."

"Respect? Eight people came close to losing their lives within the first three weeks. Holes were literally burned in their guts, crippling them forever. Mr. William Hayes died in jail, Lydia."

She cringed at the thought of the pain those people endured. "But . . ." She turned to Spencer. "But your father said he didn't know, correct? That he was taken advantage of?"

Spencer lowered his eyes. "Mother said he told her not to eat the bread. He never brought it home. No biscuits for Nell. Ever."

Lydia searched between the men for some sort of saving grace. She pulled on Spencer's sleeve. "But *you* didn't know, right? You didn't know what your father was doing."

He kept his eyes on the ground.

"Spencer?"

"Mother wrote to me, suspecting that he was involved in

something underhanded." He pushed his hands through his hair. "I didn't want to know. I was angry. Resentful. It wasn't until accusations were made and he was arrested that I realized how truly bad it was. Even if he didn't know, he had to have turned a blind eye."

"And would you?" Andrew spat out. "You promised my sister she would be investing in motorcar *safety*."

Spencer frowned in confusion. "I didn't—"

"*Feeding* upon her emotional tie to our parents' demise—"

"No."

"Would you turn a blind eye to *that*?"

"Andrew that was *my* idea," Lydia cut in while trying to find truth in all this muck.

Andrew turned on her. "Was it? Are you going to trust this veritable stranger with your bright future—trust that he won't 'turn a blind eye' to whatever sort of *promise* he's made you?"

Something in her snapped, and she stepped away from both of them, slipping from Spencer's grasp. "You mean the same way I trusted my own brother with my *bright future*?"

Andrew's eyes widened.

Spencer turned to her, eyes pleading for her to believe him. "I'm not my father, Lydia. I swear, that isn't who I am."

Lydia's chest ached. For those injured people. For this animosity from Andrew. And for Spencer, and the truth he'd withheld from them. For the truth about his father. For the truth about hers.

"I'm tired," she whispered.

Andrew looped his hand around her arm and pulled her to him. She came limply.

He glared at Spencer. "You will pack your bags and leave. You are no longer welcome."

Spencer shook his head, his chest moving up and down. "You can't mean that."

"You have nothing to offer here."

"Andrew," Lydia said, pleading in her voice. "Where is your compassion?" Tears burned her eyes.

He rounded on her. "It dissolved when I walked in here and found you in a compromising position. Your judgment is addled. You will go to your room and stay there until I say otherwise."

"*My* judgment is addled?" Lydia wrenched her arm free and backed away. "Where is Ruby?" she asked.

"Cyril stopped by to retrieve her on his way home from town. He thought it would save us a trip in this weather. She wanted to wait, but Cyril insisted."

She spun to look at the house, as if she could determine at a glance whether her friend remained or not. Numb and already feeling terribly alone, she tugged Spencer's coat off her shoulders and held it out to him by her fingertips. The chill of the afternoon's storm took advantage of her exposure once more, and her skin immediately prickled in the breeze.

He stared at her. "Wear it to the house," he whispered. "You'll be cold."

She shook her head, steadying her emotions. "I'm full of fire, remember?" When he still didn't reach for it, she dropped it to the stone floor. She stared at it a moment, caught in the sensation of abandoning something precious. Caught in the sensation of abandoning him. She wasn't used to abandoning anything.

"Come, Hero," she said roughly, then turned. As the dog met her and stayed at her hand, she felt the initial burning twist of her first real heartbreak. But the men wouldn't see that. They would see a woman walking away, tall and untorn.

Upon entering the house, she climbed the stairs to her room and stood dripping in the middle of it, the newly unveiled events of the past whirling in a different kind of storm above her head. She lifted the linen throw off the end of her bed and wiped her face and hands. She walked to the table at the window and picked up the portrait of her mother.

The click of the door opening startled her from the quiet. Fallon slipped into the room and shut the door behind her.

"Miss?" she asked in her quiet way. "You're quaking with cold. Shall I draw you a bath?"

She met the woman's soft eyes. "Fallon?" She could say no more, choking to get air through her silent sob as Fallon's arms drew around her, and they both sank to the floor.

"Shh, miss. Shh. All will be well in time. Shh."

After her bath, Lydia dressed and dried her hair in front of the fire as Fallon brushed it. Her skin felt raw beneath her clothes, as if she'd shed her old skin and exposed this new layer too soon to the elements.

"I should like to go to Florrie's for a few days. I shall leave tomorrow. Will you accompany me?" She needed her friends, and Florrie's home had space. Violet's mother hovered, and Ruby's house was out of the question with all those men about.

Fallon paused. "Of course, miss. Shall I call Grantmore Hill?"

"Yes, please. They'll need to send a car." Oh, how she wished she knew how to drive. If so, she could leave now. She winced. The roads would be muddy. "And Fallon? Don't tell my brother. He'll be out when we leave, and I'll send him word when we arrive."

Fallon lifted a brow.

"I'm not running away. I just need . . . distance."

"Yes, miss."

After several more brush strokes, Lydia gently cleared her throat. "Has Mr. Hayes gone?"

"I believe so." Fallon set down the brush and reached into her pocket. "He asked me to give you this after he left." She held out a folded sheet of the crisp parchment they kept in each bedroom for guests.

Lydia stared at the note, then quickly took it before her mind changed. She pressed it to her lap.

Without another word, Fallon began braiding and twisting Lydia's hair upon her crown, leaving the back down. She then rolled the back portion up in strips of muslin. "I'll leave that to finish drying, miss. The curls'll be right soft. I'll be calling at Grantmore Hill now."

When at last the door closed behind her maid, Lydia picked up the note. Its weight had been tremendous as she'd waited for the chance to read it alone.

With trembling fingers, she opened it and willed herself to read it calmly and carefully.

Lydia,

I don't know if I'll have the chance to prove myself to you, but please know I am innocent of the wrongdoing your brother accuses me of. My father, in his pursuit of status and increase, was blinded and guilty, and in the end, the weight of his choices killed him. He did take my idea, but he twisted it, and that betrayal has brought me as much pain as his actual death. Despite all this, I know my father loved our family. That is the thing about family, I suppose. We cannot dictate the way they show us their devotion. I've worked hard to remove all of his debts and provide for my mother and sister, though their circumstances are humble. We carry on. I will carry on.

I did not in any way try to romance you into investing your money. The romance came all of its own accord. I struggled against it until I forgot why I was fighting it. I cannot regret it. I only regret the pain I've caused you.

Lydia, it appears I've flown too close to the sun, and like Icarus, my wings have fallen apart. Perhaps I should have chosen a different character for comparison. Perhaps Peter Pan.

Your brother is right in one thing: I have nothing to offer you. I'm a Brummie from Ward End, starting from nothing, and you are my lovely Lydia of Briarwall.

I wish you everything bright and warm. Do not ever settle. That is not what you were made for.

When I smell lavender and rain and woods, I shall forever be filled with memories of you. Forgive me.

  S. Hayes

Lydia pulled the letter to her chest, bowed her head, and wept.

On Monday, the drawing room at Kinthwaite Park was filled with large, frothy hats, day gowns of all colors and stripes, and the hum of female reformation. After discussing and planning the May Day march, the attendees had been divided into groups and given a task in preparation for the event which would take place in exactly one week.

Mrs. Whittemore, as mistress of Kinthwaite Park and hostess of the weekly suffrage meetings—held beneath her husband's notice as he attended his London clubs on Mondays—had selected the

Wendy League to help make dozens upon dozens of tissue paper flowers into nosegays to pin on ladies and gentlemen in the park.

It was Lydia's and Ruby's job to gather three blossoms made at another table by other fingers, wrap them together in brightly colored ribbon, and shove a pin into the "stems." Then it was Florrie's and Violet's job to attach a small "Votes for Women" tag, fluff up the flowers, and toss them into a basket. To Lydia, a mindless job that included *stabbing* was just what she needed to finish out this day.

Andrew had attempted to "collect" her from Florrie's house, which had resulted in a heated confrontation between her brother and all three of the girls, who'd gathered at Grantmore Hill as soon as it was possible for them.

Lydia hadn't left her room during his call, but she'd heard the varied tones of voice volleyed around the drawing room, and then the scuffle on the stairs when Andrew had attempted to climb them. The three girls *and* the butler had created a human barrier that Andrew—being a gentleman—could not bring himself to breach as it would require too much touching. At least, that's how Florrie had described it. Andrew had become flustered and red-faced. He had left without a word to his sister, though he had several for her friends.

Lydia stabbed another pin in its place. "Do we still call them 'nosegays' when they're made of paper and have no scent to make our noses as such?" She picked up another bunch and stabbed.

"Have a care, Lydia, you'll stab your finger, and we've enough red blossoms already." Ruby focused on tying her ribbons.

"Well, *that* was quite morbid," Florrie said.

"Says the girl who asked all the questions about mummification at the Egyptian exhibit last month," Ruby replied.

Florrie pursed her lips, unrepentant.

"You may call them 'posies' if you wish," Mrs. Whittemore said as she walked by, looking over their work. "We can't use real flowers and make them up this far ahead of time, now can we? They'd be withered and dead, and that is quite the opposite of what we fight to portray in our movement, is it not? Alive, girls. Alive, vivacious, and—"

"Fragile as tissue paper?" Violet finished for her mother.

Mrs. Whittemore playfully narrowed her gaze at her daughter. "*Bright*, is what I was going to say, Violet Grace. Though a dash of vinegar never hurt anybody, either."

Violet grinned and tossed another finished posy into the basket. "I've vinegar in spades."

Mrs. Whittemore sighed. "Don't I know it. Use it for good, dear girl. Now, Lydia, I understand you are staying at Grantmore Hill at the moment, but I was hoping you and the girls would join us for dinner this evening—I've already rung your mother, Florrie—as I wish to ask you questions about this motorcar supply shop business."

Lydia put down her pin and swallowed. "Me? Shouldn't you take your questions to . . . Mr. Hayes?"

"I was under the impression he'd left Albury."

Lydia looked to Ruby, who drew herself up. "Mr. Hayes is staying at Little Oakley, in our carriage house by invitation of my brother Oscar."

Lydia had learned the news as soon as Ruby had arrived that morning. Apparently the two men had run into each other in town, and when Oscar learned what had happened—to what extent, she was not sure—he'd invited Spencer to stay until his business was complete. Ruby had conveyed to Lydia the fact that Spencer had been surprised to learn his business proposition was indeed still viable, though tenuous, and on the table. At least with the Burkes and a few of their friends. She had no idea what Sir Lawrence would do, or what Andrew would tell him.

"In that case, I'll invite him to dinner as well," Mrs. Whittemore said.

Lydia froze.

"Mama, don't you think it's a little late to invite Mr. Hayes to dinner tonight?" Violet asked.

"It's what he's here for, is it not? To procure investors? In any case, extending the invitation can't hurt. If he's busy, we can simply arrange a better time. You yourself are interested in his proposal, are you not?"

Violet sat back in her chair. "I am." She gave a look of apology to Lydia.

"We women need to act on our brilliant impulses if we are to hitch our wagons to the stars—to borrow a phrase from that Emerson fellow. I rather like the Americans. Quite modern about things." She bustled away. "Let's fold those banners neatly over here, Mrs. Lindquist. We are making quite a nest! Miss Hayward, I know you are passionate in the cause, but kindly remember this is a peaceful demonstration during a beloved holiday. There will be no need to chain yourself to the May Pole. . . . Yes, I realize that, but the children will be performing!"

Violet leaned over to Lydia. "I'm sorry, Lydia. Perhaps he cannot come."

She pushed a pin into another posy. "You've considered it, then? What I told you about Spencer's father? And mine?"

"We all have," Florrie said quietly.

"What I find most unsettling," Ruby said, her head still bowed over tying a ribbon, "is that Andrew spent years in Spencer's company, and it took him only minutes to believe the worst of him. Each of us has spent a matter of hours with him, and it is fairly easy to see that Spencer is a good man. A good person. He is human, and his loyalties have been stretched to their limits. What would you or I have done in similar circumstances? And then, when you throw the cacophony of love into the mix—"

Lydia stood abruptly, her chair nearly tipping all the way over. "I cannot," she said hoarsely, flickering a glance at the startled expressions from the room. She pasted on a brief smile and stepped aside as if to excuse herself.

She leaned forward, steadying herself with her chair, and whispered, "I cannot hear how good he is. Not when he is lost to me." She straightened, projecting her voice outward as she left the table. "I've poked myself with a pin after all. No, I'll get the bandage. It is minor. Hardly a mark."

She made her way to the nearest water closet and shut the door, drawing in deep breaths and pushing them out. Going to the sink, she splashed water on her face and neck, then sank to the edge of a porcelain washtub.

Ruby had referred to love as if it had been decided—that *love* was what she and Spencer had fallen into. Not flirtation, not friendship, not infatuation. It was *Ruby* who said it. Not Florrie or Violet, who threw those words around like bread to ducks. But steady, quiet, observant Ruby, who only spoke when she was certain of her words.

Love.

She held to the edge of the sink and rested her forehead on her hand.

Andrew's voice echoed in her memory: *"You are no longer welcome."*

If love was not welcome in her own home, what would be? Sir Lawrence? The thought left her chilled.

"Andrew," she whispered. "What have we done?"

CHAPTER 17

Spencer paced the small front room of the carriage house, invitation in hand. An invitation to dine at Kinthwaite Park with Mrs. Whittemore and Violet's friends. Including Lydia. The note contained no undercurrent of matchmaking or maneuvering. Simply an invitation to share his ideas. Cyril, Oscar, and George had been invited, as Mrs. Whittemore wished to have even numbers of men and women.

"You'll wear a path through the carpet if you continue like that," Oscar said. "Shall I answer for you?"

Spencer halted and pushed the note at Oscar. "Please."

Oscar held his hands up, refusing to take the paper. "Rhetorical offer, my friend. Honestly, I don't see the problem here. Mrs. Whittemore suggests this is a business dinner. Very progressive of her, which is no surprise. Her wealth is her own, so you've no husband to contend with if she wishes to invest. You will also have the ear of Florrie Janes, who tells her father everything of interest, and he snaps his fingers to make it happen for her. As for Lydia, she'll be surrounded by her friends, who will likely shelter her from you as much as possible. What could go wrong?"

Spencer lifted a brow in response.

Oscar lowered his head in a chuckle. "Alright, yes, those four are unpredictable at best. But what have you got to lose?"

That was the pivotal question, wasn't it? What did he have to lose? He'd lost Lydia. He'd likely lost Sir Lawrence's investment and those of his associates. He'd lost Andrew's trust and friendship. He was starting at the bottom again. Only this time, instead of nursing a broken heart from a shallow American heiress, he was aching over the loss of a good portion of his past, and what might have been his future.

He still faced a future, with or without Lydia Wooding in it. *We carry on.* He'd acknowledged that determination in the letter he'd written her, and it had given him strength.

"You're right. It won't matter that Lydia is there. I need to move forward, and Mrs. Whittemore's investment will be as appreciated as anyone else's."

"There's the spirit I hoped you'd have. Considering you'll have mine and my brothers' interest backing you as well."

Spencer crossed to the writing desk, scribbled out a response, and handed it to Oscar.

"I'll make sure this is hand-delivered and tell Cyril and George. You muster that confidence, and I'll stop here with the car in an hour to pick you up."

Spencer reached his hand out, and Oscar took it. "Thank you, Oscar. I don't deserve your trust."

"We'll see about that," Oscar said. "Give Andrew some time. The old codger will come around." He grinned, then left.

If only it were that simple. He'd told Oscar the bare facts, while keeping Lydia's reputation intact. Oscar had been brutally optimistic. But so many layers were buried beneath those few simple truths he'd shared.

With Oscar gone, the thought of an hour pacing the room alone soured in Spencer's gut. He retrieved his hat from a hook near the front door and stepped out into the spring evening. The sky had been clear all day and remained so, though the sinking sun painted it pink.

The Burkes' brick manor house—as well as the carriage house on the road front—was situated on the edge of the town of Albury and across from a municipal park with paths, a large gazebo, plenty of sprawling old trees, an expansive lawn, and a meandering stream.

Spencer crossed the road and entered the park through the towering wrought iron gate. He needed to walk off this anxiousness over the Whittemore dinner and seeing Lydia again. Had it only been yesterday when she'd walked away from the temple like a world-weary goddess?

Few others were in the park at this time of day. He allowed his mind to still as he strolled, barely taking note of his surroundings but for the gentle breeze, the evening songbirds, and the bubbling of the stream.

His solitude was short-lived.

"Mr. Hayes."

Spencer paused at the familiar voice, closed his eyes, and released a breath. He turned. "Sir Lawrence. How do you do?" He glanced at the young lady on Sir Lawrence's arm and the older woman not far behind them.

"Better than you, so I hear."

The finely dressed young lady giggled and covered her mouth.

Spencer smiled. "Is this your daughter, perhaps? I don't believe I've had the pleasure."

Sir Lawrence's haughty expression cooled. "I don't have a daughter."

"Oh? I must've misunderstood when Mrs. Piedmont referred to her grandchildren the other evening after the musicale." The woman had made thinly veiled boasts of what kind of husband and father her son would be with the right woman, pointedly nodding to Lydia. To say the remainder of the evening had been uncomfortable would be an understatement.

"That was a reference to *future* grandchildren."

"Ah. Forgive me. That makes much more sense." He looked between the man and the girl.

Sir Lawrence hesitated, but then straightened, his nose lifting into the air. "Mr. Hayes, this is Glorianna Jasper, and her mother, Mrs. Jasper, from Savannah."

Spencer blinked, his eyes wide. To his surprise, his mouth twitched to fight a smile. "From America?"

Sir Lawrence nodded, and the young woman curtsied, her yellow hair coiled up beneath her enormous hat.

Spencer stepped forward and took her offered hand with a short bow. "A pleasure, miss." He studied her. "How are you enjoying your stay here?"

She peeked at Sir Lawrence, and her cheeks flushed. "Very well, sir. Thank you."

Mrs. Jasper caught up to them.

"How do you do?" Spencer said with a bow.

"Very well, thank you," the woman answered, studying him to ascertain his status, no doubt.

Spencer turned his head to find Sir Lawrence watching him warily. He'd not yet let go of the girl's hand. "And how long have you been in Sir Lawrence's acquaintance, Miss Jasper?"

The girl opened her mouth to answer, but Sir Lawrence reached out and removed her hand from Spencer's. "Perhaps, my dear, you will wait for us by the stream with your mother while I have some words of business with Mr. Hayes?"

Spencer watched with interest as Sir Lawrence escorted the ladies to the shady bank of the stream, then returned and motioned Spencer toward a nearby tree. Likely the stream would muffle their conversation.

"I could have sworn she was your daughter. Forgive me. Of course, when I first met your mother, I thought she was your *wife*." Spencer held out his hands as if helpless to fix it.

"I beg your pardon?" Sir Lawrence asked, his nostrils flaring.

"We got it sorted, though, didn't we? Please do continue."

The man collected himself, which did not take much time, as he went from an irritated plank of wood to a composed plank of wood. "I've learned you've had a bit of a falling out with the Woodings."

"A bit. I've just learned you've been courting an American heiress at the same time you've been intended for Miss Wooding. Or have I misunderstood that as well?"

Sir Lawrence kept his expression bland, though a muscle twitched at his jaw. "A man must keep his options open. A dowry is a dowry. On that note, as I was under the impression you'd left Surrey, I was going to have my solicitor contact you, but since you are still here." He cleared his throat. "I'm afraid I'll have to decline you the funds for your little shops. Some . . . unsavory revelations have forced me to look elsewhere for investment. Who knows? I may open my own motorcar supply chain. After all, I know I can trust myself, eh?" His chuckle sounded like a hen stuck in her laying.

Instead of feeling defeated by this pompous and expected pronouncement, Spencer was filled with a deep sense of challenge as well as self-assurance that he could run circles around this top-hole blackguard.

If only he had the funds to do it. "I wish you all the luck with that." Spencer would truly be starting from scratch, and with a marred reputation on top of it.

The man bent his head in false deference. "As for Miss Wooding," Sir Lawrence continued, gazing about the park as if it were his own, "her brother wisely dissolved our understanding yesterday. Such a shame for her. She'll be quite on the shelf."

Spencer's heart pounded, and he pushed his hands in his pockets to keep himself from wrapping them around the man's throat. "What makes you say so?"

"Come now, you can't say you haven't witnessed her propensity for the ridiculous. Everyone knows she is brash. Outspoken and wild."

Spencer's eyes narrowed, recognizing those particular words. "Who has told you this?"

"Nobody. I have always said so. Granted, in my pursuit of Miss Wooding, I used the phrase to discourage other men from seeking her out, but now that there is no need, her reputation will do the job. Shame, really. Such a fetching girl. Mother always said her father did her such an injustice getting himself and his wife killed and leaving Miss Wooding's upbringing in the hands of strangers. My pursuit of her was an act of charity."

Spencer's fists clenched hard in his pockets, but his masked fury must've shown on his face, because Sir Lawrence stepped back from Spencer. "It is my understanding that her upbringing was left in the hands of *your* parents, and your mother—a dear friend of Mrs. Wooding—took no more interest in Lydia than she would a housefly. Thank heavens for your father's steady hand at teaching *Andrew* what he could before his demise, and for a flurry of loyal servants, tutors, and friends."

"Of course," the man said, removing his handkerchief, "I mean—who wouldn't step in in such a dire situation?" He patted his forehead.

"Indeed," Spencer ground out. "Who wouldn't?"

The beep of a horn sounded behind him. He found the Burke brothers had pulled up alongside the edge of the park, George standing and waving his arms.

"Come on, Spencer," the younger man called. "Give him a kiss and let's be off!"

Oscar reached up and pulled his laughing brother back down in his seat.

Spencer couldn't help admiring the lack of decorum. He'd take real and brash over this pompous giraffe every time.

Brash. Outspoken. And wild.

He tipped his hat to Sir Lawrence. "I'll send your notes along, and you can tear them up. A pleasure, Piedmont."

He turned and trotted to join the others.

"It's *Sir* Lawrence," the blighter called after him.

Spencer waved a hand without looking back. Poor Miss Jasper. He slid into the back seat next to Oscar, who watched him with concern.

"Sorry about George, mate," Oscar said.

As Cyril pulled back out onto the road, Spencer inhaled deeply and let it go. "Not at all. Your brother likely prevented a murder."

"That bad, eh? He withdrew his money?"

Spencer nodded but anger roiled up inside him. "That. And he's all but ruined Lydia."

The three brothers exchanged looks.

"What?" Spencer said. "What do you know?"

Oscar shook his head. "If you're referring to that 'brash and outspoken' nonsense, that hasn't ruined Lydia."

He lowered his chin. "It hasn't?"

"No."

George turned around in his seat, his arm looped over the back of it. "It's Andrew. Nobody can get past Andrew."

Spencer let that sink in and sat back in his seat.

That made more sense than anything he'd heard all day.

Dinner at Kinthwaite Park was . . . unique. To Spencer's dismay, Mrs. Whittemore had set him at the head of table. "So as to better address all present and be heard," she'd said.

Which also meant he had an unobstructed view of Lydia Wooding, though she'd been placed at the far end of the table between Oscar and George Burke. Next to George, Violet sat to Spencer's right. Opposite her, Mrs. Whittemore, then Florrie, Cyril, and Ruby finished out the side of the table to his left. A servant sat next to the sideboard, taking notes, and to whom Mrs. Whittemore would dictate additional thoughts as the discussion progressed.

Spencer had explained the bulk of his business plan during the first and second courses and had been answering questions—mostly from Cyril, Violet, and Florrie—through the third. Mrs. Whittemore had reached such an understanding of his idea that she, too, endeavored to answer questions as they came up. Indeed, she had a sharp mind for organization, and the way she prodded

Violet to consider the possibilities impressed him. He'd also disclosed his father's history, come what may.

During a pause that allowed him to take a few bites of his meal, Mrs. Whittemore leaned toward him, her voice lowered. "Thank you, Mr. Hayes, for being so transparent with your family's plight and leaving it to us to judge. Not an easy thing to do, but admirable."

He'd had many opportunities to be square with Andrew, and he'd been cowardly. Look where it had gotten him. "I'm learning, Mrs. Whittemore."

"We all are, dear boy. We all are." She sat up. "Now," her voice resumed company-level volume, "I should like to know one more thing, Mr. Hayes."

He swallowed a bite of his duck and crabapple stuffing. "Yes?"

"How do you feel about the women's movement?"

All discussion ceased. Even the servants froze.

He cleared his throat. "The women's movement?"

"Yes. I should like to know if you would take issue with a bevy of female investors who also happen to wear sashes, march on the capitols, and raise their voices to demand a vote."

Spencer set down his knife and fork and patted his mouth with his napkin, his mind scrambling as to how to answer the question with tact.

Mrs. Whittemore's brows remained lifted in expectation.

He squeezed his hands together in his lap. "Any female investors would be treated with the same respect and gratitude as their male counterparts, with the same returns, and with the same understanding that the shops' name, branding, and quality not be brandished for use in politics, social leveraging, or illegal gain. It is in the contracts, Mrs. Whittemore."

Her eyes narrowed, and her lips pursed.

"Tell her what you told me."

Spencer looked down the table where Lydia leaned toward him, her eyes meeting his for the first time that evening. Her russet-and-gold gown set off her brown eyes and the soft highlights in her hair. He'd allowed himself only a glance earlier and could hardly remove that glance once placed. But he had. And here she was, addressing him directly. And he could only take in her dark eyes. Her pert mouth. The heightened color of her cheeks.

"Tell her," she repeated. "About women and motorcars."

All eyes turned to him, pulling him out of his daze. "Yes," he said, remembering. He addressed Mrs. Whittemore, shifting in his seat. "I believe, with everything in me, that women are an inevitable part of the future of the motorcar industry." He looked about at the women around the table. "Musicians, shopkeepers, teachers, secretaries, nurses, farmers, artists, cooks, sporting enthusiasts, archaeologists, *shareholders*, you know I can go on—"

Mrs. Whittemore smiled wryly at him as he took a breath.

"These women will earn money and buy motorcars and use them as they are intended to be used: as a quicker, more efficient means of getting from point A to point B and back again. And who knows, with the interest some of these women show"—he glanced at Lydia, and once again was held by her gaze—"that they won't be installing the auto parts themselves—"

"Or owning the companies that make them," Violet interjected.

He gave her a nod. "That's right—simply because they are capable of it?"

Lydia finally dropped her gaze, and Spencer exhaled.

"Well said, Mr. Hayes." Mrs. Whittemore drew his attention, and she began to clap her hands. "Very well said."

The applause spread, even from the men, and Spencer felt the knot in his chest begin to ease. For the first time in a very long time, he felt that the odds of succeeding might just be tipped in his favor.

He glanced at Lydia, whose eyes remained lowered.

At least in matters of business.

CHAPTER 18

The ninetieth weekly meeting of the Wendy League took place in Florrie's private sitting room at Grantmore Hill. The minutes had been read, but the arrival of the post had drawn everything to a halt. The air was more subdued than usual.

Lydia had just learned that her "arranged understanding" between her and Sir Lawrence had been dissolved and the Piedmonts would no longer be regular guests for dinner at Briarwall. Her brother's missive had been short and to the point, ending with a plea for her to return home soon. To say she was dazed would be accurate. To say the news was not enough would be an absolute understatement.

The letter hung limply in her hand as the girls lounged in the plush pink furnishings of the room. The tall windows were open and, though framed with heavy cream damask that reached the towering ceiling, light sheer drapes swayed in the breeze all the way to the marble floor. Florrie had put a record on the Victrola, and Lily Elsie sweetly lilted through love songs that Lydia tried not to apply to a certain gentleman with clear hazel eyes.

Lydia had always loved this room; the confection of pink and cream softened the formidable architecture, topped by a ceiling painted with clouds and a sunrise sky. A person could dream in this room.

"Are you going to return home, Lydia?" Ruby asked from her velvet wingback chair as she gazed out the window to the labyrinth garden below.

"Someday," Lydia replied, half-serious. "I do miss Hero."

"Hero is a darling. But you're welcome to stay as long as you like," Florrie said from a pink-silk settee, Nibs at her feet. "It's been marvelous having you here. And I must admit, I do like being close to the action. That visit of Andrew's was priceless."

"I am glad none of us missed it," Violet said from another chair. "I don't think anyone of us could describe the look on Andrew's face when he realized the only way to move us out of the way was to lift us out of the way. I'd counted on his overdeveloped sense of decorum, and it paid off."

"I despise Andrew's overdeveloped sense of decorum," Lydia said, lying on her stomach on a settee matching Florrie's, her cheek resting on the back of her hand. "It's what put me here in the first place."

"Well, that and a—how did you phrase it? A bone-melting kiss?"

Lydia sighed. "Something like that, yes."

The other girls sighed.

"If it had been anybody but Cyril who had come to pick me up that evening, I would've insisted on staying until your return," Ruby said. "Alas, Cyril possesses some kind of sorcery that forces me to see reason. I wish I'd been there for you."

Lydia shook her head. "No, he was right. The roads were horrid, even the next day. I missed you—all of you—but Fallon was a champ. I was in good hands."

"I'm glad to hear it," Ruby said, leaning her head against a wing of her chair.

"Would you forgive him?" Violet asked.

"Who, Andrew?"

"No. *Spencer*. After last night. It was quite a good show of his . . . integrity."

"It was," Lydia agreed, thoughtful. However distant she'd kept herself, she'd paid careful attention to Spencer's actions and words. His entire presentation had been, well, *trustworthy*. And she could not ignore that, though he respected her distance, the few looks he gave her were contrite, searching. Warm.

She let her hand drop toward the floor, and Nibs trotted over to lick her fingers. She stroked his neck, and he settled down. She didn't answer Violet's question. She couldn't see how she could forgive Spencer and keep her brother. And forgiving Andrew wouldn't bring Spencer back. Her connection with Spencer had been immediate, and so brief. She'd dreamt of where it would go, if only given a chance. But that chance had been broken, like a spiderweb.

A distant knock was heard at the front door. After a few moments, male voices carried up the staircase.

Florrie sat up. "I wonder who that could be."

"It sounds like someone for your father," Violet suggested.

Mr. Janes's authoritative voice had joined the mix, and Florrie sat back. "Probably his solicitor. It usually is."

Lydia closed her eyes. "Does anyone have any news that does not have to do with men, motorcars, or money?"

"I heard Mama order Empress Pudding tonight."

"I love Empress Pudding," Violet said.

The clock on the mantel ticked loudly.

"Good heavens," Lydia said. "Are our lives so shallow that we cannot converse of anything other than men, motorcars, or money?"

"Don't forget pudding," Violet said.

"How could I forget pudding?"

Florrie huffed. "Food is a perfectly viable subject for a literary club such as ours."

The clock persisted in its ticking.

Lydia sat up. "Are we to be forced to discuss . . . books?"

"Anything but that," Ruby said with a small grin. "Somebody come up with a subject, quickly."

Florrie snickered. "Now I can't think of anything but men, motorcars, and money."

Violet bobbed her head back and forth. "It sounds like a book title."

"I would read that," Lydia mused with all sincerity.

Her sincerity did not prevent the room erupting in laughter.

She covered her eyes with a groan. "Blast it all to Hades in a skirt, I would read it from cover to cover."

Spencer had followed Mr. Janes to his study, the distant sound of female laughter drawing his focus just as Mr. Janes shut the mahogany door. The gentleman strode to his large, immaculate desk and threw his hand out in invitation for Spencer to have a seat.

"You can doubtless guess why I've asked you here, Hayes."

"While I can guess, I do wonder at the timing, sir."

The man scrutinized him. "I've had word that Piedmont has withdrawn his backing of your venture. Is this true?"

Spencer straightened. "Yes, sir."

Mr. Janes nodded, then pulled a note from a drawer in his desk and commenced writing. "This," he said, finishing with a crossed *T* and a flourished signature, "is my contribution to your motor supply shops." He pushed the note toward Spencer, and Spencer cautiously reached for it.

Reading it, he swallowed dryly. "Sir." He could think of nothing to say. It was three times what Piedmont had gathered. *Thank you* did not cut it.

"Hayes Motor Supply," Mr. Janes said. "Has a nice ring to it, don't you think?"

Spencer nodded, staring at the note. "As does Hayes and Janes Motor Supply."

The man nodded considering. "About time I put my own name on something," he muttered.

"Sir, you ought to know—"

"About your father." The man put his pen aside. "I know."

"You would attach your name to his?" Spencer asked, feeling like he should make it perfectly clear what Mr. Janes was getting into.

"Honestly? No. But I would attach it to yours." He folded his hands in front of him. "It is every father's hope that his children turn out better than he is. And in this case, wiser. That is what I see, Hayes. That is what I'm counting on."

The gravity of that vote of confidence moved him. "Thank you, sir. If I may ask, how does Sir Lawrence's withdrawal factor? He took his associates' pledges as well."

"Something you should know about me, Hayes." He sat back in his chair. "I don't involve myself with idiots." The man's brow rose a fraction as he waited for that statement to hit its mark.

It did. Spencer released a breath, doubly grateful for Piedmont's idiocy and his withdrawal. "I'll take that as a compliment, sir."

"You should."

"There's one more thing you ought to know," Spencer said.

"Confound it, are you trying to shake me loose?" Humor flashed in the man's eyes.

He stifled a laugh. "No. No, sir. I only mean to be up front from the start."

"Hmm. Can't dismiss that. Go on, then."

Spencer leaned forward. "A portion of my investors are suffragettes."

Mr. Janes leaned forward as well. "A portion of my family are also suffragettes." The man smiled.

Spencer smiled back. "Very well, sir. You've been warned."

"As have you."

Spencer chuckled. He liked this man very much.

"Now, my Florrie tells me you've gotten yourself into a bit of a scrape with our Lydia. Or rather, our Andrew."

Spencer's ears burned. "Yes, sir. Both, sir."

"To put it bluntly, there is a severe lack of father figures in this scenario. So. Let's put our brains together and see what we come up with to remedy the situation, hmm?"

Spencer stilled as he realized how much he wanted that guidance. How much he had missed it. He cleared his throat. "I'd appreciate that, sir. More than you know."

"And, son?"

Spencer's gaze darted to the man, the endearment unexpected and piercing. "Yes?"

"Your father went about life his way, but he'd be proud of the way you'll go about yours."

Spencer swallowed hard. "I'll do my best, sir."

"Of that I have no doubt."

A knock at the study door preceded it opening. "Mr. Andrew Wooding is here, sir."

Spencer stood abruptly.

"At ease, Hayes. Show him in, Stafford."

Before Spencer could say a word, Andrew strode in, then slammed to a halt. He looked between Janes and Spencer and scowled. "What is this?"

Mr. Janes stood. "An intervention. Gentlemen, if you'll excuse me." Spencer watched as he calmly crossed the room. He paused at the door and looked back at them both. "Don't break my study." He slipped through the door and was gone with a click.

For a moment, Spencer and Andrew looked everywhere but at each other.

Don't ever let 'em see you weak.

Spencer drew his hands behind his back. "I spoke to Piedmont."

Andrew's sharp gaze met his, his jaw stone. "Did you?"

"He admitted he's the source of Lydia's so-called reputation. The same reputation you threw in her face the other day. He used it to keep other suitors away."

"Why should I believe you?"

Spencer huffed. "You're her brother. You should be the first to believe me."

Andrew had the decency to look chagrined.

Spencer picked up a round, jade paperweight from the desk and inspected it. "He's also been courting an American heiress, likely for some time."

"What? How—"

Spencer shrugged, returning the paperweight to its place. "I met her. They were strolling in the park together. He was reluctant at first, but then seemed to warm up to the idea of using it to show off his ingenuity. Said he'd needed to keep his options open and expressed *pity* now that Lydia would certainly be on the shelf."

Andrew's eyes darkened with anger as he scrutinized him. "That sounds like him." He walked to the window and looked out over the formal garden. "What was I thinking?" he muttered.

"A lot of us have been wondering that very thing." He watched his friend at the window. "I find it ironic that you should blow like Vesuvius upon finding me and Lydia together, but you maintain this calm after learning of Piedmont's betrayal."

"I didn't lay a finger on you," he said darkly. "But heaven help that *peacock* next time I find him alone."

Spencer let that statement simmer, finding some odd comfort in it.

Andrew took a deep breath. "I heard he withdrew his funding."

"Does *everybody* know?"

"Oscar paid me a visit."

"Did he?" Spencer considered the things Oscar might've shared, the things that had transpired in the last twenty-four hours, let alone the past week. "Did he tell you that you were a right *git*?"

Andrew dropped his head. "Among other things."

Spencer lifted his brow in surprise, but schooled his features as Andrew turned to face him.

"Do you really believe it of me?" Spencer asked. "That I could be so underhanded? That I would treat you, after all you've done for me, with such *deceit*? I did not plan on anything with Lydia—as a matter of fact, I swore up and down I would not allow any woman in my life for some time. I attempted to talk her out of her investment, but she *persisted*. She is *so* persistent. But Andrew—" He paced a step in one direction, then another, pushing a hand through his hair. He stopped. "She is *wonderful*." He threw out his hands and let them drop to his sides. "She is wonderful to me." He shrugged, unable to express himself further. "That is the sum of it."

Spencer let that declaration float on the silence that followed.

Finally, Andrew shifted. "I've watched her," he said in a low and gravelly voice, "change from a carefree butterfly-of-a-child to a grounded bird stripped of all sense of safety and security. Wild-eyed and questioning when her upturned world would be put back to rights. For months she asked me when Mama was coming home. She would ask if we could use the motorcar to go find her."

Spencer closed his eyes in sympathy.

"I finally took her to visit the grave. She hadn't been allowed to attend the burial. Mr. Piedmont was too protective of her and Mrs. Piedmont too unconcerned. But I couldn't stand her asking to get in a blasted motorcar any longer." He paused and huffed, likely at the irony that Lydia had never stopped asking to get in a motorcar. "But I did take her. Warren accompanied us. And I explained to my six-year-old sister that Mama was never coming back. That Papa would never tell her stories again. And that I would do my very best to keep her safe. It was the last time I ever cried."

Spencer believed it.

Andrew's gaze remained on the floor, his expression clouded. "Have you ever tried to keep a bird whose wings have healed from taking flight again? It's exhausting." He chuckled, and Spencer lifted his brow at the accuracy of the mental image.

Andrew ran both hands over his face. "It seems I've allowed fear . . . and loss . . . to get in the way of everything. In my attempt to safeguard Lydia, I've lost her." He swallowed hard. "And a good friend."

Spencer shook his head. "I'm still 'ere, ain't I?"

Andrew suppressed a grin. Standing up straight and tall, he looked Spencer square in the eyes. "Can you forgive me? For being a right git?"

Spencer felt his shoulders relax, and he folded his arms across his chest. "I suppose I could manage it. If you forgive me for kissing your sister." He suppressed his own smile, knowing they were through the worst of it.

Andrew narrowed his gaze. "What kind of brother forgives that?"

Spencer mirrored the look. "I'm not actually sorry."

"Hmph."

"About that," Spencer hedged. "You'll be interested in knowing I've taken on a full partner."

Andrew glanced around the richly furnished office, and his gaze landed on the papers on the desk. "Have you, now?"

Spencer straightened. "I have. Hayes and Janes Motor Supply."

Andrew considered that. "Has a nice ring to it."

"That it does. And though nothing is for certain, I've got a new grip on my future." Realization struck him again, and he felt a thrill of hope. "A *solid* future. And you can be certain of this, Andrew Wooding—I'll be seeing Lydia. As in, I'll be courting her." He leaned forward, his brow arched. "Just so you're aware."

Andrew shook his head. "Is that so?"

Spencer gave a single nod.

"You always were headstrong."

"I learned from the best."

Both men smiled.

Spencer looked above him. "She's somewhere in this massive house, and I intend to find her. But before I go, I ask you one thing."

"Oh, you're going to ask? How considerate of you."

"On second thought, I'll tell you." He took a step forward and gripped Andrew's shoulder. "You teach your sister to drive, or I will."

Andrew screwed up his mouth, then huffed. He held up his hands in surrender.

Spencer gave his shoulder a firm shake before striding toward the door.

"Wait!"

Spencer threw his gaze heavenward and turned around. "*Jove*, what is it?"

Andrew's look intensified. "Do you love her? *Really* love her?"

Spencer sobered, shaking his head. He shrugged. "How could I not?"

Andrew gave him a nod, and Spencer turned at a run.

"Best of luck getting up there," Andrew called after him.

He took the stairs two at a time, shouting Lydia's name.

"Sir," a slightly frazzled butler followed him, though not as swiftly. "Sir, this is highly improper."

"Lydia!" He paused at the top of the huge staircase, looking all directions.

"At least allow me to announce you."

"I believe I've already covered that part, thank you. Lydia!"

The butler reached him, out of breath, as a door banged open far to Spencer's left. A flurry of footsteps pounded down the corridor, then Lydia skidded around the corner, followed closely by her friends. She paused, causing those behind her to bump inelegantly into one another. A small dog barked raucously at the commotion while the girls tried not to step on him.

But Lydia only watched him. "You . . . bellowed?"

"Yes." He was suddenly as out of breath as the butler.

"Forgive me, miss," the butler said. "He just blasted through."

"It's alright, Stafford," Florrie said, scooping up Nibs. "This one is allowed."

Stafford looked between Spencer and the girls, then threw his hands up and returned down the stairs.

To Spencer's chagrin, Florrie, Violet, and Ruby remained, flanking Lydia like avenging angels.

"Spencer," Lydia breathed. "What are you doing here?"

"Let me guess," Violet said behind her.

Lydia's cheeks turned charmingly rosy. "Hush." She faced Spencer. "You can't be here," she said, though the protest was weak.

Weak enough for him to step forward. "Ladies, may I be here?"

"Yes," all three friends said.

Lydia turned, eyes wide. Ruby took her arm and turned Lydia back toward him. "Don't worry about Andrew," she whispered. "He will grow up soon enough."

Lydia visibly swallowed and stepped forward, her voice stronger. "What are you doing here?"

"Mr. Janes asked me here."

Florrie gasped and squealed, hugging Nibs to her.

Spencer cleared his throat. "And then Andrew came—"

Below them, the front door opened and shut.

Lydia's eyes grew wider. "Andrew is here?" She darted a glance toward the staircase.

"I believe he just left."

"You . . . you spoke to him?"

He nodded. "Loudly."

She pressed her lips together. "Was he angry?"

"At first."

"At first?"

"Yes." He noted the familiar tendrils escaping the loose knot at the back of her neck. A silk flower was pinned in her hair above her ear. "I like your hair that way," he said.

Her hand immediately went to her hair, and he wanted to touch it, too. "Fallon felt that a flower would be cheerful."

He frowned. "Has your stay been difficult?"

She shook her head, then slowly nodded. "I miss—Hero."

He squelched a smile, his pulse leaping around. He took another step forward. "Would it help if I told you that I'm sure Hero misses you?"

"Do you think so?"

He nodded, taking another step. "I can't say that I blame him. There is so much to miss."

Violet nudged Lydia another step closer.

"Like what?" Lydia asked.

"Like talking to you about birds or motorcars. Tending to cows. Taking bicycle rides and tripping over logs. Or hearing you sing."

"Hero abhors it when I sing. He howls and howls."

"I don't."

She took another step toward him. "You don't howl?"

"I don't abhor it when you sing."

"Oh."

He closed the distance between them, still afraid to touch her. "I also don't abhor it when you insist you know what's good for me. Or when you ride astride instead of sidesaddle." A dreamy look grew in her eyes, so he continued. "I don't abhor it when you quote literature or talk about the suffrage or try to mimic my dreadful accent."

She lifted her hand and placed it over his pounding heart. His words grew unsteady.

"I especially don't abhor it when you tell your brother you'd sooner marry a tree than a knight."

She smiled, biting her lip, which drew his gaze to her mouth.

He reached, finally, and touched a curl of her hair. "There is another thing I don't abhor," he said quietly, the thick, silky threads sliding between his fingers.

Her gaze dropped to his mouth. "What is that?"

He cradled her face, his thumb smoothing over her lower lip. "Anytime I get to do this . . ."

She met his lips, closing her eyes and gripping his shirt. Her soft mouth explored his, taking his breath away with her evident willingness to be near him again, to want him again.

She pulled back abruptly, her fingers covering her mouth, and his heart dropped. She spun away but pressed her back against him. He felt her sigh. "Oh, good," she said.

His fear dissolved. He turned her back around. "They left sometime during my speech."

"That's too bad. It was a pretty speech."

"Would you like me to call them back? I believe they're just around the corner."

A giggle and a hush confirmed his suspicions.

She shook her head, pressing herself against him, gripping his shoulders. "Don't you dare. I have some business to discuss with you."

"Now?" he asked.

"Yes, now. I need to know." Her brown eyes held his. "Will you, Spencer Hayes, accept my investment in your motor supply shops and make me part of the future of the motorcar industry?"

He studied her, bewildered and confident at the same time. "I would be honored, Lydia Wooding."

A squeal from around the corner caused them both to grin.

"You may show me your appreciation now," she said.

In answer, he caught up her mouth with his, expressing as much appreciation as he dared.

"You said this couldn't happen," she said between kisses.

"I was wrong."

"I knew you were."

He rested his head on her forehead and laughed.

She grinned. "I knew it when you didn't balk at my trousers. Not once."

He pursed his lips. "I think I was done for when you asked me if I had a favorite clock."

She laughed, and the sound of it filled him.

He set her back a bit, taking her hands. "I told your brother I'll be courting you."

"You *told* him?"

"Yes. It seemed the best way to go about it. I was quite direct."

"Very wise."

He tugged her closer. "Am I to assume, then, that I may see you, regularly, Miss Wooding?"

"You *tell* Andrew, but you ask me?"

He nodded, bringing up her hand and placing a kiss on her wrist, lingering there at her scent.

She sighed. "Have I told you how much I like you, Mr. Hayes?"

"Please, tell me again."

She nodded, her smile growing, drawing him to her once more. She whispered in his ear. "I like you better than thunderstorms in the temple."

A pleasant current moved down his arm. He smiled and whispered back. "I like you better than motorcars."

She pulled back with a gasp, her mouth a perfect *O*.

He made good use of that pretty formation.

CHAPTER 19

A band sat in the gazebo playing the traditional songs of May Day as locals strolled by carrying branches of blossoms and young men danced with strings of bells tied to their legs. Florrie had just crowned the new May Queen, as she had once been, and the rosy-cheeked young girl was now paraded around the park in a flower-covered cart while children followed in their promenade to the Maypole. Linen-draped tables filled with sweets, pastries, and more flowers lined the walking paths and beckoned merrymakers to sample the tastes and scents of spring.

Lydia walked with Violet and Ruby, a basket over her arm filled with suffragette posies. Among the stern looks they'd received, they'd also handed out many posies in a happy exchange.

"Hello, ladies," Oscar Burke called out from behind.

The girls turned, finding Oscar, Cyril, and Spencer in their sack suits, high linen collars, and handsome derby hats.

Lydia found herself expecting Andrew to be with them, but quickly squelched that idea. She had always attended the festivities with her brother, but Andrew wasn't altogether thrilled with her involvement with the suffrage, tolerating it out of respect and gratitude for the Whittemore women.

Plus, she was still at Florrie's. Andrew had sent her another letter containing his approval of Spencer's romantic suit and an apology for being an overbearing antique. Her reply had simply promised that she would return to Briarwall after the May Day celebration.

Spencer's voice sounded in her ear. "What can I do to clear your head of whatever unhappy thoughts have caused you to frown?"

The scent of cedar drew her in, so her cheek met his ever so briefly before he pulled away from her ear. His hand found hers, and he lightly squeezed her fingers.

"That's a good start." Her smile lifted, and her pulse picked up as he threaded his fingers with hers. It was all they were allowed in public, but she adored any touch of Spencer's.

"As long as you realize it's just a start." He lifted a roguish brow, and she laughed, flushing at the same time.

"I'm starting to regret pairing you two for that impromptu musicale." Violet scrunched her nose.

"You don't get to take all the credit," Florrie said, joining them. "If I hadn't kept Andrew away while they searched for that clock key, who knows how long it would've been before they realized they were meant for each other."

Lydia smiled at Spencer, knowing they'd both already felt a spark of something before then. But would they have had the courage to do something about it?

"And who do you think challenged Andrew to that rousing game of chess so Lydia and Spencer could make nice, hmm?" Violet said.

"Ah, but the perfume was *my* idea. Let's not forget that," Florrie said with a triumphant grin.

"Oh, for the love," exclaimed Cyril. "Shall we get you each a crown of flowers and declare you both Queens of 'I'm Better Than You at Matchmaking'?"

"Well, what would that prove, if we *both* had crowns?" Florrie rolled her eyes.

"I've a better idea," Violet said, setting her basket on the grass. She stepped to Cyril, who startled back half a step. "Oh, come now, you big brute, hold still."

Cyril held one hand on his hat, watching warily as Violet worked at his lapel.

She stepped away. "There. Better than a crown, I say."

Cyril looked down at the posy now pinned to his coat and, somewhat pink-cheeked, narrowed his eyes at Violet.

Violet shrugged innocently. "Votes for Women."

Florrie leaned forward. "Hard to resist, isn't she?"

Oscar leaned into his brother and laughed. "You know, ladies, *I'm* the one who told Andrew to get his head out of his—" He ducked as Cyril knocked his derby to the ground.

"Hold on, that's a new hat." Oscar went to fetch it before it was stepped on in the crowds.

Cyril smoothed his fingers over the rim of his own derby. "I'll be at the lemonade stand, showing off my posy, should anybody need me." He strode away.

"Well," Violet said, putting an arm around Florrie's waist, "I guess I'm not *that* hard to resist."

"Sweetie," Florrie said, "that man just turned four shades of red in your honor."

Violet watched after him thoughtfully. "Shall we go make ourselves crowns?"

"An excellent idea we ought not to waste." She took Violet's arm, and they headed to one of the nearby flower stands.

Lydia glanced at Ruby, who remained quiet, watching her friends with a smile. It was Ruby who'd suggested love was in play. Actual love. Love worth fighting for.

Oscar returned, dusting off his hat. Nodding to Lydia and Spencer, he offered his arm to his sister. "Miss Burke, would you care to leave these lovebirds to themselves and join me for some lemonade with our surly older brother?"

She took his arm. "I should like nothing better." She grinned at Lydia and Spencer, who removed his hat and bowed to her as Oscar led her away.

"Ruby is a dear," Lydia said.

"Yes. Astounding, actually."

"Because she's grown up in the middle of all those brothers?"

"That, and because she still manages to fit in so well with you, Florrie, and Violet."

Her mouth flew open as he laughed, and she reached for his hat.

He stepped back in time, but she pursued.

"You'll pay for that," she said, laughing.

He took her basket from her. "I have an idea," he said, still evading her reach. "Why don't you pin one of these on me, and I'll turn four shades of red?"

She paused, then her mouth quirked. "Very well." They'd stopped at the edge of the park, near the road. "Hold still, you big brute."

He laughed and stepped close to her, holding very still. She pulled a posy out of the basket and, with her heart pounding, took her time pinning it to his lapel, enjoying the chance to be so near him. Would she ever tire of it? She couldn't imagine. And they were just beginning.

She looked up to find him watching her.

"There is only one thing keeping me from kissing you right now," he said.

"Do you like kissing me, Mr. Hayes?"

His eyes flashed. "Fully, wholly, and completely."

She would be the one turning four shades of red. "What is stopping you, then? Propriety?"

He shook his head. "It takes something much stronger than that to resist you, my lovely Lydia."

She smiled at the way he said *lovely*. "What is it?"

The beep from a motorcar just on the other side of a low hedge of boxwoods made her jump.

Spencer nodded toward the Singer tourer. *"That."*

She focused her attention on the vehicle with a furrowed brow. "Andrew?"

Indeed, her brother was climbing out of the car, approaching through the break in the hedge, his cap crushed in his hand. He nodded. "Spencer." He glanced nervously at her. "Lydia."

"Andrew" she said. "You came."

"I did. But I'm not staying."

"You're not?"

"Neither are you," Spencer said, grinning.

"You seem unsettlingly happy about that," she said to him.

"Lydia?"

She turned to Andrew, who was holding out his hand. "Would you like to go for a drive?"

It slowly dawned on her what he was asking. She was unable to speak for a moment, then she nodded. "Yes. Yes, very much. I would very much like to go for a drive. With you. My brother. In a car."

Andrew couldn't hide his amusement, and he stepped aside as she joined him, grinning widely. He led her carefully through the hedge.

"Don't be gone too long," Spencer called after them.

"We'll be gone as long as it takes," Andrew replied.

She looked up at him. "As long as it takes for what?"

He led her to the driver's side and moved to help her up. "As long as it takes to teach you to drive this contraption."

She halted and stared up at her brother who had given up his last years of boyhood to care for her and their home and their future. She pushed up onto her toes and wrapped her arms around his neck. "Oh, thank you."

He squeezed her back. "You're quite welcome."

After another moment, she let go and climbed into the driver's seat. Andrew took his time explaining the parts to her—the steering column, the brake, the shifting mechanism. She let him show her even though she already knew it all.

Then he went around and climbed in next to her. He put his cap on, and she started the motor, barely containing her excitement.

She checked for any cars nearby and, finding it clear, pulled out onto the road, Andrew talking her through it the entire time. After a few practice starts and jolty stops, they turned onto a long, open stretch, and she could feel the breeze and the rumble of the engine as they passed under canopies of trees and skirted fields of sheep and cattle.

"That's right, Lydia. You're doing splendidly. Mind this turn. Slow down and make sure no one is coming the other direction."

She did as he directed, slowing to pass a milk lorry.

"I did it!" she yelled.

"Well done!"

"Andrew?" she asked.

"Yes?"

She grinned. "It's like flying, is it not?"

Andrew released his smile. "Yes, Lydia. Very much like flying."

ACKNOWLEDGMENTS

Thank you, Lisa Mangum and Heidi Gordon, for planting the notion of an Edwardian rom-com in my beleaguered brain and then letting me take off with it. I look forward to more flying with you and my Wendy League!

Thank you to my alpha readers—the talented and knowledgeable Arlem Hawks and Megan Walker. Your feedback has been invaluable, and I've loved getting to know you better. Keep writing your lovely stories!

Thank you, Shadow Mountain Publishing, for entrusting me with your label. I will always give you and my readers my very best. Another thank you to my editor, Lisa, for your eagle-eye editing and laughing at the funny parts.

Thank you, Story Spark Staff, Storymakers, and all my writer friends for life. I'm so blessed to be part of this incredible community. Thank you, Adventure for Women, for giving me balance and trees and mountains, and a place to breathe.

To my children and grandchildren, thank you for inspiring me to create worlds where laughter, love, hope, and determination overcome fear, doubt, and pain. I love you, I love you, I love you.

Thank you, Brandon, my love and sometimes Lost Boy. I

treasure every one of our adventures together—even the ones without fairy dust.

Thank you, Sir James Matthew Barrie, for giving the world such a unique and wondrous story in your play, *Peter Pan; or, The Boy Who Wouldn't Grow Up*, and for the line, "'Wendy,' Peter Pan continued in a voice that no woman has ever yet been able to resist, 'Wendy, one girl is more use than twenty boys.'"

DISCUSSION QUESTIONS

1. *Hearts of Briarwall* is set in Surrey County, England, in 1906, after the Victorian Era, and during the reign of King Edward VII.
   Between the years of 1901 and 1914, the Edwardian Era was also
   referred to as the "Gilded Age." Why do you think it received
   that name?

2. J.M. Barrie's play *Peter Pan; or, The Boy Who Couldn't Grow Up* de-
   buted at the Duke of York's Theatre in London on December
   27, 1904. After the girls see the play, they form a club and call
   themselves "the Wendy League." How does the club's motto,
   "Seize the opportunity to fly," drive the story? How many other
   nods to the story of Peter Pan can you find in *Hearts of Briarwall*?

3. When we meet Spencer, he steps off a train at Paddington
   Station, admires several motorcars, then meets Andrew and
   boards the horse carriage awaiting them. How does this imag-
   ery reflect where Spencer is in his life? What other technologi-
   cal or modern wonders are appearing at this time in history?

4. Floris is a London perfumery that has been creating scents
   since 1730 and is still in business today at the same location on
   89 Jermyn Street. (They have a lovely website.) Many of their
   scents are still in circulation, including those I've given to the

Wendy League. Which scents are you drawn to? Which Floris perfume would you choose for yourself or a loved one? Why?

5. Compare and contrast social norms of the Regency, Victorian, and Edwardian eras. How did things like courting, manners, a woman's place, and class systems change? What things stayed the same?

6. Lydia dreams of learning to drive a car. Spencer dreams of building a company. What odds are stacked against each of them? What works in their favor? Do you have a dream, but the odds are stacked against you? What might work in your favor?

7. *Hearts of Briarwall* takes place during the Second Industrial Revolution. While the First Industrial Revolution's focus was on the steam engine and textile manufacturing, the Second focused on steel, electricity, and the automobile. What new inventions do you see appearing in Lydia and Spencer's world? What old inventions were still in use?

8. Lydia, Violet, Florrie, and Ruby have a special bond, as do Spencer and Andrew. What are some enduring qualities of lifelong friendships? Name some of your other favorite literary friendships.

9. The Women's Suffrage Movement was in full swing during 1906 with varying degrees of intensity. How did the movement impact the women and men of Lydia and Spencer's world? How has it impacted your own?